A Cornish Encounter

A tale of interrupted passion

Clare Allison

This novel is a work of fiction
This paperback edition 2020
1
First published in Great Britain by Clare Allison 2020
Clare Allison asserts the moral right to be identified as the author of this work.

Chapter One

'I know!' declared Iris triumphantly. 'Sally can ask Justin Trevelyan!'

Suddenly pandemonium broke out. Sally, struck equally by shock and panic, choked on her tea, spraying a liberal mouthful over Bob Helmsworth. Bob, as Chairman, desperate to get out of her line of fire and hang on to what dignity he could, shot backwards in his chair his foot catching the leg of the ancient rattan table and sending the teapot flying. A scalding river of brown gushed towards the ladies at the far end who rose as one, shrieking and clutching their neatly typed agendas. Coughing and gasping, Sally jumped up and rushed into the kitchen for kitchen roll and cloths.

Buying time with some desperate mopping action, Sally got control of her breathing and gathered her wits. Ask Justin Trevelyan? Over her dead body! Typical of Iris to remember her past connection with Justin. And to blurt it out like that with no warning.

'I'll just make some more, shall I?' Sally asked brightly, brandishing the teapot and beating a hasty retreat. She refilled the kettle and reached for the teabags, her mind buzzing as she went through the familiar motions. Now that her initial panic had faded, she could admit to herself that, if you needed a local celebrity to give some kudos to a fundraising campaign, Iris's idea of inviting Justin Trevelyan back to the village wasn't at all bad. It was just that Sally would rather have all her teeth pulled without anaesthetic than be the one to do it.

Justin Trevelyan was the latest in a line of classical musicians with sufficient charisma and glamour to appeal not only to the aficionados but to mainstream audiences too. Sally could clearly picture him as the poster-boy for the Last Night of the Proms the previous year; smouldering deep blue eyes, wickedly charming grin, broad shoulders filling his tail coat beautifully and all topped by a shaggy mane of tousled black curls. No wonder the viewing figures had gone up.

'Everything all right, Sally dear?' Sally jumped guiltily as Iris Girton's quavering voice interrupted her train of thought. 'Only we'd best get on. Bob has promised his wife he'll be back in time for the Over 60s bridge club.'

'Sorry,' Sally pushed the handsome face of Justin Trevelyan firmly out of her mind. 'It's all ready, Iris. I'll just bring it through.'

She passed round eight fresh cups of tea, made sure everyone had the right amounts of milk and sugar and, finally, sat down again.

'Right then,' Bob, who revelled in his role as Chairman, cleared his throat importantly. 'Back to business then, eh? Iris, you were saying something?'

'Yes! Justin Trevelyan!' Iris beamed. 'I can't imagine why we didn't think of him before. Do you suppose he'd come?'

Pandemonium broke out again. Everyone had an opinion and felt obliged to give it. Sally's, now that she'd chance to think, was that there was no chance of Justin being free at this short notice. She offered up a quick prayer that she was right. None of the other committee members really had much of an idea. Some felt that a world-renowned conductor of his standing would have his diary filled well in advance. But surely, argued others, when he heard how the winter gale had ripped off the roof of the village hall, threatening serious damage to the tower of the adjoining church in the process, the very church where he had given his earliest performances, he would be sympathetic? And when he heard the impact this was having on the village as the brownies, scouts, playgroup, Women's Institute and Over 60s Club, to name but a few, now had nowhere to meet, surely then he would feel compelled to give something back?

Sally thought not. As she remembered it, all the village had ever done for Justin was complain that his music was too loud, too modern or both, but she held her tongue while the discussion ebbed and flowed around her. Just as they reluctantly decided it was probably pointless even asking him and Sally was breathing a secret sigh of relief, Iris once again exclaimed,

'Yes, but we've got a connection, someone who can make a personal appeal. Haven't we, Sally, dear?' Peering over her reading glasses, she turned her gimlet gaze on Sally, 'You and he were rather close at one time, weren't you?'

Sally allowed the shining, dark brown curtain of her hair to fall forward, hiding her burning cheeks. She took a deep, calming breath.

'We...were...uh...friends at Uni,' she admitted. 'But that was years ago. I haven't seen Justin in...oooh...ages.' If just saying his name caused such a horrible constriction in her chest, how could she possibly bring herself to contact him? 'I don't think he'd even remember me now, really I don't.'

Iris peered at her even more intently. 'Are you sure dear? I quite clearly recall your poor dear mother telling me that you and he,' she paused, leaning in, lowering her voice to a dramatic and gravelly whisper, 'flat-shared, in your London days. However famous he now is, I'm sure Mr Trevelyan isn't quite as absent minded as that!'

No, quailed Sally inwardly, not absent-minded at all, just arrogant, stubborn, judgemental, cruel....and those were some of his more attractive qualities. Even if he hadn't been all those things, surely Iris could see how impossible her suggestion was? What was Sally supposed to do? Call him up and say, 'Hi, remember me? We were lovers once and on the strength of that I'd like you to give up a week of your time, unpaid, to raise money for the church hall of the village where neither you nor any of your family live any more'? Sally, squirming in embarrassment at the very idea, swept her hair back from her face and twirled it into a long rope over her right shoulder.

'I can see it might be a little difficult, Sally dear,' Iris conceded. 'However, sometimes it is necessary to make a small personal sacrifice for the greater good. And think how pleased Peter will be when he hears what you have done!'

At the mention of her fiancé, Sally's spirits plummeted further. She twined her fingers more tightly still in the loop of her hair. Being vicar of the church in question, Peter would undoubtedly want her to do everything within her power to raise the finance needed to pay for the repairs. But it was unreasonable to expect him to be pleased when he discovered that this meant her begging a favour from an ex-lover about whom she'd given him only the sketchiest of details.

But why get worked up? Briskly, she tossed her ponytail back out of the way, quite convinced that no personal appeal from her would cut any ice with Justin Trevelyan, not after the way they had parted for the last time. In any case, as she knew that orchestral concerts were booked sometimes years in advance, she couldn't imagine he'd be able to take time out of his hectic schedule at this kind of notice; it was inconceivable that he would be available. So, she might as well give in with as much grace as she could muster, invite the wretched man, then sit back and wait for the inevitable refusal.

'That's settled then,' having received no further objections from Sally, Iris beamed happily round at her fellow committee members as if their worries were already over. 'We'll hold a grand fund-raising music festival in the week leading up to the Easter weekend with Justin Trevelyan as the star attraction. Sally will write the letter of invitation.'

Even though the business of the meeting was officially over, it still took a while before everyone had finished helping Sally tidy up her conservatory and actually left. Finally, all the dirty crockery returned to the tiny kitchen and offers of washing up gently but firmly refused, Sally found herself alone.

She was a great believer in getting jobs done as soon as they arose, particularly if they were nasty ones and she had every intention of putting something down on paper to Justin Trevelyan that very evening. She was extremely grateful that Iris and Bob, being of the age they were, had considered a letter the only appropriate way of contacting him. Had they been of a younger generation they might have suggested an e-mail or, heaven help her, a phone call. As it was, she could take her time getting the wording just right.

She filled the sink with hot water and added a squirt of washing up liquid, mentally composing the opening paragraph. How to strike the right tone? It had to sound like a genuine invitation. On the other hand, pride dictated that he should understand it was only as secretary of the fund-raising committee that she was writing to him, not from any personal desire to see him again. And of course, as she no longer had any idea of Justin's private address, the letter of invitation would have to go through his agent so whatever she wrote would have to hit exactly the right combination of previous acquaintance and professionalism. The irony was not lost on her.

To be asking a favour of Justin through a third party! Justin, of whom she could once have asked anything.

As soon as everything was washed, dried and put away, Sally opened up her laptop. Her first job was to find the name and contact details of Justin's agent. And the most obvious way of doing that was by googling Justin. No sooner had she typed in his name than thousands of results appeared instantly.   Goodness! Justin Trevelyan was even more famous than she'd thought! Intrigued, she clicked on the link to a video masterclass and Justin appeared, full-screen. Sally recoiled. Suddenly, it was as if he was right there, in her living room! Smiling directly at her. Deep set blue eyes crinkled at the corners just as she remembered. His hair, a few flecks of distinguished grey at the temples, a little shorter now than he'd worn it in his youth, just brushed his collar, the same wayward lock sliding endearingly across his left eyebrow. Realising his lips were moving, Sally fumbled to bring up the sound icon and unclick mute. And then he was speaking to her.

The intervening years had added a little depth, a little gravitas to the timbre of his voice and the international travel had given it a slightly drawling inflexion, but the essence of it was recognisable to anyone who had known him as well as Sally had. She listened mesmerised. The clip was long and detailed. As it reached its conclusion and the image died abruptly, Sally exhaled slowly the breath she had been unconsciously holding throughout and gave herself a mental shake. This wasn't getting any letters written.

But that brief taste had piqued her curiosity; she couldn't help herself. Having saved the contact details of his agent and read his latest reviews, Sally scrolled down and continued clicking entries at random. She was not impressed, yet not surprised either, by what she now read. Justin Trevelyan, prize-winning, sought-after, highly-talented conductor, had also gained himself quite a reputation as a tyrant, terrorising unfortunate musicians and impresarios who failed to live up to his exacting expectations. One head-line caught her eye, 'Bully with a Baton', causing her lips to curl with distaste as she scanned the article describing how he had reduced the principal cellist of a major orchestra to tears. Not only that, 'Two-timing Trevelyan', as she already knew to her cost, was quite the ladies' man and his name had been linked to a series of female celebrities both single and, to Sally's definite disapproval, married. Having had all her worst fears about him confirmed, she was even more convinced that there was no way a letter from her would persuade him to renounce this playboy life-style in favour of

5

village life even for just a week. Poor Iris was destined to be sadly disappointed. And the sooner that happened, the better, as far as Sally was concerned.

She opened a word document and settled down to write the hardest letter of her life. After a good couple of hours of painful effort during which she nearly wore out the lettering on the delete and backspace keys, Sally decided to settle for what she had achieved, pressed print, signed it and quickly sealed it into an envelope, before she had chance to change her mind. She would post it first thing in the morning, first class.

Chapter Two

For the fourth time, Justin ran back across the stage and jumped nimbly onto the podium. The majority of the audience was still standing, clapping enthusiastically, some even cat-calling and whistling. He acknowledged them with yet another bow then turned away to face the orchestra. Indicating with his baton, he drew individual musicians to their feet to receive their share of the acclaim; the principal woodwind players, the first trumpet, the timpanist. Then he gestured towards the wings. The soprano soloist, resplendent in an off-the-shoulder gold creation which swept the floor as she walked regally forwards to a further wave of wild applause. She bowed. Justin leaped from the podium, clasped her hands in his and kissed her soundly on both cheeks. This time the band joined the audience in calling and whistling.

'Well,' he thought wryly as he lead her from the brightness of the stage into the gloom of the wings. 'That will provide a little grist to the rumour-mill.' He was well aware of the current speculation about the nature of his relationship with the Scandinavian blonde but at that particular moment, he guessed he was the only one who knew for certain that the relationship had run its course. He had every intention of informing the lady concerned of his decision later that evening. Gently, he detached her hand from his arm. 'Well done, darling! You were superb!' His compliment was genuine. She had sung beautifully, as ever.

'Yes,' she agreed complacently, as she swept towards the dressing rooms, ignoring lesser beings who were trying to add their praise to Justin's. 'It was good concert. We make great team.' She paused at the large cream door to her own room and regarded him archly, placing a long, smooth, white hand on his shirtfront. 'And not just on concert platform. You are coming in?'

Justin hesitated. A night spent in her cool yet willing arms would be a perfect way to round off a very successful tour but.... He caught the slightly desperate plea in her eyes and realised that, for him at least, the prospect was less than appealing. There had been, was still, a strong physical attraction between them. Why wouldn't there be? She was blonde, beautiful and very talented. And given the nature of the music they'd been working on and the fact that they were both young, free and single, it had almost been inevitable that they should get together. But, Elisabetta was back to Sweden in the morning and, after a couple of days in London catching up on things with his agent, Justin himself would be off to the States for almost two months. Suddenly the logistics of maintaining a long-distance relationship with her, with anyone, just seemed like more effort than it was worth.

He assumed an expression of reluctant regret. Why postpone the inevitable? 'I think not, Elisabetta,' he said calmly, taking a slight but unmistakeable step back.

'I see.' She removed her hand from his chest and pushed open the door. 'You are done with me now, yes? All that passion, all that ardour, was just for the music. And now we have performed for the last time, you have no more need of me. I see I have been very stupid. You are user, Justin Trevelyan. And that is not nice.' She paused, clearly waiting for him to respond to her accusation but, when he made no move to do so, she slipped into her dressing room, closing the door firmly behind her, tears glistening at the corners of her eyes.

Justin shrugged and moved slowly to his own dressing room. Maybe she was right? He hadn't intended to 'use' her, whatever that meant. He'd met her and liked her and, as far as he was concerned, they'd both gone into the affair with their eyes open. But there had never been any more to it than that, on his part at least. There never was.

'Max,' As he stepped over the threshold, he acknowledged his manager's presence in his dressing room.

'Great show, JT! In fact, according to all the crits I've read, great tour!' Max O'Donaghue, one of the first to spot Justin Trevelyan's prodigious potential, had been his agent since his first professional gigs and one of his closest friends for almost as long in spite of the difference in their ages. Now, Max clapped him on the back and shook his hand, then peered at him more closely. 'Why the long face? Everything went swimmingly, didn't it?'

Justin slumped down onto a chair, whipped off his bow tie and loosened his shirt collar. 'Elisabetta.'

'Ah,' Max nodded understandingly. 'Just given her the brush off have you?'

Justin looked up quickly. 'What makes you say that? Maybe she's dumped me.'

Max gave vent to a short, sharp laugh. 'No way. Besides, I saw it coming. It's always the same with you. You get close, they get keen, you get bored. Don't fret, JT. She'll be fine in a day or two.' He rose and poured them both a drink. 'Here. Get that down you.'

'Thanks,' obediently, Justin took the glass Max handed him. 'I didn't mean to hurt her, you know.'

'I know,' Max reassured him gently. 'You never do. You just don't seem to be able to help yourself. Anyway, cheer up. At least she's not the type to go running to the tabloids about it.'

'I suppose I should be thankful for small mercies,' Justin agreed and downed the remainder of his drink. 'I hate having my relationships all over the papers.'

'Relationships?' queried Max sardonically, resuming his seat. 'Not sure any of your brief liaisons would actually qualify as relationships, old man.'

'What do you mean?'

'Well, most of them are over before they've begun. You've had nothing longer than a quick fling in years. Not since I've known you. In fact, not since....'

'Yes, OK!' Justin cut short his ruminations angrily. 'Not since I went to Stockholm. Point taken. Well, if that's how a,' he paused and waggled his index fingers indicating inverted commas, 'relationship' works, you can count me out. I'm perfectly happy with quick flings!'

Max raised an eyebrow. 'Perfectly happy? Really? That'll be why you're moping round in here picking over what went wrong with Elisabetta, then?'

Justin leapt to his feet and shucked off his dinner jacket. 'I am not moping and you are the one doing the picking over.' He threw the jacket at his manager. 'For God's sake make yourself useful, Max, and hang that up, will you? I'm going to get changed so we can go and get something to eat.'

Max did as he was asked, aware that Justin's rare mood of introspection was over. Maybe JT would find what he was looking for in the USA? Max, happily married and emotionally settled, hoped for his friend's sake that he would.

Chapter Three

There it was. A slender, pure white envelope lay on her doormat. Sally knew immediately what it was. She withdrew her key from the lock and closed the door behind her, picking the letter up and tapping it meditatively, allowing herself a moment to think about how she would feel if by some miracle its contents were positive. What would it be like to see Justin Trevelyan again in the flesh? Would he remember her? Could they put their differences behind them in the interest of the common cause?

Decisively, Sally flipped the envelope over and slit it open. Just as she had thought! Justin and his agent regretfully declined her kind invitation due to prior engagements. So that was that. It would be nice to think Iris and the committee had a Plan B for raising the funds necessary for the repair work to the church hall but Sally knew that they had put all their eggs in the one basket; Justin Trevelyan. The festival would still go ahead of course. Heavens, it would have to, numerous groups and choirs had already been practising hard in anticipation, but without the draw of someone of Justin's calibre, ticket sales would be severely limited and they would be almost as far from the total they required as they were at the moment.

She refolded the letter and tucked it back into its envelope, dumping her bags in the living room and going through to the kitchen. Time and enough to break the bad news to Iris and the rest of the committee. She'd had a long and particularly hectic day at school what with practice SATs all morning and parents' evening afterwards. All she wanted now was a cup of tea, her feet up for five minutes and to forget all about roofs and fund-raising. She tucked the envelope into her jacket pocket, filled the kettle and dropped a tea bag into a mug, relishing the peace and quiet of her little cottage.

Sally eased off her shoes, picked up her mug and made her way into the conservatory, gratefully subsiding into one of the well-cushioned wicker chairs. As she nursed her tea, she couldn't stop herself wracking her brains for other ways of raising money. There were all the usual old standbys of course. Sponsored walks, sponsored silences, willing helpers wielding charity boxes outside the post office and in the pub. But they needed serious money and fast before the hall fell down completely taking the church tower with it. If Justin had agreed to take part, the local media would have gone wild and ticket sales would have been guaranteed even if they'd upped the prices. They might even have been able to persuade him to give some exclusive pre-concert talks for really serious amounts of money.

'Sally?' The was a gentle rap on the back door and Peter's voice brought her back to the present as he appeared in the doorway.

Sally slid her feet off the chair she'd been resting them on and raised her face for a kiss. 'Peter! Sorry, I didn't hear you coming up the path. How are you?'

Peter Laity, Vicar of St Piran's and the surrounding five villages, was a mild-mannered man some ten years Sally's senior, quite good looking in a rather sandy sort of way and much-loved by his generally elderly parishioners. He leaned down and touched his lips to her cheek then, giving it a little brush first, took the seat her feet had just vacated. 'Day dreaming?' he queried with a smile.

Sally shrugged. 'Not really. Attempting to conjure up inspiration on the fund-raising front. I got the reply from Justin Trevelyan's agent.' She extracted the letter from her pocket and slid it across the table. 'Not good news I'm afraid.'

Peter cast his eyes over the brief missive. 'Oh dear. That's a bit of a blow. The committee will be disappointed, especially Iris. But perhaps it's just as well, eh?'

Sally frowned, 'Just as well how exactly?'

'Well, you know,' airily he waved a hand. 'I was never all that keen on the idea of someone like that just waltzing in for the week and taking all the credit.'

'Someone like what?' Sally asked knowing that Peter being 'never all that keen' was a huge understatement.

When they had first become close, Sally had been completely frank with him about the fact that she'd had a previous, serious relationship. Peter had been won over by her honesty and, in spite of his own deeply held belief that committed Christians, and particularly vicars, should not have sex outside of marriage, had assured her it made no difference to his feelings for her and that there would be no need for them to refer to the matter again.

No need, that is, until Iris had hatched her evil plan and Sally had felt it necessary to explain the exact nature of that previous relationship and who it had been with. As she had anticipated, Peter had not been best pleased. Whilst the vicar in him had welcomed the plan for raising funds for the repair of the church hall, the man in him had clearly resented the idea that the person responsible for its success would be his fiancée's ex-lover.

'Well, you know,' he continued. 'Someone so used to having everyone fawning over him. We'd have put in all the hard work but I doubt he would have given credit where it was due. And, well, it might have been awkward for you.'

Awkward for you, you mean, Sally thought, but had the self-restraint not to say. 'If Justin had, by some miracle, been free, I am sure we could all have managed to behave like civilised adults for a week or so,' she assured him instead. 'And as for him not giving credit where it was due, I wouldn't imagine for a minute he'd care a fig whether he got the credit for our insignificant little festival or not.' She got abruptly to her feet and busied herself with testing the soil in the plant pots that lined the window sill. 'How you can say it's just as well he's not coming, I don't know. It's your church that's practically falling down, after all.' Sally knew she was being snappy and irrational. Peter was merely articulating what she had been saying to herself daily for the past couple of weeks. 'It's all academic now, anyway. He's not coming so the festival will just have to go ahead without him.'

'I know it's disappointing and we won't make anything like as much money but I think we'll be much more comfortable this way,' said Peter, consolingly.

Sally, suddenly and inexplicably, found herself of the opinion that comfort could be very much over-rated. But, as there was nothing she could do about it either way, she held her peace.

Peter came to stand behind her, wrapping his arms around hers, and hugging her to him. 'Don't let's fight about it, Sally. Not when he's not even coming.'

Sally accepted his embrace, leaning into him and allowing her head to fall back against his shoulder. That was one of the nicest things about Peter. If ever they'd had a disagreement over anything, he was always the first to make it all right again. He never held grudges and Sally had never heard him raise his voice.

'You're right,' she let her disgruntlement melt away as she turned within his arms and kissed him lightly on the mouth. 'I'm sorry for biting your head off. It's been a long day.'

Peter, encouraged by this demonstration of affection, showed every sign of turning her casual kiss into something more significant but the shrill ring of the phone broke the mood. Peter muttered a mild oath as Sally moved to answer it.

'That'll be Iris again, asking if I've heard anything yet.'

Peter, reluctant to relinquish her in the optimistic hope that, once she'd filled Iris in, they could carry on where they'd left off, followed her across the room and resumed his hold around her waist.

Chapter Four

'And finally, there's this,' Max gathered up the contracts they'd been going over and pushed two sheets of paper towards his client. 'That's the invite and my reply. Standard sort of thing.'

Justin picked up both and scanned their contents quickly. The name of the village and the church had piqued his interest but it was as he recognised the signature at the bottom of the invitation that his stomach lurched and his mouth went suddenly dry. S Marsh. His pulse quickened and he glanced up.

'You didn't think to consult me?'

'What am I doing now?'

'Presenting me with a done deal. Consultation is where opinions are sought. Usually.' He threw himself back in his chair, tossing the letter onto the desk in disgust.

Max rolled his eyes. The number of times he'd asked Justin to consider just such a charity gig! And the answer had always been exactly the same. No way. So, why was he creating a fuss over this one?

'Well, I know it's your neck of the woods, JT. That's why I'm keeping you in the loop, old chap. But as you never go for these kinds of things, I just fired off the standard 'prior commitments' letter, letting them down lightly.'

'It didn't occur to you to ask me first?'

'Why would I? I don't usually. Don't tell me you're actually considering doing it? Why?'

'Because she's asked me.'

'She? She who?' Seeking enlightenment, Max scooped the letter off the desk and studied it carefully. Justin regarded him, brows drawn in a classic and recognisable scowl of disapproval. Their eyes met. 'Ah…. S. Marsh. That wouldn't be S for Sally, would it? THE Sally?'

Justin, arms folded his arms across his broad chest and gave something which could have been a grunt of acknowledgment whilst his narrowed eyes under their stark, black brows challenged Max to make something of it.

Sally Marsh. He could see her now, in his mind's eye, quite clearly even after all this time, long, shimmering chestnut hair cascading over her shoulders, those deep, fathomless brown eyes gazing directly, intently into his. She'd written to invite him back.

And his agent had sent his apologies!

'Listen, old man,' Max leaned across the desk towards him. 'I know it's signed by her and all that but it does say she's the secretary of this committee. I wouldn't read too much into it if I were you. It's not as though it's a personal invitation or anything. She's probably acting under instructions, just doing what the chairman chap has told her to do.'

Justin straightened up impatiently, snatching the paperwork back. 'No-one could make that woman do something she didn't want to. I should know! No, if she's signed her name to that and had the nerve to mention 'our past close relationship',' he jabbed his finger at the offending passage, 'it's because she wanted to. Well, that's fine by me. In fact, it's given me the perfect excuse to do something I've been wanting to do for a very long time.'

Max, far too good an agent to believe the old adage that any publicity is good publicity, shifted uncomfortably in his chair. 'Just be careful, JT, eh? We've had a nice run of quiet from the tabloids. Don't want to do anything to rock the boat, do we? And revenge is a tricky thing, y'know. Nasty habit of backfiring.'

'Revenge?' Justin repeated the word musingly, rolling it around his mouth with relish. 'Now there's an idea…..' Then he caught Max's expression of consternation and allowed himself a saturnine smile. 'Nothing so melodramatic, Max. Let's just say this is something I need to get out of my system once and for all. An itch that has to be scratched.'

Max allowed himself a smile of nervous relief. 'A little piece of unfinished business?'

'Exactly. Couldn't have put it better myself.' Once more, Justin tossed the letter onto the desk. 'Call them and say I've changed my mind.'

Max blanched visibly and, in response, simply slid the schedule they'd been working on earlier towards him. 'Impossible!'

'Make it happen,' Justin pushed the schedule back at him.

'JT!' Max remonstrated, indicating the dates in question. 'You can see for yourself, you're booked solid. It can't be done.'

'Make it happen,' Justin repeated, deadly quiet. 'That's what I pay you for.'

'This is a charity gig,' Max muttered darkly. 'You do know that fifteen per cent of nothing is nothing?'

'Whereas fifteen per cent of the rest of the year is a tidy little sum,' Justin reminded him curtly. 'This isn't up for discussion, Max. Make it happen.' And flattening the letter of invitation on the desk so he could read it clearly, Justin picked up the phone and punched in the telephone number written at the top.

At the second ring, Sally answered, 'Hello?'

'Sally.' The single word confirmed he had recognised her voice instantly just as she had his. Even without her recent foray into the world of internet video links, Sally would have known immediately who was speaking.

'Justin?' she croaked, her mouth suddenly dry and her heart beginning a tattoo which threatened to deafen her. She pulled free of Peter's embrace and held him away from her, fending him off with her free hand. She had a sudden and ominous feeling that she was going to need to focus all her concentration on this call.

'I'm ringing to confirm arrangements,' Justin informed her brusquely.

'But..,' Sally stammered, 'The letter...Your agent....'

'Should have known better than to make any decisions regarding my schedule without consulting me first! A mistake I don't think he will be making again. However, that's irrelevant as far as you are concerned. What you need to know is that I am accepting the invitation to appear at your festival, subject, of course, to certain conditions.'

Of course, thought Sally now she'd recovered from her initial shock, there would be conditions. Get your pound of flesh, why don't you?

'Well that's very good news,' replied Sally's polite and infinitely more diplomatic alter ego. 'The committee will be delighted.'

17

'They haven't heard my conditions yet,' he observed dryly. 'Obviously, I am anxious that my name should be linked only to performances of the highest musical standards and I therefore have to insist that I appear not as guest conductor but as musical director of the entire festival. To ensure that everything runs to my satisfaction, I have cleared my diary for the three weeks preceding the festival weekend in order that I can oversee and where necessary lead the final rehearsals and thus guarantee the quality of the performances involved.'

Hundreds of miles apart, Max and Sally gulped simultaneously.

'But that would give you complete control over every aspect of the festival!' squeaked Sally.

'Three weeks, old boy?' Max's whisper was anguished.

Justin's reply was terse and uncompromising, 'Yes.'

It was clearly a 'take it or leave it' stance and totally non-negotiable. Whilst her brain was screaming at her not to accept under any circumstances, Sally found her treacherous mouth accepting his terms without demure. 'On behalf of the committee, I'm delighted to be able to accept those conditions. We're very grateful to you for giving up your time so generously.'

But Justin wasn't interested in her platitudes. 'You have my agent's number and e-mail address. All discussions regarding the programme for each concert will have to go through him. I also want to see biographies, or at least some idea of the background, of each performer or ensemble,' he dictated, rapidly. 'Performance times of the festival week itself and rehearsal schedules and venues for everyone taking part in the three weeks preceding it. I'm assuming the venue will be the church as the hall is, by your account, unusable at present. That will mean the nave will have to be cleared sufficiently to fit the full orchestra in and flexible seating arranged for maximum capacity. Oh, I also need your range of ticket prices. Don't worry about programmes, posters or fliers. If you forward the information I've requested promptly, someone at this end will deal with all of that.'

Sally managed to pull herself together sufficiently to claw back a little ground. 'We'll want to see proofs of any printed material before they go to press, just to ensure all the details are accurate.' And, she added to herself, to make sure this remains OUR festival and doesn't just turn into the Justin Trevelyan show.

Justin harrumphed in displeasure, 'Yes, I expected you would. Just don't spend too long dithering over them. We're on a very tight schedule for this and you'll need all the publicity you can get. Of course, your team will have to be responsible for distribution at your end.'

At this rate, thought Sally, 'my team' aka yours truly will be run ragged long before we get to the stage of putting up posters. Aloud she said, 'No problem. I'm sure we can manage that.'

'Good,' Justin didn't sound too convinced. 'I'm going to be out of the country from now on, so, as I said, any further arrangements will have to be made through my agent but I think we've covered all the essentials. Unless there's anything else you can think of?'

'No, I think you've been pretty thorough.' Though it was nice to be asked, finally.

'Fine. Good. Well,' Sally sensed a momentary and uncharacteristic hesitation on Justin's part. Then he said, 'Goodbye, then, Sally.' And the line went dead.

In London, Max O'Donaghue was clutching his head in disbelief having heard the deal his client had just struck.

In Cornwall, Sally Marsh felt very much the same. It was as if she'd just had a hefty blow to the solar plexus. She staggered to the chair nearest to her and sat down heavily. 'Goodness!'

Peter, philosophical in the face of her unusually brusque rejection of his advances, took the seat opposite. 'Problem?'

'No…' Sally sounded surprised, even to herself. 'At least, it depends on how you look at it.' Rapidly, she recounted the salient points of the phone conversation. 'So,' she concluded. 'He's coming for nearly a month all told and basically will be in charge of everything.

'Well,' said Peter, attempting, and failing, to judge exactly how Sally felt about this. He fell back on his default setting of finding the good in every situation. 'If he's going to sort it all out, that will mean less work for you. Which,' he placed his hand over hers and smiled diffidently, 'has to be good.'

Sally slid her hand out and placed it firmly in her lap. 'Hmm, possibly.' Personally, she was pretty sure having Justin 'in charge' would mean he would make impossible demands which someone, and she had a fair idea of who that someone would be, would have to see were met. 'That remains to be seen,' she told Peter doubtfully. 'He doesn't know anyone down here except me any more or how we do things. It'll probably mean I have to spend a lot of time with him, at least, for the first few days.'

Peter straightened up frowning, 'I'm not sure I like the sound of that. I think, if there are any meetings to be held, I should be included.' He caught the look Sally shot him across the table, 'or at any rate,' he amended, hastily, 'one of the other committee members. You can't be expected to shoulder all the responsibility.'

Sally regarded him through narrowed eyes, easily interpreting the sub-text. 'What's the matter, Peter? Don't you trust me?'

Peter took both her hands in his and held them fast, 'I trust you implicitly, you know that, but, after what you've told me about him, I wouldn't trust Trevelyan as far as I could throw him!'

Standing abruptly, Sally took her mug back to the kitchen and rinsed it out. 'Honestly Peter, get a grip. There is no way someone like Justin Trevelyan is going to be interested in a provincial little nobody like me.'

'He was before,' Peter pointed out reasonably, trailing after her.

The cupboard door slammed to as Sally replaced her mug. 'Thanks,' she answered wryly, noting he didn't dispute the phrase 'provincial little nobody', 'but that was years ago when we were both hardly more than kids. Justin moves in completely different circles now. He's famous, well-travelled, well-off and well-known for being difficult and demanding. I teach in a primary school and I'm engaged to a vicar. The only thing we still have in common is that we once happened to live in the same village.'

As the words left her lips, Sally was aware of a momentary pang of regret for her younger self. She had felt so full of excitement back then, had had such optimism that her life would be rich in experiences and full of happiness. And the plans that they had made together! Places they would visit, things they would do. Looking back now it seemed to Sally that Justin had achieved all his former goals and more, whilst her teenage dreams appeared destined to remain largely unfulfilled.

Get a grip, Sally Marsh, she chided herself sternly. Until that evening when Iris had had her stroke of evil genius, Sally had been completely content with her lot, busy and fulfilled, at the heart of village life with people who trusted and depended on her and a good, honest, straightforward man who loved her. Thoughts of jet-setting around the world hadn't crossed her mind in years and no good would come of indulging in such flights of fancy now. She gave herself a little shake. No, the sooner this whole festival thing was over and life returned to normal, the happier she would be. She wiped the sink round and turned slowly, drying her hands on a towel.

'So, what are your plans for this evening? Because,' she continued, barely giving him time to draw breath let alone answer, 'We've got tons to do now to get things ready in time and I need to get over to Iris's to fill her in so we can get started.' Sally smiled at him brightly, 'That's OK with you, love, isn't it?'

Resigned to an evening of his own company, Peter rose obediently, pecked her cheek and told her not to let Iris keep her at it too late.

As soon as he had left, Sally was galvanised into action. She switched on her laptop, logged on and opened up a fresh document. First, she made a list of all the items Justin had instructed her to e-mail to his London agent, Max O'Donaghue. After that, she made an additional list of things which she knew needed organising which the agent wouldn't get involved with such as ticket sales, distribution, refreshments, extra venues for when the church was in use, setting up and moving chairs, extra toilet facilities. She chewed her lip meditatively. Maybe the pub would help them out with that last one? She added 'ask The Pump about toilets' to the list and printed the whole lot off in duplicate. Then she put the pages neatly into a plastic wallet and headed over to Iris's.

In London, Max was still shaking his head and regarding his ruined schedule with an air of rueful desperation.

'I hope you know what you're doing, JT,' he sighed anxiously. 'Because I sure as hell don't.'

'Easy, I'm giving something back to the community that raised me.'

As Max had heard Justin's pithy comments on said community many times, he stared at him now in disbelief. 'Why?'

'Or,' Justin acknowledged the improbability of his last statement, 'think of it as a holiday.'

'A holiday?' queried Max.

'Yes, you know, a restful break between periods of work,' Justin adopted a patronising tone. 'You have them. Why shouldn't I?'

'Don't act the martyr with me, JT' Max admonished. 'You have holidays, jolly nice ones.'

'Yes, well, I'm due another one and this is it.'

'Except it won't be a break, will it? And given the emotional angst that's likely to be involved, I can't imagine it will be restful either.'

'Emotional angst?'

'Well, that's why you're going, isn't it? To see this Sally woman again? To rake over what went wrong and who said what to whom? More of a nightmare than a holiday, I'd have thought.'

'Like you said, I expect she's just the secretary. Probably has very little to do with the actual running of things. I'll probably hardly see her.'

'Well, if that's really what you thought, you wouldn't be bothering to go, would you? Clearly you intend to see her but I can't for the life of me work out what you hope to gain by it. What are you going to do? Ask her where it all went wrong before? Beg her to take you back and try again?'

'No!' Justin barked, slamming a hand down on the desk so sharply, Max jumped in his seat. 'I have no intention of doing anything of the kind! It's just....' A deep and ragged sigh welled up from deep within him. He raked a hand through his by now unruly hair and slumped back in his chair. 'It all happened so quickly, Max. One day, we were planning to spend the rest of our lives together and the next....it was all over. We had this row....we both said things and then, that was it. I never saw her, never even spoke to her again.'

Max regarded his client and friend closely. Never before had Justin spoken of any of this to him. Indeed, Max strongly suspected he'd never talked about it to anyone. Small but important pieces of the complicated puzzle that was Justin Trevelyan began to fall into place. Several long moments passed, then he came to a decision.

'OK. You're going to lose a serious amount of goodwill here, JT but, 'he raised a hand to cut off Justin's remonstrations, 'I know, you don't care what people think and if they don't want to book you again it's their loss not yours blah, blah blah. What I was going to say was, sometimes you just have to do what you just have to do and this appears to be one of those times. So, I'll back you. I'll rejig your schedule, I'll search out the stand-ins and I'll smooth all the ruffled feathers. I'll even liaise with Sally Marsh, get the publicity material up to scratch and generally do anything I can to make sure all the technical stuff runs smoothly. The rest, old man, is up to you.'

Justin thanked Max, briefly but sincerely. In a very few more minutes, their meeting was wrapped up. As he made his way outside and hailed a cab, Justin found Max's words echoing in his head. What did he hope to gain from this? Was he hoping she would not have aged well, that he would feel completely indifferent to her, that one sight of her would confirm to him that he had had, they both had, a lucky escape? Or perhaps they would just slot into the old, well-remembered camaraderie, the easy jokes, the shared silences that had preceded their sexual relationship? And although he hadn't been a complete innocent when they had got together, Sally Marsh had been his first proper sexual relationship, so would there be some latent attraction still lingering between them?

And what about the rest of them? He was honest enough and self-aware enough to admit that it would afford him no little pleasure to return to the village now as something of a hero, now that he had made good, proved so many of them wrong and achieved what he had set out to, professionally at least. There were others too, that whilst it was inevitable he should have lost touch with, he would be pleased to see again. Old school friends, rugby colleagues. How many of them were still living locally, he wondered? Sally's Mum too. He'd always got on with her and though of course she'd have taken Sally's side in any argument, he was pretty sure she wouldn't hold a grudge and, if Sally could bring herself to welcome him, her mother would follow suit. All in all, he found himself looking forward to his month or so in Cornwall with a feeling of pleasurable anticipation. And let's face it, if things didn't quite according to plan, he could always come back early. It would be no skin off his nose, would it?

Chapter Five

Sally had known Iris her whole life. When, in her early forties, Gelda Marsh found herself a delighted but rather bewildered first-time mother, their next-door neighbour had become an invaluable source of friendship, support and hands-on baby-sitting. And when Sally had suddenly lost her father, to an undiagnosed heart condition, and had then nursed her mother through cancer, Iris had become more like a Grandmother to her than ever. Sometimes she drove Sally mad with her unsolicited advice and rather fussing manner. But as the advice, however unwelcome, was always very sound, and her fussiness hid a sharp intellect and dry sense of humour, Sally willingly tolerated both. Equally, Sally knew that she often drove Iris to distraction with her easy acceptance of life in the village and her role within it.

'I worry about you, Sally dear, I really do. You're getting middle-aged before your time,' Iris was used to say, shaking her head in despair.

Sally laughed at her concerns. Although she had a few close female friends of her own age, having had elderly parents, Sally naturally gravitated towards the older inhabitants and happily served alongside them on most of the village clubs and committees.

Now, seated in Iris's over-crowded, over-heated front parlour, Sally lost no time in bringing her old friend up to speed with the latest events.

'I must say, everything seems to be turning out incredibly well, dear, better than I'd dared hope,' said Iris, pleased as punch that her original idea had borne so much fruit. 'I have to say too, that I never knew him well but Justin Trevelyan always struck me as a rather wild young man and, of course, I assumed something dreadful must have happened for you to have broken with him so completely...' she paused giving Sally ample opportunity to enlighten her. An opportunity Sally had no intention of taking. What would be the point of stirring it all up again now? She simply smiled and waited for Iris to continue. 'But he can't be all that bad to be giving so freely of his time and expertise, especially as he doesn't stand to gain anything personally.'

In the short walk to Iris's house, Sally had herself pondered Justin's motives. Why would he give up a month of his time, clearing his diary as he'd said, to help raise funds for a village with which he had no current connections? She had finally decided it must have been a decision rashly made in a fit of pique with his agent when he discovered that unfortunate individual had turned down Sally's invitation without asking him first. But, as Iris currently seemed to be so much in charity with him, and it would help if at least one of them was, Sally did not share this theory with her. Instead she said, 'Well, whatever the reason, I think we should just grab what he's offering with both hands and get as much as we can out of it.'

Iris nodded. 'A little crudely put, my dear, but I agree whole heartedly with the sentiment.'

They settled down to a serious discussion of Sally's notes and within a very short time, the bulk of the plans were laid. All that remained to be done was to run them past Max O'Donaghue and Bob Helmsworth for the official seals of approval and then put them into action.

Over the next weeks, Sally developed a strangely obsessive love-hate relationship with her gmail account. She found herself scouring her phone for e-mails as soon as she woke up, checking it again as soon as she came through the front door at the end of the day and at regular intervals throughout the evening. Justin, and by association Max, did not like to wait for an answer and appeared to expect immediate replies to every query. It was with some difficulty that Sally had explained to Max that there was no point trying to reach her on her mobile during the day; she could hardly take a call with twenty-eight pairs of little ears listening in, and she didn't think her Headteacher would be very pleased about it if she tried to! So, Max e-mailed her. He e-mailed her incessantly.

When the idea of a music festival had first been muted, Sally had fondly imagined it would be a case of asking a variety of good local musicians what they would like to play and then simply writing out a list of their chosen pieces. Apparently, it was a lot more complicated than that. Apparently, certain pieces couldn't be played next to each other because they were in the wrong musical key. And others required completely different groups of performers and seating arrangements so couldn't be scheduled one after the other for risk of boring the audience whilst all the chairs and music stands were moved around.

Then, Peter put his foot down and, as Sally knew, when it came to his religion, his was a very heavy and intractable foot indeed, particularly with the added weight of the Bishop behind it. There were only certain pieces he would countenance being played in the church, especially at Easter, and on that he was absolutely immoveable. As he was too, on the timings of the church services on Good Friday and Easter Sunday. Justin, whose music was his religion, appeared to think Peter was being deliberately obstructive and a lengthy four-way correspondence ensued during which Sally and Max displayed all the skills of international peacekeepers.

Eventually, mutual agreement was reached on the pieces for the sacred days of the Easter weekend. Good Friday would see the key services taking place as usual, with an unobjectionable programme of classical chamber pieces in the afternoon and Bach's solemn and sacred St Matthew Passion being performed in the evening. Following evensong on Easter Sunday, a classical concert of Mozart in the first half would be rounded off by the joyous Choral Symphony by Beethoven after the interval.

By the time all this had been sorted out, Sally and Max were firm virtual friends; he seemed to have taken the whole project to heart. It was Max who arranged for the television trails of the festival with footage of the idyllically pretty church, marred by a glimpse of the currently dilapidated hall in the background, interspersed with stills of Justin looking broodingly handsome or wielding a baton with panache. And, when Sally had done the maths and realised that, even if every ticket for every performance were sold, they would still be a long way off their required total, it was Max who persuaded Justin to agree to host 'celebrity' lunches before the preconcert talks.

'Jesus, they'll be wanting blood, next!' Justin exclaimed, pacing round his hotel room with a score in one hand and his mobile in the other.

'But you'll be there anyway, you have to eat and there's little point going to all this trouble and still ending short of the total,' Max reminded him persuasively.

'I know! I know! Just so long as I'm not spending the whole time kowtowing to a bunch of cloth-ears with more money than musical sense. I'll need all the rehearsal time I can get, God knows what kind of standard

I'm going to find when I get down there, and I won't stand for celebrity lunch stunts getting in the way!' he'd insisted.

'You're going to have plenty of time to rehearse. The lunches only happen right at the end just before each afternoon performance so you'll have had all the rehearsals by then. You just have to turn up, look sexy, smile a bit and sound intelligent. Nothing you haven't done before, old man.'

'Yes, I'm really going to feel like doing that, aren't I?' Justin continued to complain. 'And when am I going to find the time to write these pre-concert talks, Max? I've got back to back rehearsals and shows here and then I'm straight down to Cornwall!'

Max didn't point out that Justin had the option of putting the phone down and starting straight away. He didn't point out that Justin had only himself to blame for getting involved in the first place. Instead he said,

'I know, old man, tough schedule. But you'll get it all done, same as you always do. And just think how pleased the lovely Ms Marsh will be when all that money comes rolling in!'

'Hmph! She bloody better be,' Justin muttered darkly.

Max couldn't resist adding naughtily, 'And grateful too.'

'That's NOT why I am doing this!'

'No? Remind me again just exactly why you are doing it then.'

'I'm doing it because…because,' he floundered. 'Because an old friend has asked me to help them out. And because I can.'

'No ulterior motive then?'

'Max!' Justin growled warningly.

'Of course, I haven't met the lady in question but she sends the sweetest e-mails and, for someone not in the business, is incredibly on the ball and organised. I'd say she has a lot going for her. You could do worse, old boy.'

'Oh, fuck off, Max!' Justin jabbed at the off button, slung both his mobile and the now redundant score roughly onto the bed and collapsed heavily beside them. He stared at the ceiling wondering, as he had done a hundred times since speaking to Sally on the phone, just exactly what he did hope to gain by going back, by doing this damn stupid festival.

He'd be lying if he said he hadn't thought of her over the years. He had. Not frequently, certainly not daily. But often enough. More often, if he was honest with himself, than he thought of any other of his exes. More often than he wanted to, really.

27

He wondered why.

He was long over her, of course he was. Had replaced her easily, almost immediately and had hardly been single since. But Max was right. Somehow with the weird, unsociable hours, the travelling and never being with the same group of people for more than a few weeks at a time, he'd never formed such a close relationship with anybody since. When it seemed as though he might, it was almost as if Sally Marsh was there, looking over his shoulder, inviting some kind of idealised comparison that other women stood no chance of living up to. And now, a seemingly endless stream of e-mails and phone calls fielded and forwarded by Max were keeping her constantly at the forefront of his mind.

So. Justin sat up suddenly as if reaching a conclusion. It would be good to see her again in the flesh, to remind himself, to remind them both, of how utterly unsuitable they had been for each other, what a lucky escape they had both had. To finally…., what was that Godawful expression Americans used? That was it; closure. To finally bring some closure to their ancient affair. Well, the best way of doing that as far as Justin could see was to make sure that he spent as much time in her company as he possibly could.

And he knew exactly how to do that. Bring it on.

Chapter Six

Sally awoke, immediately aware of an almost overpowering feeling of dread. She blinked, giving her eyes time to become accustomed to the dawn light filtering in round the edges of the curtains and her brain time to remember just what it was that was causing her such anxiety. Then it came to her. Today was the day. The day she'd been anticipating and dreading for weeks and weeks. The day that Justin Trevelyan would be arriving.

In a few short hours, she'd drive to the station to meet him, then they would travel in her car, with him sitting right there, next to her as she ferried him to the best hotel in the area. Today was the day that she would see him in the flesh for the first time in years.

She pulled the duvet over her head wanting nothing more than to go back to yesterday or wind on to tomorrow, or, better still, fast forward to a month's time when the whole festival would be over.

Ten minutes, she promised herself. Just ten more minutes of not thinking about anything, before I get up. She closed her eyes again, snuggled down into the delicious warmth of her bed and willed herself to relax. But her mind was less obedient than her body and, in spite of her physical comfort, it refused to settle on any subject other than Justin Trevelyan.

As a child he had slid in and out of her life, on the periphery of her acquaintance as his family followed his naval father. They lived in quarters on longer postings, returning to the family home in the village if Commander Trevelyan was going to be based at the local air station, RNAS Culdrose, for any length of time. Then, one day, Justin Trevelyan had become much more than a passing acquaintance. Sally remembered it as if it had been yesterday.

Back from Uni for the Christmas holidays, she'd been using the playing fields as a short cut home from the bus stop, her mind full of shopping and parties, totally oblivious to what was going on around her. As she'd stepped through the bushes lining the footpath onto the edge of the field, Justin had come thundering up the left wing of the rugby pitch, flung himself full length onto the ball and skidded to a halt at her feet, spattering her legs with mud. She'd squealed in surprise and looked down to see him grinning wickedly up at her through a thatch of sweat-slicked black curls. He'd got to his feet, and stood looming over her, six foot two of muscled male beauty. Subjecting her to a long, lingering appraisal, he'd tossed the ball nonchalantly from hand to hand before lobbing it casually back towards his team mates.

'Hi, sorry about that, didn't see you there,' he attempted to wipe his right hand clean on his thigh, before extending it her. 'Justin, Justin Trevelyan.' He'd paused, obviously waiting for her to supply her own name but Sally, heart still pounding from the shock of seeing him skidding towards her, furious at the state of her new jeans, and becoming uncomfortably aware of the shouts and jeers of his fellow players, backed quickly away from him.

'Whoa!' he'd stepped towards her, laying a restraining mud-caked hand on her arm. 'Don't rush off like a frightened rabbit....' Then he'd paused, coolly looking her over once again from head to toe. 'No, not a rabbit, more a fawn, yes, Bambi, all huge eyes and long legs.'

He'd accompanied it with a devastating smile, clearly expecting his easy compliment to have its usual winning effect. Sally, loathing the endless legs which placed her head and shoulders above her girlfriends, had bristled at the comparison and retorted stingingly, 'I'd rather be a fawn with at least some pretentions to intelligence than an...an ox, wallowing in the mud!' And she'd whipped away out of his grasp and back the way she had come, his casual laughter ringing in her ears.

No wonder he'd laughed. The moment she said it, she'd realised that her quick rejoinder hadn't come out slick and sophisticated as she'd intended but snobbish and pretentious. All the way home, cheeks burning in embarrassment, she had comforted herself with the thought that she would probably never see him again so it really didn't matter.

Later that evening, she'd realised just how wrong she'd been. The doorbell had rung and she'd been amazed to find Justin on the front step. Justin, in pristine white T-shirt and dark jacket over fashionably baggy blue jeans, clutching a small posy of pink rosebuds and looking even more impossibly handsome now that he was showered and shaved than he had in his rugby kit.

'The Bambi comment was crass,' he'd admitted without preamble, holding the flowers out to her. 'I apologise.'

Sally had opened her mouth to apologise in her turn but as her limpid brown eyes met his piercing blue ones fully for the first time, the words had died on her lips and she'd been totally lost…

Enough! Sighing impatiently, Sally threw back the covers and got up. Today was going to be difficult enough without all this misty-eyed reminiscing. Whether Justin had been, or indeed still was, gorgeous, should be neither here nor there to her.

She wandered out of her bedroom into the tiny bathroom and switched on the shower. Undressing, she caught sight of herself in the mirror and stopped, suddenly, turning this way and that to look at herself more closely. In spite of her good resolutions, she couldn't help but wonder what Justin would make of her now.

She still had the same wide-set, dark brown eyes, thickly lashed and rounded with just the hint of a smile line appearing at the corners; the same endless long legs that she'd had at school. He'd been right, of course. She had been all huge brown eyes and gangly legs. She recognised now that both were a positive asset but though she had got used to her height, she'd never grown to like it. She leaned forward, peering at her face, noting the creamy complexion framed by the same almost waist-length, silky brown hair. Her gaze travelled downwards. She'd been skinny back then. She smoothed her hands over her still flat stomach then up and under her breasts. Sally wrinkled her nose, critically. She'd definitely filled out a bit on top though and got a bit curvy over the hips too. But the last time she'd seen Justin, she'd still been a student, just a slip of a girl. Now she was a woman, with a woman's figure and, she reminded herself sternly, with a woman's self-control. Something told her that, over the next few weeks, she was going to need as much of the latter as she could muster.

Shivering, Sally turned away from the mirror and jumped into the shower. It shouldn't matter to her what Justin thought of her now. He was nothing to her, after all. But honesty forced her to acknowledge that it did matter. It mattered very much. If his images on the internet were anything to go by, the years had been very kind to him. He was even more impossibly attractive now than ever and Sally was woman enough not to want him to compare her too unfavourably with her younger self.

With some difficulty, she managed to stop herself dressing up. Just her usual jeans, vest top and little cardigan would be quite appropriate for chauffeuring Justin Trevelyan around. The same lick of mascara and touch of lip gloss as always, a casual twist of her hair into a low bun to keep it out of the way. There. Once more she surveyed herself in the mirror. Not bad, she acknowledged. Not glamorous, not beautiful but certainly acceptable. Now, only four and half hours to get through before he was due to arrive.

Chapter Seven

Sally felt far too restless to do anything that required concentration like marking books or checking ticket orders. But there were still a couple of boxes of posters and fliers that needed distributing so she decided to get on with those. Driving round the countryside asking anywhere with a display window to advertise the festival should help take her mind off things a bit. It was a beautiful spring day, bright but chilly. She slipped on a jacket and pair of gloves, loaded up the car and set off.

It was a time-consuming business. It was usually not too difficult to get posters and fliers displayed in larger venues and public spaces. Owners of smaller businesses though, were not always so ready to sacrifice a large slice of window space without a thorough explanation of the cause. It often required all Sally's well-honed powers of persuasion and a good few minutes' discussion before she got the result she wanted. Lunchtime was approaching and Sally was just thinking about stopping for a break when her phone bleeped. The text was simple and to the point.

'J not getting train. Pick up from Perranporth airfield. eta 2.15pm. Max.'

Sally flung the phone down in disgust. She had exchanged umpteen e-mails over the train booking, first class, of course. Now Max was telling her to pick Justin up from the airfield! And she'd have to really get a move on to be there by 2.15. Typical Justin, she fumed. Changing arrangements at the last minute, expecting me just to drop everything and come running. She turned the car around and drove off. Lunch would have to wait.

Just as Sally was pulling up into the airfield car park, a small private plane was making what looked to her like a perfect landing. She watched for a moment, fascinated, as it drew smoothly to a halt and the pilot alighted. She had never been to the airfield before, let alone picked someone up there and she had no idea what the procedure was. She got out of her car, locked it and began walking towards the only building which didn't appear to be an aircraft hangar, a low, single-storey box so square it could have been constructed from lego. A shout behind her made her turn back to the open field, and stop dead in her tracks.

And there he was, silhouetted against the skyline, tall, broad and moving rapidly towards her.

A small part of her brain registered that the scene was just like a clip from a film, an old one, Top Gun or some Bond movie. The remainder of her brain was entirely taken up with Justin Trevelyan. He halted in front of her, his powerful, six foot two frame looming over her, one eyebrow raised quizzically, studying her closely. Sally's mouth went dry, her stomach knotted and she found it inexplicably difficult to breathe. She could not have spoken if she'd tried.

The airfield was not busy. A single light aircraft buzzed overhead. In the distance a lone male voice called out. Birds sang and the trees rustled gently in the breeze. But Justin was oblivious to everything except the woman standing before him.

When he'd thought about this moment, as of course he had over the past month or so, he'd limited his imaginings to the purely prosaic, what they'd say, where they'd be, how she'd look. He'd never dreamed that just the sight of her would affect him like this. God, but she was beautiful!

Instinctively he moved, seizing her by the shoulders. He pulled her roughly to him and clamped his mouth firmly on hers.

Momentarily, Sally tensed, fought the kiss. Then her body relaxed against his, moulding itself to the well-remembered contours, her lips parted of their own accord and all conscious thought was suspended. He released his savage hold and swept her into his arms, deepening the kiss as his tongue found hers. Mindlessly, Sally wound her arms around his neck, her fingers twined amongst the unruly curls as her body surrendered itself to his.

Finally, they drew apart. For a long second, she remained within his arms, staring up at that handsome face, into those darkly intense blue eyes. Then, as she regained control of her breathing and discovered to her surprise that her legs would, in fact, still hold her weight, she struggled upright and released herself from his hold.

Justin stepped back too, watching her carefully, realising her response to him had been as visceral and instinctive as his to her. Maybe getting her out of his system wasn't going to be quite as straightforward as he'd imagined. Exercising iron self-will, he regained control of his breathing, tipped his head to one side and treated her to his most disarming grin.

'Hi, Sal,' then, when she didn't answer his nonchalant greeting, 'What's the matter? Cat got your tongue?'

'Huh!' stung by his casual tone, Sally managed at last to find her voice. 'My ability to come up with a suitable response appears to have gone the same way as your manners and good taste!'

Well, what was she supposed to say to someone who, having not even spoken to her for years and years, suddenly reappears out of the sky like some avenging angel and kisses her senseless? Angry with Justin but even more so with herself for responding to him so wantonly, Sally stomped off towards the car, unlocking it from a distance as she approached. A minion appeared from somewhere and put a considerable number of cases and bags in the boot before backing off with a friendly wave. Justin paused to call out a word of thanks then swung himself into the passenger seat beside her.

'So,' he continued conversationally. 'What's the problem? Is it my mode of transport or my greeting that's put your back up?' Sally remained resolutely silently. 'Sal?' He turned in his seat to face her and, even side-on, she could feel the heat of his mega-watt smile. 'You're clearly desperate to let rip so, please, don't let any consideration for my feelings stand in your way.'

Desperately, she tried to hold her tongue but she just couldn't do it. As she backed out of the parking space, words exploded from her. 'Your choice of transport is monumentally ostentatious and your greeting was presumptuous to say the least!' Oh God, what was she saying? It was just like their first encounter all over again! What was it about him that made her so….pompous?

The sharp crack of his laughter rent the air. 'Nicely put, Sal,' his tone was admiring. 'You always did have a flair for words. But, as ever, your reasoning is flawed. You can't deny the greeting was both pleasurable and appropriate.'

'Appropriate?' Sally couldn't believe her ears. 'You call that… that… kiss an appropriate way of saying hello to someone you haven't seen for God knows how long?'

'Making up for lost time, sweetheart. And I note you didn't attempt to deny it was pleasurable,' his smug tone had Sally almost incandescent. 'As for flying,' he continued smoothly, ignoring her gasp of rage, 'it's simply practical. It takes half the time, I need to keep my flying hours up and it's convenient to have my own plane handy should I wish to make a quick getaway.'

'Why would you want to do that?' Angry as she was, the thinly veiled threat was not lost on her. Surely even Justin Trevelyan wouldn't back out on them at this point?

'Ah, Sally,' finally, caressingly, he used her full name. 'We both know there's only one reason I'm here and only one reason I'll be staying,' he paused tantalisingly.

'Well?' she demanded abruptly.

'Curiosity, of course, about you.'

Sally tutted in exasperation. 'Then I'm afraid you are going to be sadly disappointed. I live a very dull life, the details of which would doubtless bore you stupid.'

He subjected her to a long calculating stare, the kind of stare that made Sally's skin grow hot. 'On the contrary, if the last ten minutes are anything to go by, I don't think I'm going to be bored at all. At least, let's hope not. You wouldn't want me heading back prematurely now would you?'

Sally slapped down the left-hand indicator and screeched to a halt in a passing place, causing the car behind to swerve wildly. She took a deep breath, drew the remaining shreds of her dignity around her and turned to face him.

'Personally,' she informed him, fighting to keep her tone even, 'I couldn't give a damn whether you stayed or not but,' she went on quickly, not giving him time to respond to that statement, 'as a lot of other people have worked extremely hard to make this festival a success, I'm not going to be the one responsible for ruining it. Well, don't worry. I've got the message loud and clear. You're happy to stay as long as I do exactly as I'm told. So, you tell me how high and I'll jump.'

Having got that off her chest, Sally indicated once more and pulled out carefully onto the road.

'Good. In that case, you won't mind turning round and heading back in the other direction.'

'What?' In spite of the narrowness of the winding road, she risked a quick look at his face. His expression was utterly impassive. 'Justin, you wouldn't really dump us in it like that, would you?'

'Well, that remains to be seen, doesn't it? Entirely depending, as you so correctly surmised, on how well you meet my needs,' he let that particular phrase sink in before continuing, 'but I haven't been away so long that I don't realise you are going in the wrong direction.'

'But I'm not. I booked you into Lawncrest, as directed by your agent.'

'Oh no, sweetheart. I spend forty weeks of the year in hotels. I have no intention of slumming it in some two-star backwater for the next four of them.'

'It's not two-star! It's five and it's got that TV chef, you know the blonde one, running its restaurant. Max said that would be acceptable. I had the devil of a job getting you in there as the season's already started and it's so much in demand. I'm sure you'll be very comfortable. Heaven knows its going to cost enough.'

'You should be pleased I've changed my mind about it then, shouldn't you?'

'So where are you staying? I didn't realise you still had connections in this area.'

'Only one connection, Sal,' he corrected her, his eyes glinting ominously.

'Oh no!' Sally remonstrated as his meaning became clear to her. 'No, you can't mean…'

'Absolutely,' his tone was almost unbearably self-assured. 'I'm going to stay with you. I always did get on well with your mother.'

'But she's….,' Sally broke off. She didn't want to have that conversation with him at this point, for some reason feeling inexplicably disappointed in him that he didn't already know. It was still too raw and painful to talk about and she needed to be strong at that moment to deal with his impossible demands.

She subsided into silence, victim of a bitter internal wrangle. She knew she should tell him, about her mother, about the move, about the fact that he really should take the room at the hotel. But he'd been so unreasonable, so highhanded since the moment he'd stepped out of that plane that, instead, the desire for vengeance got the better of common sense. At the next available turning, she indicated yet again, swung the car round and headed back the way they'd come. Fine, Justin Trevelyan, if you want to stay with me instead of in a luxury five-star hotel, you can. On your own head be it!

Aloud she said casually, 'Could you possibly call Lawncrest then? If they're able to book the room out again, we may not get charged a cancellation fee.' Justin complied and soon Sally had the satisfaction of knowing that his boats had been well and truly burned.

A short time later, Sally was pulling up outside her little cottage. She was amused but not surprised to note the puzzled look on Justin's face.

'Here we are then,' she trilled, as she got out and went to get his bags from the boot. 'Home sweet home.'

When Justin had known her before, she had lived with her parents in a spacious bungalow next door to Iris Girton. What he had no way of knowing was that it had been sold off long ago to pay the fees on her mother's care home and Sally was now the proud owner of a mortgage on a tiny cottage.

Realisation was beginning to dawn as Justin got out of the car, grabbed the remaining luggage and followed her in, needing to bend his head as he went through the front door. Sally went straight up the stairs to the spare room.

She loved her little house. Granite-built over two hundred years ago, there was a kitchen and main living room downstairs and she had had the conservatory built on the back across the width of the house. This, much the largest room in the cottage, had been the regular meeting place of several committees, ever since the church hall had been placed out of bounds.

Upstairs were two small bedrooms separated by a miniscule bathroom. Sally's room had a single bed and therefore room for a narrow wardrobe and chest of drawers as well. The spare room had a four foot six bed and a hanging rail to the left of the small but decorative fireplace. Apart from that, there was no storage space for clothes and only just enough room to edge round the bed on either side. Dumping her load on the only available floor space, Sally crossed to the window and drew the curtains back fully.

38

'A bit cramped I'm afraid,' she informed him unnecessarily, turning just in time to see him crack his head painfully on one of the low beams.

He swore under his breath. If only he'd read that damn letter more carefully! How had he not noticed her change of address?

Because once he'd seen her signature, he'd felt …. What? Surprise? Shock? Hope, maybe? And he'd decided instantly to accept her invitation no matter what obstacles Max might put in his way. Just as seeing her again in the flesh had confirmed instantly his half-formed idea that staying at her place would be infinitely preferable to being put up in a hotel. So here he was. Trapped by his own impetuosity into living in a doll's house for the next four weeks. Of course, he could still leave and go to a hotel, if he wanted to…But where would be the fun in that?

Sally felt a momentary pang of guilt as she watched him ruefully rubbing his forehead. 'That's karma, Justin Trevelyan!' she thought and an irresistible bubble of laughter welled in her throat. Their eyes met. She recognised in his, an unmistakeable glint of appreciation and suddenly she couldn't help herself. As the bubble surfaced and broke, a fully-fledged giggling fit took hold of her. Justin's lips twitched in response and suddenly the tension which had crackled between them ever since he'd stepped from the plane, ebbed away and with it the passage of time. His throaty chuckle filled the room and they were both nineteen again.

'You little bitch!' he accused without rancour, 'I'm going to get you for that.' Still smiling, he reached out for her but Sally was too quick. She squealed, leaped onto and across the bed, making it to the door just as he did.

'No, you don't,' he blocked her exit, lunging towards her, catching her in a rugby tackle that brought her down heavily onto the pillows. Effortlessly, he flipped her onto her back and held her pinned beneath him.

'Let me go, you brute!' Sally laughed up at him, wriggling helplessly under his weight.

Suddenly, they were both still.

He could smell minty toothpaste on her breath and the well-remembered delicate scent of her skin. Her eyes held his briefly, synchronised as they widened, the pupils dilating. Then he allowed his gaze to travel over her face, drinking in the details. The slender, arching brows, the flawless skin taught over high cheekbones, the delicate, aquiline nose. Finally, they came to rest on her lips, moistened, slightly parted. His stomach contracted and he dipped his head, touching his mouth to hers, permitting himself an exquisite butterfly kiss of infinite tenderness. He saw her eyes close, felt her body melt beneath his, and gave himself up to the moment.

'Sally?' A male voice called up from downstairs.

Suddenly, Justin found himself ignominiously tipped off as Sally leaped into guilty action.

'Up here, Peter,' she answered, hastily straightening her jacket. 'Stay there, I'm just coming.' Sally pressed gloved hands to her burning cheeks and hissed at Justin to get up, her eyes pleading silently with him to comply.

'What the fuck's going on, Sal?' he demanded in a whisper, obediently rising to his feet as Peter's steps sounded on the stairs.

'Sally? What's going on?' echoed Peter as he reached the doorway, taking in the suitcases and Justin's towering presence. Sally cleared her throat and began a slightly rambling explanation.

'I'm going to be staying with Sally,' Justin cut her off. 'It's pointless paying out on expensive hotel bills when Sally and I are...' there was the briefest hesitation, 'old friends.' He extended a hand. 'Justin Trevelyan. And you are?'

It was dislike at first sight. Justin squared his shoulders and narrowed his eyes. Peter drew himself up to his full height, which still left him a good few inches short of Justin. He gave the proffered hand a single abrupt shake.

'Peter Laity. Vicar of St Piran's, the church we're raising funds for. And,' he paused, looking from one to the other, obviously feeling the need to stake his claim, 'Sally's fiancé.'

Justin, receiving this news with complete impassivity, made no comment. Peter, however, had more to say, to Sally at least. 'Is that entirely appropriate, Sally? To have Mr Trevelyan staying with you?'

Once again Sally began a rather convoluted reply and once again Justin cut her off.

'Entirely appropriate. We've known each other since we were children. And, as Sally is engaged,' he emphasised the word heavily, causing a blush to rise on Sally's cheeks, 'to you, Vicar, there can be no question of any impropriety, can there, Sally?'

Sally, only too conscious of the impropriety that there had been only minutes before, shook her head furiously. 'No, of course not, absolutely.'

'Now,' Justin moved towards the door, holding it open and smoothly ushering Peter and Sally out onto the landing, 'if you don't mind, Sally and I have a lot of sorting out to do and we really need to get on.'

Outmanoeuvred, Peter retreated down the stairs. 'Well, I expect I'll see you later then, Sally. Goodbye Mr Trevelyan.'

'Justin, please,' responded Justin suavely, then closed the front door behind him and turned to face a red-faced Sally. He raised one eyebrow in mocking enquiry, 'Engaged, Sal? To a vicar? At what point were you thinking of filling me in on that minor detail?'

Sally found to her surprise that she was no longer feeling guilty. No, what she was feeling was a deep and seething anger that he had put her in the position she was in. She folded her arms across her chest and faced him squarely.

'Maybe I'd have told you when you stopped giving me orders and actually took the trouble to ask me how I was! Maybe it would have come up in conversation, if we'd had any. Then maybe you'd also have found out that actually both my parents are dead, that I had to sell the bungalow to pay for Mum's care home fees and that's why you've invited yourself to stay in something only marginally bigger than a caravan!'

Sally turned on her heel and marched into the kitchen. She wrenched open the cupboard door, took out two mugs and slammed them onto the worktop. Then she overfilled the kettle and flicked its switch on so hard it bounced and shot water everywhere. Damn him! Damn Justin Trevelyan and his deep, dark blue eyes and his chiselled good looks and his bloody charming smile. Give her Peter any day. Calm, honest, good-natured Peter who was always there when she needed him and never, ever made her feel so murderously angry!

'Sal?' Justin's voice broke into her furious internal monologue. She placed her hands flat on the work top, took a couple of deep breaths and turned round to face him.

'It's Sally, actually, Justin. Not Sal. No-one ever calls me that any more. It's Sally, OK?' she watched as a strange expression flitted momentarily across his handsome features.

'Sally,' he repeated obediently. 'I'll try to remember. Anyway, I'm sorry. You're right. I've been appallingly inconsiderate all day,' he raked a hand through his hair and gave a slight, self-deprecating laugh. 'It's a bit of a weird situation you have to admit.'

Sally regarded him suspiciously, 'Not made any less weird by you insisting on staying here.'

'Would it surprise you to know I was actually looking forward to that?'

'It would, actually, when Max made such a song and dance about you staying in a hotel.'

'Oh Max,' he flicked his fingers dismissively. 'That's his job, to get the best deal out of things. It would be stupid me staying in a hotel with you still living here.' He folded his arms and rested a shoulder against the door jamb. 'I always remember such happy times at your place. And I really did feel I got on with your parents.'

A smile softened Sally's face. She remembered happy times too. And he was right, her parents had adored him. His own mother, whose family owned several local farms of substantial acreage, had been, as Justin sardonically put it, 'frightfully county' and had liked to entertain lavishly. During the long holidays, when he wasn't practising the piano or throwing himself round a rugby pitch, Justin had escaped her frequent social gatherings by hanging out in Sally's room, on his back at the bottom of her bed, legs vertical against the wall, listening to music on his iPod and ostensibly working, whilst Sally, curled up at the pillow end, scrawled pages of essays and devoured her set books. And Sally's Mum, an inveterate nurturer, had kept him supplied with huge plates of wholesome food and her father had taken a real interest in his future plans.

'It would just have been nice to have been asked in advance,' she chided him gently, now.

'I wanted to keep my options open. Let's face it, it's been a long time and I wasn't sure what kind of a reception I was going to get.'

It crossed Sally's mind to ask him what kind of reception he thought he deserved but she was anxious not to say or do anything else controversial. Not yet, anyway.

'Well, you're here now, so I suppose we'd better both make the best of it,' Sally turned her attention back to the kettle. 'Still milk and one?'

'Ah, no. Half-caf, Colombian, skinny latte, hold the sprinkles for me, please, Sal.'

She turned, about to give him a piece of her mind, then as she caught the wickedly teasing gleam in his eye, she realised he was taking the rise out of her again, and she couldn't help but return his smile. He always did know how to make her laugh.

They carried their drinks through to the conservatory and had just sat down when Sally's stomach grumbled loudly. She clutched a hand to it, embarrassed.

'Goodness. I've just realised. I missed out on lunch and I'm starving. I'll have to go and make a sandwich or something. How about you?'

Justin admitted that he was as hungry as she was having also skipped a midday meal. 'But listen, it's my fault you missed out and I'm well aware I'm causing you loads of trouble,' he held up a hand to silence her as she would have disagreed with him. 'No, you weren't expecting me. I foisted myself on you, so the least I can do is take you out for a meal somewhere nice to make up for it.'

'No, honestly, there's no need. I can easily make us something here,' knowing the contents, or rather lack of them, in the fridge, Sally admitted to herself that that was going to be something of a challenge but there was no way she was telling him that. Something in her expression must have given her away.

'You weren't expecting me,' he remonstrated. 'You probably don't have much in. It makes much more sense for us to go out.'

A tiny part of Sally was tempted, sorely tempted, but she knew she mustn't give in. 'Justin, we can't! I can't! You've just told Peter we have tons to do. I can't go swanning off for dinner with you.'

'Ah,' he leaned back lazily in his chair and surveyed her through narrowed eyes. 'Now we're getting to it. Afraid of upsetting the Pious Peter, are you?'

Sally flushed angrily. 'Of course not. But you must admit it would look a bit odd, us going out for dinner as soon as you've arrived, especially as you practically threw him out on the pretext of us having work to do.'

'Being engaged to someone doesn't mean you can't go out for dinner with an old friend, you know, Sal.'

'It's Sally, for the hundredth time!' she reminded him tetchily. 'And of course, Peter wouldn't mind me going for dinner with an old friend. It's just…' she floundered, suddenly unable to put her fears into words.

'It's just what, Sally?' he asked quietly, steepling his fingers and studying her intently.

She threw herself back in her seat, angrily, 'Well, you're hardly just an old friend are you?'

43

'No?' his voice was barely audible now. 'Then how would you describe me?'

A strange stillness descended on them. Sally drew in a huge shuddering breath. She looked up slowly, her eyes meeting his directly.

'You broke my heart, you bastard!'

If she'd hoped for a dramatic response, she got none. He merely smiled slightly and answered, in a voice so neutral they could have been discussing the weather, 'Strangely, that's not quite how I remember it, Sally.' Then he rose and headed for the doorway. 'We still have to eat,' he pointed out in the same colourless tone. 'Give me your car keys and I'll head into town and get a takeaway of some sort.'

Mutely, Sally uncurled herself from the chair where she had been huddling, foraged in her bag and handed over the keys.

'Chinese, alright?' he asked, pausing by the front door. Sally shrugged. It didn't matter to her what, or even if, she ate. Her hunger seemed to have vanished.

'Chinese it is, then,' he told her, opening the door and disappearing into the gloom.

He was, he acknowledged to himself as he slammed the car into gear and shot off up the High Street, very angry. Angry with the sort of deep down, primal anger the like of which he hadn't experienced in years. Not since, in fact, the last time he'd spoken to Sally Marsh. Now, he vented his anger on Sally's poor car which squealed in distress as he floored the accelerator, swerving wildly into the outside lane of the by-pass. Broke her heart, indeed! As if he'd been the one who…. Determinedly, he stamped down on that particular line of thought. There was no point going over old ground. That would only fuel this anger and cloud his judgement. Clearly, she blamed him for what had happened. Had been, or so it seemed, as hurt as he had been.

So where did that leave him now? What did he hope to gain by being here, opening up old wounds, raking over the past? Especially in the light of her engagement. Did he really want to cause more heartbreak, more pain? No. He might be a lot of things but he wasn't deliberately cruel. Justin began to wish he had never come. But now he was here with rehearsals only days away, he had passed the point of no return and would just have to stick it out till it was over. The prospect did nothing to improve his mood.

Chapter Eight

Supper was a cheerless affair. Justin, hungry when he had ordered, had bought enough to feed half the village but Sally, having all but lost her appetite, could not do the food justice. She nibbled some prawn crackers and picked pieces of chicken out of the chow mein. They barely spoke. A coldness had settled between them since Sally's hasty accusation, dampening the atmosphere and smothering the glimmer of reconciliation which had flickered between them.

Having wolfed down an enormous plateful in record time, Justin rose and stuffed the empty containers into the takeaway bag, scraped and stacked the plates and carried them through to the kitchen. Sally trundled after him, reluctant to spend any more time in his company than she had to but at the same time feeling that she could hardly let him wash up as well.

She moved to the sink and rinsed off the plates. 'Thank you for supper, Justin,' she had meant to sound sincere, and really was grateful that she hadn't had to provide a meal for him but, even to her own ears, her thanks sounded as empty as those of a child, made by its mother to thank the hostess of a birthday party it hadn't much enjoyed. 'I'll wash up,' she told him, desperate to have him out of the kitchen and well away from her. 'You go and…do whatever you need to do. Unpack or something.'

Justin stopped in the act of putting the rubbish in the bin. 'Unpack?' he repeated, straightening up to face her and arching a brow in query. 'I'm staying then, am I?'

Sally shrugged again. At this rate, she was going to lose the power speech entirely by the end of the month. Besides, they both knew the question was academic, for tonight at least. He'd cancelled his reservation and it was now quite late.

'Well, thank you, Sal,' he replied in answer to his own question, his thanks sounding no more sincere than hers had a moment before. 'I'll do as you suggested then. Unpack. It should take quite some time. After all, it's going to be quite a challenge fitting everything onto one two foot rail.'

Against all reason, Sally rose to the bait. 'Whose fault is that? You're only here for a few weeks but you've brought more luggage than the queen!'

'That's because nobody informed me about the dress code for the festival. I had no idea what was expected. It would have looked pretty stupid if I'd turned up in tails if everyone else was in casual dress, wouldn't it? I had a half a day's turn around when I got back from the States so I packed for every eventuality; tails, dinner jacket, lounge suit, informal. Hence the quantity of luggage.'

'Oh,' said Sally in a small voice, knowing that the oversight was entirely down to her. The one thing, at least she hoped it was just the one, that she, and Max too for that matter, hadn't thought about. 'Sorry. We'll have to ask the musicians taking part what they usually wear, I suppose. I'll get onto it tomorrow. Anyway, at least you came prepared.'

'Yes, I did,' Justin agreed, adding enigmatically as he headed for the door, 'on the clothes front anyway.'

As soon as he was safely in his room, Sally left the dishes draining, retrieved her car keys from the conservatory table where he'd deposited them on his return and headed out to her car. She glanced at her watch. Late but not too late. Thank heavens it was a Saturday, not a Sunday.

She pulled out into the main street heading towards the by-pass. Although the holiday season was just about underway, the traffic at this time was minimal and she was soon bowling along on the edge of the speed limit anxious to get things over with as soon as possible. After a good twenty minutes, she saw the bright neon signs up ahead, pulled off onto the slip road and slid the car easily into a space. Jumping out into the chilly evening air, she grabbed a trolley and set about her late-night shopping spree.

The out-of-town supermarket was fully stocked still and had everything she could possibly have needed. Having lived alone for so long and before that only with a mother with the appetite of a sparrow, Sally

46

found it difficult to remember what a healthy, obviously active, and demanding male would consume on a weekly basis so she settled for tons of fresh fruit and veg, went heavy on the carbs in the form of rice, pasta and various breads to put in the freezer, with an assortment of the better cuts of meat which, in the normal of way of things, she would only buy when catering for a special occasion. While she was at it, she loaded up dairy stuffs for the fridge, a family pack of toilet rolls and some extra cleaning materials.

Checking out took her ages, and a huge number of plastic bags in addition to the reusable ones which she kept in the boot. It also cost more than she would usually spend in a month. At last, with the boot crammed full, she sped back the way she had come.

It took just as long to put everything away and, by the end, her cupboards were groaning and her fridge would barely close. She slammed the last door shut with a sense of satisfaction and bundled all the bags together into one, safe in the knowledge that Justin could eat his own bodyweight and there'd still be food to spare.

Groggy from a combination of the emotional ups and downs of the day and being dog-tired, Sally made her way gratefully up the stairs to her own room. Of Justin there was no sign.

Chapter Nine

Sally awoke suddenly. She peered into the inky blackness.

There was only one street lamp in the village at the entrance of the school. Otherwise there was no artificial lighting to be seen. This was a conscious decision of the Parish Council which the whole village agreed with as it kept both expenditure and the carbon footprint down. They were all used to going nowhere after dark without a stout pair of shoes and a torch. Now, however, it meant that the only thing Sally could see in her bedroom was the green tinged numerals on her alarm clock showing ten to four in the morning.

Having registered this, she became aware of what had woken her, a noise from downstairs. Sally lay absolutely still, listening intently. Yes, there it was again! She slid out of bed, picked up the old warming iron she used as a doorstop, crept onto the landing and down the stairs. She paused for no more than a second, took a deep breath, wielded the iron aloft and flicked on the light.

Justin Trevelyan, earphones in position and iPod in hand, spun round so fast, he nearly throttled himself. Both exclaimed at the same time; Sally with an admirably restrained, 'Oh my god!' whilst Justin let fly with a string of obscenities. He was the first to regain his composure.

'Sorry, I didn't mean to disturb you,' he took a step towards her, hand outstretched.

Sally, rigid at the bottom of the stairs, one hand still clutching the warming iron, the other pressed to her chest as if trying by force to return her pounding heart to its rightful place inside her ribcage, backed off rapidly.

'Disturb me?' she shrieked. 'Damn near frightened me to death! Have you any idea what the time is?'

Justin had the grace to look sheepish. He removed the earphones and switched off the iPod. 'I know. Middle of the night. Couldn't sleep. I've been in half a dozen different time zones in the past ten days and my body clock's all over the shop.' Sally relaxed a little. She remembered something about an American Tour.

'I see. Tricky for you. Well, don't let me stop you doing whatever you need to do to relax,' she waved a hand, 'feel free. Now I know you're not a mad, axe-wielding murderer, I daresay I can sleep easy in my bed. I'll just get myself a drink first though, while I'm up.'

Justin, wearing what looked like a pair of tracksuit bottoms and nothing else, padded into the kitchen in her wake, watching her as she reached for a glass and filled it. Anxious to discover the source of the noises in her living room, Sally had slipped out of bed wearing just her pyjamas. These consisted of a tiny little top with shoe string straps and a very short pair of shorts.

Now, her proximity to Justin in the confines of her little kitchen made her acutely conscious of the amount of bare flesh she had on show. Surreptitiously, she hitched up the front of the vest to cover her cleavage and tugged at the legs of her shorts. The movement did not go unnoticed.

She heard Justin's swift, impatient intake of breath. 'Credit me with a little finesse, Sally, please. Attractive as the prospect might be, I'm not about to jump you.'

'Well, it wouldn't be the first time,' Sally muttered to herself but Justin, hearing finely tuned due to years of practice, picked it up.

'If you are referring to yesterday, I will admit that things got a little... physical. Put it down to a temporary lapse of self-control due to the excessive pleasure of seeing you again after so long.' His tone was sarcastic and she was about to utter a pithy retort when she read the mischievous glint in his eye. He struck a comical pose.

'Forgive me, Sal,' he begged, melodramatically. 'I just couldn't help myself.'

'You are such a liar!' she replied, lips twitching against her better judgement. 'You knew exactly what you were doing. The only reason you kissed me was to see how I'd react and you know it.'

Having no intention of correcting this misapprehension, Justin held up his hands in a gesture of submission. 'Guilty as charged. But it was worth it. You are such good value when you're angry!' He flicked her a quick, up and down look of assessment. 'Almost as good value as when you come downstairs in the middle of the night. What were you thinking of anyway rushing in like that waving lethal weapons?' He indicated the smoothing iron, now resting harmlessly on the worktop. 'Surely you must have known it was me down here?'

Sally shrugged, feeling more than a little silly at the way she had reacted. 'I wasn't thinking...,' she admitted. 'I just woke up, heard a noise and thought it was a burglar or something, so I grabbed the first thing I could find and came down to investigate.'

'Dressed like that?' Justin's tone was scathing. 'Not very bright was it? A little tip, Sal, next time you're thinking of tackling a burglar, on your own, in the middle of the night, for God's sake wear something a little less...' he lowered his tone, and moved, almost imperceptibly towards her, 'tempting.'

Suddenly the atmosphere had changed from one of friendly banter to something decidedly less comfortable. Time to scotch this conversation here and now, thought Sally. If she let it run any further, it just might run into trouble. She turned to face him squarely and waggled her left hand at him affording him a clear view of the solitaire on her ring finger. 'I'm engaged now, remember?'

'So you are,' he captured her hand and subjected the ring to minute scrutiny. 'A solitaire. That figures.'

'What do you mean?'

'Well, it's not exactly original is it? Or even a particularly good stone, come to that. But just about what one would expect of the Pious Peter.'

'Don't call him that. Anyway, it suits me, it's pretty and tasteful.'

'It's small and unimaginative,' Justin let go of her hand dismissively.

'Well,' she retorted, stung by his criticism, folding her arms firmly in front of her and removing her poor ring from view. 'I'd rather have this than the kind of vulgar rock you would probably go for.'

'If, in the unlikely event of me ever finding a woman I thought I could spend the rest of my life with, I was to choose a ring, I would match the stone to her personality and ensure it was as big as she was beautiful.'

'Hah! Then like I said, it would have to be a rock, though probably a tasteless one. Nothing on earth would persuade me to wear a ring like that.'

'Don't flatter yourself, sweetheart,' he drawled, smoothly. 'Nothing on earth would persuade me to offer you one, vulgar or otherwise. Let's face it, you're just like your solitaire. The packaging may be pretty but the contents really aren't up to much. You and Pious Peter are well-suited to each other.'

'Don't call him that! And yes, for your information, we are well-suited. He's a good man. He's calm and dependable and honest and...' Sally spluttered to a halt.

'Me thinks the lady doth protest too much. Who're you trying to convince, Sal? Me or yourself? Calm, dependable, honest...,' he mimicked her cruelly. 'Hardly a ringing endorsement is it?' Suddenly, he lowered his voice to little more than a whisper. 'Does he turn you on though, Sally?' his eyes bored into her, hypnotising her as he reached out a hand, touching his forefinger, feather-light, to her cheek.

'I love Peter!' she asserted defiantly, swatting his hand away. 'And he loves me! There's more to a relationship than lust, you know.'

'True,' he acknowledged silkily, his finger now gently caressing the swell of her lower lip. 'But it'd be a very dull relationship without it.' He moved his finger lower, burned a stinging trail along her jaw-line, across her collar bone. 'Does Peter make you go weak at the knees when he looks at you?' Sally trembled at the contact of skin against skin. 'Can he set you alight with one little touch?' his finger came to rest on the soft rise at the top of her breast. Slowly he moved towards her, his eyes holding her captive, till his lips were just millimetres from hers. 'Does Peter make you feel like this?' he whispered.

Sally shivered, waves of sensation washing over her, her treacherous body responding to his every movement.

'Justin!' she begged, desperately. 'Stop it, please.'

'Why?' he bit out savagely, wheeling away, putting feet of cold empty space between them. 'Why should I stop now, Sally? I'm just beginning to enjoy myself.'

Sally gasped at the sudden contrast in his mood, then straightened up, gaining strength from an answering anger rising up within her. 'I'm engaged, Justin! It might not mean anything to you, but it does to me. Don't make things difficult!'

'Difficult for whom?' he demanded, turning on her once again. 'You might be engaged but that places no restriction on me, does it?'

'No,' she agreed, bitterness tainting the words she spat back at him. 'If your past record is anything to go by, it doesn't. But just because you have the morals of any alley cat, please don't assume the rest of us are the same. If you thought you could waltz back in here and pick up from where we left off, you've got another think coming. It's just not going to happen, you can trust me on that!'

'Pick up where we left off?' his tone was incredulous, disbelieving. 'I wouldn't put myself through that again if you were the last woman on earth. As for trusting you, I'll not make that mistake again, either!'

'What are you talking about? I've only ever been completely honest and up front with you, Justin Trevelyan!'

'Honest? Oh, you mean like yesterday? When you all but seduced me before the Pious Peter walked in?'

'I seduced you?' She couldn't believe how he was twisting events to suit his own argument. 'How can you say that after the way you just behaved? None of this is my fault, none of it! If you'd gone to a hotel like you were supposed to none of this would have happened. You insisted on coming here, remember?'

'I thought you lived in a sprawling great bungalow!' he yelled, accusingly. 'I thought your mother would be on hand to act as chaperone. D'you really think for one moment that I would have put myself in this position?'

'Well, I'm sorry if my humble abode isn't good enough for the great Justin Trevelyan! Feel free to leave anytime you like,' Sally's hands clenched, chest heaving and face flushing as years of pent up rage erupted from within her. 'It wouldn't be the first time you walked out on me, would it?'

They faced each other like a couple of cats, hackles raised, hissing and spitting. Long moments passed, the tension crackling between them.

Finally, Justin gave a long rasping sigh and turned away. 'You should thank me for that. I probably saved us both our sanity!' He shot the words over his shoulder at her as he turned on his heel and strode back upstairs leaving Sally with nothing on which to vent her anger. Only when she was back in her bed, thumping the pillow in a vain effort to get to sleep did his words come back to her. 'As if I'd put myself through that again,' he'd said. And it occurred to her to wonder if their estrangement had hurt him almost as much as it had her.

Chapter Ten

Though she'd had a disturbed night's sleep, Sally woke early the next morning and knew immediately that she was not going to be able to lie in. The fact that Justin Trevelyan was lying, large as life and twice as vicious, just yards away in her spare room, somehow made it out of the question that she could remain in bed a moment longer.

She got up, tip-toed into the bathroom clutching her dressing gown tightly round her, and showered and dressed as quickly as she could. There was no way she was going to risk encountering him again other than fully dressed. The house was silent as she crept downstairs into the kitchen. She didn't, as she normally would have, put the radio on. She couldn't help but think that the longer Justin slept, the better it would be for both of them so she didn't want to do anything that might wake him up before he was ready. She did not want to have to spend her day dealing with a tired and potentially bad-tempered Justin. She'd had enough of that last night.

She made her tea and toast and was just taking it into the conservatory to eat it in comfort when the front door opened. She glanced at her watch. Twenty past seven. Surely Peter wasn't up and about at this time? Curious, she poked her head round the kitchen door to see Justin, bent double, removing his running shoes. He straightened up and peeled off his T-shirt, revealing a rippling, sweat-slicked torso. Sally gulped. He looked up, catching sight of her.

'Sorry. Did I wake you?' He wiped his face in the crumpled Tee.

'No! I didn't realise you were up,' she came further into the room. 'How long have you been out?'

Justin shrugged noncommittally. 'About an hour or so, I guess. I ran down to the beach and out along the towans.'

Sally did some rapid mental maths and worked out he must have been gone for a lot longer than an hour. 'Goodness, Justin. Don't you ever sleep?'

He shrugged again, 'Sometimes it's harder than others.' He moved towards the stairs, clearly not willing to discuss his sleeping habits with her. 'Mind if I shower?'

'No, go ahead. I'm done in the bathroom.' Sally wasn't sure which she disliked more, the snarling snapping Justin of the previous night or this morning's icily polite version. 'Do you want breakfast?'

'Just coffee, thanks,' he paused at the foot of the stairs. 'Then I'll need to meet with the committee as soon as it's possible. Please,' he added as an afterthought.

Sally was puzzled by the request. 'Why d'you want to meet with committee?'

'Because,' he began with exaggerated patience, 'in case you had forgotten, I'm here to direct a music festival. I need to meet the organising committee so they can bring me up to speed on what's been done already and what's still left to do. I need the rehearsal schedules, programmes etcetera, etcetera.'

'But,' Sally was about to explain to him that there was no need to meet with the whole committee as she had all the information he could possibly need.

'Sally,' he interrupted, wearily, drawing a hand across his brow. 'Please just do as I ask. We don't need to discuss it. Just round them up and get them down here as early as they can make it. I've a lot to do and I want to get on.'

Sally, torn between wanting to explain that he was about to waste everyone's time and not wanting to argue with him yet again, capitulated.

'Fine. No problem. I'll ring round and get them here straight away.'

By nine o'clock, all eight members of the festival committee plus Justin, shaved, showered and glowering in a black t-shirt and jeans, were squashed into Sally's conservatory and seated with some difficulty around the old rattan table.

Sally handed round the obligatory cups of tea and, it being so early on a Sunday morning, halves of buttered crumpets she'd taken out of the freezer and defrosted under the grill. Justin, controlling his impatience with some difficulty, refused everything and waited, arms folded, frown fixed firmly in place, for the meeting to begin.

'Maybe we could start now?' he asked eventually, when it seemed that no more passing, pouring or stirring could possibly be needed.

Bob Helmsworth cleared his throat, 'I'll open the meeting, lad. Chairman's role and all that.'

Sally risked a quick glance at Justin's face to see what effect being addressed as 'lad' had had on him. Justin, stony-faced still at his end of the table, appeared either not have to have noticed or to be taking it in his stride.

Bob allowed his gaze to roam around the table, looking at each member in turn, before coming to rest on Sally, seated at his right hand. 'Ready with the minutes, Sally?' He was nothing if not a stickler for protocol.

Keeping a straight face with difficulty as Justin's brows drew yet more firmly together, Sally obediently handed round the minutes of the last meeting. A silence fell as all members studied them assiduously. Justin unfolded his arms with a barely suppressed sigh. He picked up a biro and began twining it, in and out, round and round, through the fingers of his left hand.

'Any amendments?' Bob asked at last. 'No? Fine. Minutes of the last meeting agreed.'

Sally wrote this on her pad and waited for the next instruction.

'On to today's agenda then,' Bob went on ponderously. 'Any apologies, Sally?'

'Nope. All present and correct, Bob,' Sally informed him needlessly as he could see for himself that all eight members were there in person.

'Good. In that case,' he turned towards Justin, 'I'd like to formally welcome Mr Trevelyan to this meeting of the St Piran's Fundraising Festival Committee.'

This statement was greeted by a general twittering of appreciation accompanied by a little ripple of applause started by Iris's friend, Harriet Minors.

'Thank you,' Justin sat forward in his seat. 'Now there are various questions I'd like...'

'Just a minute, lad,' Bob's booming voice once more held forth. 'Sally here's done us an agenda. We'll follow that if you don't mind.' With a noise like gas escaping from a cylinder, Justin subsided into his chair and motioned with his hand for Bob to continue. Sally was heartily glad that she had the excuse of taking the minutes to keep her eyes firmly cast downwards to her pad. If she had caught Justin's eye, she felt she might well have disgraced herself by laughing aloud. As it was, she took a deep breath and kept on scribbling her notes.

'Item one,' said Bob. 'Publicity. How far have we got with that?'

Sally handed around a single sheet showing clearly how many posters and fliers had been distributed and where to. It also outlined areas still to be covered and the plans for doing so over the next couple of days. 'We've placed adverts in the local press and Max, Mr Trevelyan's agent,' she explained for the benefit of the rest of the committee, 'has arranged for some publicity on both radio and TV.'

Justin coughed politely, 'May I ask a question?' he addressed his request to Bob.

'By all means. Go ahead.'

'Sally has organised the distribution of all the publicity material to date. I am interpreting this correctly, aren't I?' again he addressed the chairman.

Sally jumped in, anxious to spare Bob's blushes. Bob would neither know nor care who had done what just as long as she had told him it was done. 'Yes, that's right. It was easy for me to get people to take a box or so with them on their routine journeys.'

'And when you say 'we've placed adverts in the local press', who exactly does that refer to?'

'Is there a problem with the copy?' Sally asked knowing full well she'd cleared the copy with Max well before the deadlines.

'No, no problem. I would just like to clarify who is responsible for publicity.' He raised an enquiring brow in her direction.

'Me,' she admitted, avoiding his gaze. 'As I think you're well aware. May we go on now?'

'Oh, please do,' he invited coolly.

Sally was unsure of exactly why he was being so nit-picking, especially as he was the one agitating to get on with things. What she was sure of was that she didn't for one moment trust this mood of his. His body language spoke of extreme impatience but his tone was both accommodating and uncharacteristically courteous. She chewed the end of her pen nervously.

'Item two,' Bob took up the reins again. 'Ticket sales. Now these, I believe, are going really rather well.'

Sally handed round another neatly produced sheet showing ticket sales to date for each of the concerts, nine in total, with actual and projected revenue so far.

'Yes,' Bob scanned the sheet and turned to Justin, 'Four all but sold out already. Pretty good going isn't it?'

'Yes, Sally has done a very good job organising the ticket sales. Shall we minute that formally?' Was he being sarcastic? A quick look at his face gave Sally little clue as to what was going on in Justin's mind.

'Oh, by all means,' Bob was surprised at the suggestion but not averse to the idea. 'Minute that Sally,' he instructed. 'Formal thanks to Sally Marsh for excellent effort on the sale of tickets.' Obediently, Sally scribbled on her pad. Just as well no-one else could read her short-hand. If they had been able to, they would have seen that she had written, 'Justin is being a complete pain'.

'Item three, rehearsal schedule.'

This time Sally had just one sheet of paper which she handed direct to Justin. 'All of the artists and ensembles have one of these. It shows the dates, times and venues of all rehearsals whether or not you'll be conducting. The ones with asterisks need further auditioning to make sure they are up to standard, but of course, you'll want to be involved with all groups at some point before the actual festival week.'

Justin glanced over the impressively laid out schedule. 'Who has already been involved in auditioning them?' he wanted to know.

'Many of the larger groups were already well known to the committee,' Sally avoided answering his question directly.

'And who auditioned the ones which weren't?' he wasn't letting her off the hook that easily.

Sally blushed. 'Me,' she admitted reluctantly.

'I see,' his face remained impassive. 'Do let's go on. Item four, I believe.'

On they went. Past programme notes and sales, the copy of which had been agreed between the artists, Sally and Max, and the sale of which at the respective performances was to be carried out by members of the Woman's Institute according to Sally's rota. Through seating arrangements and stage set-up, which Sally had allocated to the heavies on The Pump rugby team, and toilet facilities, courtesy of Andy, landlord of The Pump, who was happy to help Sally out whenever she asked. On to refreshments, which consisted of tea and cakes for each afternoon by the playgroup Mums and wine and cocktail pasties for the evenings courtesy of the WI catering team, over glass hire and purchase of paper plates, which were down to Andy again, past the barbecue on the green on the Saturday afternoon when the jazz band, children's dance troupe and bell ringers would be performing, for which the Scout dads were happy to take responsibility, right through to item eleven noting that the darts team had agreed, at Sally's behest, to organise and install ramps for disabled access.

Eventually, Bob said, 'Right then. That's about it. Any other business?'

'Yes, I have a point I'd like to raise,' Justin's voice was ominously quiet.

Bob turned, looking at him expectantly.

Sally, fearing the worse hissed, 'Justin!' in a tone half-warning, half-pleading. But Justin wasn't about to stop.

'Just something I'd like to ask really,' he paused.

'Go ahead, lad,' Bob invited, jovially.

'What do you lot do?'

'I beg your pardon?' blustered Bob.

'We've been through eleven agenda items. None of you appear to have lifted a finger on a single one of them apart from Sally. She's running this show single-handed, while you sit round pontificating,' he appeared to be just getting into his stride when Iris, who had been unusually quiet throughout, interrupted.

'Actually, Mr Trevelyan,' she told him crisply, removing her reading glasses with a sweep of one gnarled hand. 'I feel I have had a significant role in organising this festival. You may not be aware but it was, in fact, my idea to invite you to conduct at it.' She paused, her narrow-eyed stare skewering him to his seat. 'Sally had her reservations about the wisdom of such an action and, in view of your disappointingly belligerent attitude this morning, I must say that I am rather inclined, at this point, to agree with her. Perhaps in future we'd do better to leave the ideas to Sally too. Now,' having effectively silenced Justin with this damning little speech, Iris rose to her feet, 'I think this meeting has gone on quite long enough. Thank you for the tea and crumpets, Sally dear. Come along, everybody. We'll leave them to it. I'm sure Mr Trevelyan won't mind giving Sally a hand to clear up.'

Obediently, people began gathering their things together and moving towards the door. But it appeared Iris hadn't quite finished yet. 'Perhaps, Mr Trevelyan,' she added, snapping her glasses into their case with a determined click, 'when you are feeling more settled, Sally could organise a little supper for us all, so that we can get to know you properly in more amenable circumstances. Let us know which date suits you both, Sally. I'm sure we'll be able to make it.' She turned and swept out, Harriet and the remaining committee members following rapidly after.

Sally began stacking cups and plates in silence unable to believe the scene she had just witnessed. Not only had Justin been unnecessarily rude, which for some reason felt awfully like her fault, she was now lumbered with organising some kind of genteel supper party. And she knew, without having to consult any of the written schedules, that the only evening Justin could possibly be free for it was going to be that very Friday which left her less than a week to get it sorted!

Awkwardly, Justin gathered the teapot, milk jug and sugar bowl onto the tray. 'It needed saying, Sal,' he began but she quelled him with a look.

'No, it didn't,' she put the pile of crockery down and faced him, hands on hips. 'And especially not like that. They are all just kind, elderly people with too much time on their hands but not enough energy or flair to do much with it. These committee meetings are the highlight of the week for some of them. Why begrudge them that?'

'But you do everything, Sally! And no-one even seems to notice.'

Sally dismissed this with a flap of her hand. 'Well, I could certainly do without having to cater for supper for ten this week, that's for sure. Other than that, I make a few phone calls and do a bit of word processing. It's not particularly onerous.'

'Don't underestimate yourself! You've organised a whole festival single-handed! And you work full-time too! When do you get time to do anything for yourself?'

'This,' she waved a hand at the pile of agendas on the table, 'is for me. I get as much out of it as they do. I like to be busy and fulfilled. I'm engaged to Peter. I'm going to be a vicar's wife. It kind of goes with the territory. This is what my life is now, Justin.'

Justin regarded her closely, a mixture of disbelief and admiration in his eyes. 'And you're happy with it?'

'It's a good life. I've a lot to be thankful for,' Sally scooped her hair back off her face and returned his gaze calmly.

For several moments neither spoke.

'Well, I don't know how you do it,' Justin told her finally. 'You deserve a halo or a medal at least. God knows, you'd need the patience of a saint to deal with that lot on a regular basis. Especially that old witch, Iris Girton.'

Sally swallowed a giggle. 'Justin! She's not an old witch. She's been very good to me over the years. You're just miffed because she got the last word.' She giggled again. 'She clipped your ear once, do you remember? For stepping on her delphiniums.'

'She was always on at me for something or other. It's almost like I've never been away. Although, as I remember that particular incident,' he corrected her, aggrieved. 'I was nobly trying to retrieve your book from her flower bed at the time.'

'My book,' Sally's tone made it clear she was accepting none of his excuses, 'which had only landed there because you were trying to wrestle it off me!'

'I had to do something,' Justin protested. 'I hadn't got a word out of you all afternoon because of that book.'

'Typical, you always hated it if I didn't give you my undivided attention.'

'It was for your own good. You worked far too hard. Still do by the look of it.'

'You'd better give me a hand with this lot then like Iris said,' Sally threatened indicating the dirty crockery, 'Or I'll tell on you and she'll be back to give you another ticking off!'

'God forbid!' he picked up the tray with alacrity and headed for the door.

For a while they carried things through to the kitchen in companionable silence. Then, as Sally put in the plug, turned on the hot tap and handed Justin a tea towel, he asked, 'Why didn't you tell me that meeting was going to be a pointless waste of time?

'I did try but you wouldn't listen. You said, and I quote, 'We don't need to discuss it. Just round them up and get them down here.' Sally gave a fair impression of Justin in authoritarian mode. 'I think there may have been a 'please' around somewhere but I couldn't swear to it.'

'Oh God, am I really that bad?' he asked remorsefully.

'I don't know, do I?' Sally countered, not wanting to get into an analysis of Justin's character flaws. Not when they were just getting on so well.

'Sal?' he pressed her for an answer.

She shrugged. 'Perhaps it's me. Maybe I bring out the worst in you. But telling people what to do without listening to their opinions, or even asking to see if they've got any, does seem to be a bit of a habit of yours.' She plunged her hands into the steaming water and attacked the dishes with a vengeance.

'Oh God,' he repeated, receiving a cup and drying it carefully. 'It's like you said, I guess,' he continued thoughtfully. 'It kind of goes with the territory. I'm a conductor, giving orders is what I do. Sometimes, when I'm guest conducting a major orchestra, I might only have a handful of three-hour rehearsals to get through the whole programme. I don't have time to ask the first flute politely if she has any particular feelings on how her solo should be played. I just tell her how to do it and she does.'

'Just remember, the first flute gets paid to take your crap. I don't.'

'Point taken, Sal. If I was to promise to try really hard from now on, do you think we could manage to be civil for the next few weeks?'

'I don't make promises I might not be able to keep, Justin. So all I'll say is, I'll try if you will. And for goodness sake stop calling me Sal!'

After all the dishes were put neatly away, they settled down to the proper work of the day. The smaller local groups and those playing 'lighter' programmes were to fill the lunch and evening concert slots in the week preceding Easter. To complement the sacred concerts on Good Friday and Easter Sunday, Easter Saturday was to be very family oriented with a barbeque, maypole dancing and roving jazz band on the green, a display of church and handbell ringing and a silver band concert during the afternoon as well as performances by some local dancing schools. In the evening, the Cornwall Youth Orchestra would star in the first half with Britten's Young Person's Guide to the Orchestra whilst a semi-staged performance of Joseph and the Amazing Technicoloured Dreamcoat would form the second half. To bring things to a close on Easter Monday, they would wheel out the big guns in the form of the hugely exciting Belshazzar's Feast in the afternoon and the iconic Verdi Requiem in the evening.

There was therefore a huge amount of rehearsal needed with all those involved and it was clear that everyone was going to have to work extremely hard over the next three weeks if they were to pull off the festival successfully.

'You're very efficient,' Justin told her as Sally scrolled through her database calling musicians and choral conductors to confirm exactly when and what Justin was expecting to be working on with them. 'You could do this for a living.'

'Hmm,' Sally replied sceptically. 'I can't think how the London Symphony Orchestra manages without me. Anyway, I already have a perfectly good living, thank you. Now shush, I've got through to an answer machine and want to leave a sensible message.'

Having stopped only for a quick sandwich at lunchtime, it was late in the afternoon when they finally finished pouring over the schedule. Justin, seated next to her at the small workstation set up in the corner of her living room, peered critically at the onscreen spreadsheet.

'Right! Good work, Miss Marsh,' he congratulated her. 'I think we're done.'

'Not quite,' Sally clicked onto the single empty cell representing the following Friday evening and typed in 'Supper Party with Committee @ 8pm'.

'Sal!' remonstrated Justin in an anguished tone. 'Do I have to?' He sounded like a recalcitrant six-year old.

She smothered a smile. 'Yes, you do,' she told him firmly. 'You were rude and unpleasant when you met them this morning. Iris is absolutely right, you need to meet them again so they can get to know you properly.'

'But why? I'll be gone again in a months' time.'

'You will be but I won't and neither will Iris and we both feel responsible for you. And in any case, this is the most exciting thing to happen to this village since The Pump cricket team won the county cup. They deserve pleasant memories of it.' Seeing she had not clinched the argument, she continued, 'Your mum would say you should. My mum would have too.'

'And you think I should?' he asked, his expression pained.

Sally nodded. 'Yes, I do. It won't hurt you, you won't have to miss any rehearsals, and it would mean a lot to them.'

'Alright, alright,' he held up his hands in submission. 'But don't play the emotional blackmail card too often, Sal, it will rapidly become devalued.'

Sally was pleased. It hadn't been quite as difficult to persuade him as she had feared. She clicked send and a muffled ping heralded the arrival of a file containing the amended schedule and a neat list of names, phone numbers and addresses in Justin's smartphone.

'Excellent!' she flipped the lid of the laptop shut. 'That's settled then. I'll tell Iris and do a quick ring round. After a couple of hours exercising your legendary charm, you'll have them all, Bob Helsmworth included, eating out of your hand.'

Justin shuddered. 'That conjures up a mental image too disgusting to contemplate. Now, I've been very good all afternoon. I need some relaxation. Any chance of a piano?' He looked at her expectantly.

'Sorry,' Sally peered under the table and patted her pockets. 'Don't seem to have one tucked away here anywhere!'

He raised that single, quizzical brow, 'Don't try and be smart with me, Sally Marsh. You know perfectly well what I meant. Any chance of using the one in the church?'

Sally smiled him an apology and checked her watch. 'There will be no-one there now until the evening service. That gives you an hour or so.'

'Great!' he got to his feet. 'Do I need a key or something?'

Sally, being both Peter's fiancée and on the cleaning rota, had the keys. She fetched them from a drawer in the living room.

'I'll come with you. There was a crèche for the service this morning and Sunday School this afternoon, so there'll probably be some tidying up to do.'

'Another one of your civic duties, Sal?' She shot him a livid look. Misinterpreting, he corrected himself hastily. 'Sally. Sorry. Did I keep you from church today?'

'We'll go this way,' Sally lead him out of the conservatory and down through the small, flower-filled cottage garden. 'I don't always go,' she said in answer to his question. 'It's not compulsory, you know.'

Justin, following her along the path towards the churchyard, was obviously puzzled by this. 'But I thought, as fiancée of the worthy Peter, you'd have to go every week?'

Sally didn't like the way Justin spoke about Peter but she supposed worthy was an improvement on pious. 'Peter has his degree of faith. I have mine. He doesn't mind if I don't go to church every week. Besides, he knew I was likely to be tied up with you today.'

Justin gave a derisive snort. 'I'll bet he minded that!'

'Peter,' Sally remarked heavily, making the unfavourable comparison between them clear, 'is both reasonable and understanding. He knows I'm going to have to spend time with you because of the festival and he's fine with that.'

'Really? Poor Peter. D'you know, I can almost bring myself to feel sorry for him.'

Sally, pushing some errant brambles out of her way, slanted him a querying look. 'Why?'

'You have him just where you want him, don't you?' Justin reached forward, caught the brambles and lifted them high enough for her to step under.

Sally tossed her head dismissively. 'Ours is an adult relationship, an equal partnership but I can see I'm wasting my breath trying to explain that to you. You just don't understand.'

'Dead right, I don't. You've obviously been engaged for ages.'

'Not ages,' Sally broke in. 'A few months.'

'OK,' he conceded, 'Months, yet you still live in separate houses. Then you tell him you're going to be working closely with your ex for weeks at a time and he's fine with it? He must be either impotent or stupid!'

'Justin!' Sally rounded on him, about to give him a piece of her mind. Then she stopped and made a great play of studying her watch. 'Well that didn't last long, did it?'

'What?' He demanded, baffled.

'Five hours or so, maximum.' She stepped onto the narrow gravel path wending its way through the graveyard towards the church.

'What are you going on about?' Justin gave up following and walked beside her on the grass, trying to glean some clue from her profile as to what she was talking about.

'You promised,' Sally walked on, head bent. 'You promised you'd try very hard to be civil.'

'I am being civil,' he protested, in hurt tones.

She looked up suddenly. 'You just accused my fiancée of being either impotent or stupid, Justin. That, in my book, is neither civil nor kind.'

65

'You're right,' he raked a hand through his tousled hair.

'Thank you, I think. Is that some kind of apology?'

'No, I don't mean right about Peter, or about me not being civil,' he caught her arm, bringing her to a halt. 'I mean you were right before. When you said you bring out the worst in me. You absolutely do. I would never have said something like that to anyone else.' He loomed over her, brows furrowed, blue eyes piercing. Sally, gazing up at him, shook her head, sadly.

'Great. Thanks again. That makes me feel a whole lot better.' She released herself from his grasp and moved towards the church porch. 'C'mon. We're here now and you wanted to play.'

'Sally…' Justin's arm fell loosely to his side. The heavy key grated in the lock and Sally stepped inside. Justin swore softly to himself.

He knew he had a reputation for being exacting, difficult even but he'd meant what he said, Sally really did seem to bring out the worst in him. What was it about the woman? He cast his mind back to when they'd been together before. Had it always been like this? He remembered laughs, lots of laughs. And sex, of course. The most incredible sex. But rows? Few and far between, as he recalled. Until, the last one, of course. That final brutal, eviscerating exchange which had torn them apart completely. And now, he reminded himself sternly, Sally was engaged to someone else, and all he had to do was hold it together for the next few weeks. Surely he could manage that?

He squared his shoulders and followed Sally inside.

The church was dark and cool as churches are. It smelled of old wood, polish, incense and spring flowers.

She turned with a smile as she heard his footsteps approaching.

'Sally, I…' he reached a hand towards her, his expression solemn, and would have said more but she side-stepped his touch, and interrupted lightly,

'Here you are then. You play the piano and I'll tidy the toys. Take as long as you like.' Not waiting for a reply, she made her way down the aisle and into the vestry where the morning service crèche was held.

It was better than she had expected. A few toys remained out of the toy chest, a couple of puzzles lay upturned on the floor but otherwise the morning's helpers had done a good job. She had a general tidy, putting the larger items back in their places and stacking the chairs neatly against the wall, half an ear on the music wafting through from the church. Justin was clearly working on the scores he had brought with him, playing disjointed phrases over and over till he was content with them.

Sally picked up the puzzles and, collecting all the little pieces in her lap, settled down on the floor to restore them to order. As she slotted the simple shapes into their places, she smiled in recognition. That was definitely not one of the pieces in the festival! She hummed along to one of her favourite show tunes and, as the swooping melody filled the room, Sally felt her spirits lift, as they always did, in response. She stacked the completed puzzles on a shelf and crept back into the church.

'Do you still sing, Sally?' Justin called as she approached.

She shook her head, leaning her arms along the back of the piano and resting her chin on her hands. 'Not for years. Don't seem to get the time now.'

'You know this one though,' he encouraged. 'I heard you humming it.' He sang along a couple of bars and, unable to stop herself, Sally joined in, melody and words flowing from her with no conscious effort. Justin's easy accompaniment soared and swooped around her as she held the simple tune.

Emboldened, Sally straightened up. She too began to improvise, weaving her voice in and out of the chords, as Justin followed her instinctively. Reaching the end of the song, she gave a self-conscious little laugh, 'Goodness. I haven't sung like that in ages.'

Justin, still playing, segued smoothly into another popular melody, 'How about this one?'

She shook her head. 'It doesn't seem right somehow, singing those kinds of songs in a church.'

Justin smiled, 'I don't think anyone will mind if they sound as good as the last one did. Go on, just one more,' and he modulated easily into 'Misty' knowing she would not be able to resist. Her lips parted in response and she gave in to the desire to pour her heart out.

'Sally?' She broke off abruptly, whipping round to see Peter, in his Sunday attire of dog collar and dark suit, making his way hastily down the aisle. 'I heard you from outside. I couldn't imagine who it was!' He stopped, looking bemused. 'I had no idea you could sing like that, Sally.'

'Oh, well, I'm not really very …' Sally flustered.

'Sally has a lovely voice,' Justin informed him firmly. 'It's a shame she doesn't use it any more.'

'Yes, well, perhaps she has more important things with which to occupy her time now,' and before Justin could argue the point, Peter went on, 'I'm glad I've caught up with you, Sally. There are a few things I need to talk to you about.'

'OK,' Sally leaned an elbow on the piano and waited.

'Not here,' Peter said quickly, 'We don't want to interrupt Mr Trevelyan's rehearsal.'

'Don't mind me, I'll just carry on regardless.'

'Maybe we could have a stroll outside?'

Sally glanced at Justin, who shrugged, 'I'm easy either way.'

Impatiently, Sally strode ahead of Peter, through the porch and onto the path. He couldn't have chosen a worse time to drag her away, just as she and Justin were managing to mend some bridges. She turned to face him.

'Well, Peter? What was it you needed to discuss so urgently?'

'Sally,' he reprimanded her gently, taking her by the shoulders and pulling her close to him. 'I haven't seen you properly for two days. Don't I at least get a kiss hello?' He leaned towards her, placing his lips on hers.

Obediently, Sally returned his embrace. After a moment, she pulled away. 'It's not long till evening service, Peter. If you do need to talk to me, you'd better get on with it before people start arriving.' Peter sighed, but did not relinquish his hold.

'What I wanted to ask is, when is Trevelyan going to book into Lawncrest?'

Sally looked away. Nothing further had been said about Justin moving out since their blazing row of the previous night. Sally was sure he could easily have persuaded the hotel to make a room available, the expense not really being an issue when you earned as much as he did. It was probably tax deductible or something anyway. But he hadn't referred to the matter again and Sally, not wanting to rake over the argument in which they had both said things they probably shouldn't have, didn't feel able to either. She'd said he could stay and he had. Simple as that.

'He isn't going to,' was all she told Peter now. 'We cancelled the reservation.'

'I'm really not happy with that, Sally,' his hold on her tightened. 'It could give rise to some unpleasant gossip. If he must remain in your cottage, though I honestly can't see why he should, why don't you come and stay at my house till the festival is over?'

'That really would give the gossip mongers something to talk about!' Sally was amazed that he would even suggest such a thing. 'We live apart for months even though we're engaged, then Justin appears and suddenly, I up sticks and move in with you. What would they make of that?'

'I wasn't suggesting that you move in with me, Sally,' Peter corrected her stiffly. 'Trevelyan's appearance doesn't change my opinion on that kind of arrangement. I just think it would be preferable if you were under the same roof as your fiancé rather than some playboy type who might take advantage of you.'

Briefly, humour wrestled with outrage in Sally's breast. Humour won. 'Oh Peter, you do sound Victorian!' she told him fondly. 'You are making a fuss over nothing, you funny old stick. I've told Justin he can stay, you don't want me moving in with you, so it looks like we'll all have to make the best of it.'

'It's not I don't want you moving in with me Sally, you know that. I may have strong views on sex before marriage but that doesn't mean that I don't find you attractive, that I don't want you...' his voice trailed off as his lips found hers again and his hands drew her more closely to him. Sally willed herself to respond as once she might have but it was no good, some vital ingredient appeared to be missing. Eventually, deciding she was just too strung up from the events of the last two days, she pushed him away.

'Peter, stop! What if someone sees us?'

'Let them!' he replied, recklessly, reaching for her again. 'We are engaged after all.'

At that moment, Harriet Minors rounded the corner and gave a little wave. Sally had never been so pleased to see one of Peter's parishioners. She returned Harriet's wave and moved back towards the porch, then, Peter's crestfallen expression tugging at her conscience, she returned and kissed him tenderly full on the lips.

'It's only a month, Peter,' she assured him. 'Then everything will be back to normal.'

She met Justin in the doorway, obviously on the point of leaving. 'That's good timing. We'd best go now. The service starts soon. Or did you want to stay?'

'Good god, no!' he looked aghast at the prospect. 'Unless you do?'

'No, not tonight, I think.' Sally fell into step beside him as they meandered along the path. Peter's behaviour puzzled and worried her a little. It wasn't like him to be so sexually assertive and she couldn't understand why he had picked that moment and that place, public and inappropriate as it was, to demonstrate his feelings for her.

'What's the matter, Sal?' Justin picked up on her mood. For once she didn't feel the urge to correct him. Sally scooped her hair back from her face and twirled it meditatively into a long curling rope over one shoulder.

'Nothing,' she lied. 'I'm fine.'

Justin shook his head, not believing her. 'Come on, I know you. You're doing that thing with your hair. Something's up. What is it? You and the worthy Peter had a ruck?'

She released her hair as if it had burned her. Goodness, was she that transparent? It was Sally's turn to shake her head. 'Not really. He was just...' she stopped, flushing, very much aware that it was entirely wrong of her to be discussing her fiancé's behaviour with Justin. 'Being a little odd,' she finished lamely.

'Ah,' Justin nodded, knowingly. 'Getting a bit fresh was he? I'm not surprised. You're a very beautiful woman, Sal. And, of course, it's a perfectly natural reaction of his now that I'm on the scene.'

'Justin!'

'You should be grateful to me really for putting your mind at rest. At least you know his sex drive is OK.'

'Justin!'

'That's assuming of course that you and he haven't already...' he waited momentarily for her to contradict him.

'Justin!'

'I thought not. So, what happened just now? Surprise you with his ardour, did he?'

'Justin, stop it! I shouldn't be discussing this with you.' Sally was by now desperate to stop this dangerous line of enquiry.

'But you're not discussing it, Sally,' he explained, calmly. 'I'm hypothesising and you're just shrieking 'Justin' every now and then.'

'I am not shrieking,' she moderated her tone in a belated attempt to maintain her dignity.

'Not now, no, but you were. 'Justin!'' his imitation of both her tone and facial expression were cruelly accurate, and all the more comical for that.

'You are incorrigible, Justin Trevelyan!' She told him, slapping him hard across the arm.

'Yep,' he agreed, unabashed. 'One of my many endearing qualities.'

'More like one of the few,' Sally muttered darkly.

'Good girl! That's more like it.' He smiled at her approvingly.

'What?'

'You must be feeling better now.' Sally had to admit to herself that she did indeed feel better. 'That's because you're being rude to me again,' he explained. 'Bet you don't spar with Peter like this.'

'No,' she informed him coolly. 'I don't. But that's because Peter and I very seldom disagree about anything.'

'Well, that's good, I suppose,' he sounded doubtful. 'It must be very…peaceful for you both. It's a pity though,'

'A pity?' she couldn't help but ask though she knew she would probably regret encouraging him. 'In what way?'

'Just think of all that kissing and making up you're missing out on. Oh, no, wait! I forgot, Peter doesn't approve of that either!'

'Justin!'

'Careful, Sal. You're shrieking again.'

'I am not shrieking,' she took a further hefty swipe at his arm. 'And don't keep calling me Sal!'

Justin, neatly dodging her attack, stopped suddenly in his tracks. 'I know what it is!' he exclaimed as if in the grip of a real 'Eureka' moment. 'You're hungry. You always did get dead grouchy when you were hungry.'

Sally, though she really was very hungry indeed, did not like being the subject of such a sweeping generalisation. Neither did she like the way he seized her arm and practically dragged her back down the path and across the road towards The Pump. Seeing the mulish look on her face, Justin released her on the doorstep to perform an elegant and old-fashioned bow.

'My dear Miss Marsh,' he asked in the clipped accents of an actor in a period drama. 'Would you kindly do me the honour of joining me for dinner at the local hostelry?' He bent low over her hand which he pressed delicately to his lips.

Laughing, Sally responded in kind and dropped him a neat little curtsey, 'Well, my good sir, as you have phrased your request so politely,' she replied, archly, 'it would be churlish of me to refuse. Shall we go in?'

He drew her arm through his and lead her into the welcoming warmth of the public bar.

Andy, the landlord, greeted Sally with his customary good humour. 'Evening, Sally, love. How's life treating you?' Then, before she had chance to reply, he exclaimed, 'Justin Trevelyan, as I live and breathe! It is you! I heard you were coming back for a bit.' He came round to their side of the bar, shook Justin's hand and then clapped him on the shoulder. 'Well, mate, it's good to see one of us is packing their weight in muscle not flab.' He patted his own generous belly, chuckling. 'Still playing on the wing, are you?'

'Not as often as I'd like, Andy, I'm afraid. How's the old team doing these days?' Several minutes passed while Andy and Justin chewed over current form and old times when they'd been teammates. Sally, having automatically been furnished with a half pint of cider by Andy, slipped onto a bar stool and waited, quietly sipping her drink.

Finally, a lull in the conversation gave Andy the chance to call through to the back, 'Lou! Lou! Come in here a minute love, will you? You'll never guess who's just turned up.'

His wife and co-licensee wandered through from the kitchen.

'Give over shouting, Andy, will you? Oh!' She paused abruptly, then whisked round to the public side of the bar and threw herself towards Justin almost sending his pint flying. He put it down hastily, obligingly enveloped her in a huge bear hug and submitted to having his face pulled down and soundly kissed. 'Justin! It's 'andsome to see you again, my lover!' she told him, patting her hair and smoothing her top down over her hips as he released her.

Sally couldn't blame her. Justin did rather have that effect on women. She herself was valiantly resisting the urge to go to the ladies and check her appearance but, as she hadn't thought to bring her handbag with her, there didn't seem much point. She stayed where she was.

'Well!' Lou looked from one to the other, like the proud mother of two children. 'I must say it's good to see you two in here together again.' Sally felt a tell-tale blush rising on her cheeks. 'Just like old times. You always did make such a lovely pair.' Lou leaned forward conspiratorially and addressed Sally with a wink, 'Take my advice and hang on to him this time, love. Not often you get money and looks in one package, is it?'

'That's enough, Lou,' Andy admonished his wife good-naturedly. 'Sally's got other fish to fry these days, haven't you, Sally girl?'

Sally gulped, reddening and it was left to Justin to step in nobly, saving her further embarrassment.

'Yes,' he agreed, sincerity tinged with exactly the right degree of regret. 'The vicar's a lucky man. Now, Lou,' he deftly changed the subject, 'What have you got on the menu tonight? I'm starving.'

Lou lead them to a secluded table for two in the restaurant area, furnished them with menus and pointed out the specials' board. She cleared their empty glasses. 'Couple more? Or would you prefer wine with your meal?' she asked, back in professional mode.

Justin glanced at Sally. 'You choose,' he instructed.

Lunch felt like years ago to Sally and she could already feel the effects of the cider, fuddling her brain and making her limbs feel heavy. It was incredibly pleasant to feel this relaxed after all the recent tension. 'I'll have another half, please, Lou,' she said recklessly.

Justin ordered a half for himself and they turned their attention to the menus as Lou made her way back to the kitchen, leaving her recent faux pas hanging in the air between them.

Justin leaned forward, keeping his voice low. 'She has a lot of good qualities, Lou, but tact certainly isn't one of them!'

'You can say that again,' Sally groaned, covering her face with a hand. 'I didn't know where to look. Thank you for coming to the rescue.'

'My pleasure,' he told her briskly, closing his menu with a decisive snap. 'It's not often I get to see you lost for words.'

'You're right,' Sally smiled. 'I can normally hold my own pretty well.'

'I had noticed. You've been putting me in my place ever since I got here. I know,' he added quickly as Sally would have remonstrated. 'No more than I deserved, I admit. So, how about we call a truce? I promise I'll make a real effort this time.'

Gratefully, Sally agreed. If the festival were to be a success, they both needed to concentrate on that and not waste energy sniping at each other.

Lou returned and took their orders, steak and salad for Sally, the same with chips for Justin. The food was simple but good and, as if making up for earlier, Lou's service was swift and unobtrusive. The conversation flowed easily, uninhibited and uninterrupted. They reminisced about their schooldays and Sally filled him in on various mutual acquaintances he had lost touch with. Justin regaled her with anecdotes of his travels. They talked about music they both enjoyed, books they'd read and films they'd seen.

Eventually Sally pushed her coffee cup and brandy glass away and declared that she couldn't eat or drink another thing. Yawning, she glanced at her watch. 'Heavens! I had no idea it was so late. I'm really going to struggle to get up for school in the morning.'

'Come on then, sleepy head,' Justin dropped a wodge of notes onto the table and reached out a hand to her. 'Let's get you home to bed before you doze off where you are.'

They made their way through the now empty bar, Justin calling his thanks to Andy and Lou and promising to drop in on them again very soon. Outside, it was cold and dark with a mean little nipping wind. Above them the moon slid in and out behind feathery wisps of cloud. Sally shivered.

'Come here,' Justin drew her to him and draped an arm casually across her shoulders, rubbing her arm. 'Better?'

The warm bulk of him clamping her to his side sent a glow of heat coursing through her that Sally knew had nothing to do with actual temperature. She nodded, concentrating very hard on keeping her breathing normal and even.

They walked in silence, back down the main street, skirting the wall of the churchyard and finally arriving at Sally's cottage. Justin took the keys from her fumbling fingers and opened the front door. The pallid light of the moon slanted in through the living room windows casting eerie shadows across the walls. Sally reached out to switch on the light but Justin caught her hand.

'Don't!' he whispered and Sally knew he was right. Neither of them wanted to break the spell, to risk bringing an end to this feeling of delicious intimacy.

He turned her to him, cupping her face in his hands, and drew her close. Sally's eyes fluttered closed, her lips parted slightly in anticipation. She heard his breathing quicken. Then he placed a gentle, almost avuncular kiss upon her forehead and released her in the direction of the stairs.

'Goodnight, Sal,' his voice floated up to her as she reached the landing.

She drifted into the bathroom and then into bed, feeling at once almost weightless and yet curiously leaden. Sally fell almost immediately asleep, stirring only slightly when, hours later, Justin made his own way up to bed.

Chapter Eleven

'Hiya, love,' Kath poked her head round the classroom door. 'Got time for a quick chat?'

Sally, seated in front of a pile of Maths exercise books which she'd hoped to finish marking before she went home, smiled and put her pen down. ''Course. Come on in.'

'Can't be long,' Kath informed her sauntering over to Sally's desk and perching herself on the edge. 'Got a hot date later but I just had to catch up with you before I left. I hear,' she regarded Sally closely, 'that the gorgeous Mr Trevelyan did not book into Lawncrest as planned, after all?'

'Incredible!' Sally replied, frowning in bewilderment. 'I know I should be used to it by now, but I never cease to be amazed at your ability to a) have a hot date practically every night of the week, b) still manage to get all your school work done and c) know what everyone else is doing almost before they do themselves. Go on,' she eased herself back in her chair and folded her arms across her chest, regarding her friend expectantly. 'What else have your sources told you?'

Kath, teacher of the Year Five class below Sally's Year Six, was her closest friend. They had joined the school at the same time on the Graduate Teacher Programme and both loved their jobs but there the similarity ended. Where Sally was tall, slender, brunette and tending towards the reserved, Kath was a small, voluptuous blonde for whom the description 'bombshell' could have been purposely coined. She was bubbly, she was buxom and possessed a Brummie accent so sharp it could fell trees. As she sang in one of the choirs taking part in the festival, she also had a vested interest in the comings and goings of Justin Trevelyan. Now, she leaned towards Sally and said, 'Never mind about what my sources have told me. What I want to know is what you haven't! Come on, spill!'

Sally allowed a slight pause, then confessed, quietly, 'You're right. He didn't book into Lawncrest. He's staying with me for the month.'

'Oh my god!' Kath screamed, her face a picture of incredulity. 'But I thought…you said…How on earth's he ended up at your place?'

Sally, who had spent most of the day wondering the same thing and was as anxious to get Kath's take on the weekend's events as Kath was to hear exactly what had happened, began from the beginning. Kath listened raptly, only interrupting Sally's monologue with the odd gasp or muffled oath.

When she had finished, Kath was silent for a moment or two, then said, 'Let me get this straight. You haven't seen Justin for what…six years? He arrives, literally, out of the blue, snogs you witless and somehow works it so he's staying at your place, much against your will. You're practically caught in flagrante in his bedroom by Peter, you have a furious row in the middle of the night dressed only in your naughties and then, having put up the backs of the entire committee, he whisks you off to dinner at The Pump and you end the evening the best of mates. What is going on?'

Sally, suffering the after effects of a late night and a greater than usual consumption of alcohol, knuckled her tired eyes and yawned behind her hand. She pushed the pile of books out of the way and laid her head despondently on her forearm. 'I have no idea, Kath, honestly. When you put it like that, I sound completely pathetic, I know I do. I keep asking myself why I didn't put my foot down over Lawncrest. Why didn't I just tell him where to get off? I know he's a…'

'A shit,' supplied Kath helpfully, being the one person who knew exactly what had passed between Sally and Justin years before.

'Exactly. He left me in bits and there's no way I'm going there again. I know I should have stood my ground and stuck to the arrangements I'd made with his agent. But dealing with Justin Trevelyan is like dealing with a steam roller. It doesn't matter what you say or do, he just keeps on going and you either get out of the way or he goes right over you.'

'Or snogs you into submission,' Kath added suggestively.

Sally flapped a hand at her. 'Don't keep using that word, Kath. It makes it sound so sordid.'

'Oooh, touchy!' Kath laughed at her friend's discomfiture. 'Well, if being 'kissed',' she gave the word unwarranted emphasis, 'by Justin Trevelyan isn't sordid, what is it then?'

Sally opened her eyes, glared at Kath, then closed them again. But it was a fair question. How would she describe how she felt when Justin kissed her?

'It's…it's a bit like a nuclear explosion…'

'Oh my god!' Kath interrupted again. 'You mean like the earth moving and seeing stars and stuff? I thought that only happened in books.'

'No!' Sally cried just a bit too quickly. Kath raised a sceptical eyebrow causing Sally to admit reluctantly, 'Well, yes, a bit, I suppose. But what I meant was, afterwards, there's this moment of complete calm and then, then comes the fall out. Invariably there's some kind of hideous backlash. It's almost like he was doing it on purpose to make things difficult for me.'

'Why on earth would he do that?' Kath demanded, settling herself more comfortably on the desk.

'I've no idea! If anything, the boot should be on the other foot. He left me, remember? I'm the one should be trying to make him suffer, not the other way round.'

'Hmmn. Maybe he just wants one last fling with you for old times' sake.'

'Oh yes, that's likely after six years, not!' Sally dismissed this theory out of hand. 'And even if that was the case, why didn't he make the most of it when he had the chance?'

'What d'you mean?' Kath was intrigued. Sally straightened up a little, leaning her left elbow on the desk and cupping her face in her hand. With her right forefinger she twirled a lock of hair round and round, avoiding Kath's interested gaze.

'When he brought me back from The Pump, I was more than a little squiffy,' she admitted. 'Quite squiffy enough for him to have had his evil way with me with very little resistance. But he didn't. He just patted me on the head and sent me off to bed like a good little girl.'

Kath spread her hands before her palms uppermost. 'Obviously too much of a gentleman to take advantage of you.'

'Who, Justin?' Sally swept her hair back off her face and threw herself back in her chair. 'Pull the other one!'

'People change, Sally, you know they do. Perhaps he's acquired a conscience in the past six years.'

'People might change a bit but they rarely undergo complete personality transplants. Justin has always done just exactly what Justin wants with very little consideration for anyone else. And that's another thing! I've been wracking my brains to work out why he'd accept this gig in the first place. At first, I thought he was just teaching his agent a lesson, you know, not to decline things without asking him first but the more I think about it, the more convinced I am that there's more to it than that.'

'Well, he said, didn't he? Curiosity about you!'

'I don't believe that for one minute,' Sally told her roundly. 'No, I reckon, with some of the stuff I've read on the net, he's after some good publicity for a change and staying with me is part of that. You know, Justin Trevelyan giving his services free to the community and not so grand he's above staying with an old school friend or something. But that still doesn't explain why he's been playing hot and cold with me since he got here, does it?'

'But that's exactly it! If it's good publicity he's after, he's not going to go messing on his own doorstep, is he? I mean, there was nothing stopping him trying it on with you when he thought you were still fair game but once he realised you were engaged to Peter, he worked out just how messy things could get and he backed off.' Sally shrugged. She supposed that was vaguely possible. 'Anyway, let's hope so, otherwise the next few weeks could be really interesting for all of us. And not in a good way, either!' Kath glanced at her watch, slid off the desk and headed for the door, running a hand through her curly blonde mass of hair. 'Must fly! Got to get this washed and dried ready for my accountant.'

Sally laughed. 'Accountant? I thought you were dating an electrician?'

'Well, you know what they say? You've got to kiss a lot of frogs.'

'Oh, and you limit yourself to kissing, do you?' Sally teased, raising a sceptical eyebrow.

Kath gave her a naughty smile. 'Now where would be the fun in that?' Then she stopped and turned back to face her friend, a sombre expression settling on her usually smiling features. 'I'm just killing time, Sally, we both know that, until my Peter comes along. You're really lucky to have him, to be settled like you are. You know that, don't you? And you will....' she hesitated.

'What?' Sally encouraged her softly.

'Be careful!' Kath blurted out quickly. 'This business with Justin… I know what it's like Sally, the thrill of the chase and all that, but it's not worth jeopardising something more meaningful for, so just be careful, that's all.'

'Oh, Kath!' Sally got up from behind her desk, quickly crossed the room to her friend, and giving her a hug. She knew only too well that Kath's bubbly, fun-loving façade hid a deep longing to be both a wife and mother. 'There's no need to worry about me, honestly. I've more than learned my lesson where Justin's concerned and I've absolutely no intention of going there again. And as for you, just keep kissing those frogs.' She opened the door of the classroom and ushered Kath into the corridor. 'Now, go! You don't want to keep a potential prince waiting, do you?'

Chapter Twelve

Kath and Peter needn't have worried, reflected Sally as she drove home at the end of the week. Justin had taken delivery of an expensive-looking hire car on Monday morning since when they had been like ships that pass in the night. Sally left early each morning for school while Justin was either still in bed or, judging by the absence of his trainers by the front door, out on a run. By the time she got back in the evenings, he would already have left for a rehearsal, not usually returning till Sally was safely tucked up in bed.

For all his reported playboy life-style, Justin was surprisingly self-sufficient. Although the contents of the fridge were decreasing rapidly, the only sign that he had cooked anything for himself was the appearance of the odd utensil in the wrong drawer. The brief appearance of some of his clothes in the minute airing cupboard showed he was doing his own washing too. Other than that, the disruption to her usual routine was minimal.

Their paths had crossed a couple of times as Sally was coming in and he was going out. Justin had asked politely if she had had a good day and Sally had enquired about how the rehearsals were going. Once, he'd put a large wadge of 'house-keeping' money on the windowsill and resolutely refused to let her return it. Sally had taken out his share of the shopping bill and put the rest in her underwear drawer. She'd need more supplies next week but she was determined to give back anything she hadn't spent by the end of his stay.

Peter had also been conspicuous by his absence. He had popped in as usual but did not stay long. Sally wasn't sure if this was because he didn't want to risk bumping into Justin or because he was genuinely busy. Probably the latter; Peter's parish encompassed a cluster of six villages which kept him pretty tied up. There were four services every Sunday while visiting parishioners, prayer meetings, youth groups and bible studies occupied every day and most of his evenings.

In truth, as Bob had insisted on their usual, protracted Wednesday meeting, Sally had seen more of the committee members than either Peter or Justin. Knowing she'd have heard if there'd been any problems, she assured them that Justin was delighted with their arrangements and that all the rehearsals were going brilliantly. They all agreed what a good thing it was that Sally and Justin had remained such good friends.

All that is except Iris. 'You're looking rather pale, Sally dear,' she'd said, giving her young friend a thoroughly searching look. 'I do hope you're not overdoing it. Trevelyan is an extremely good conductor, as I know from our choral rehearsal, but I should imagine he can be very exacting. I do hope having him here isn't putting too much of a strain on you. Perhaps I'll have a little word with him about it.'

'No!' Sally had implored desperately, unable to imagine how Justin would react to further intervention from Iris. 'Please, there's really no need. He's the most considerate guest. I've probably just got a bit of that bug that's been going around school.' She touched her throat slightly as if to add truth to this claim. 'And I have been a bit worried about this supper I'm hosting on Friday, you know.' She hoped that perhaps Iris would say that, if it was going to give Sally additional stress, they could forget all about it. No such luck.

'Ah yes, Friday!' Iris had perked up immediately, her concern for Sally's welfare apparently forgotten. 'We're all looking forward to it. And there's no need for you to do a thing.' Her assurances were echoed determinedly by the others. 'Everyone knows so you don't need to bother with invitations and we're all going to bring a plate of food so there will be no need for you to do any cooking. There will be a few more of us than usual though, dear, as both the Helmsworths are coming, and Peter of course, and I believe some of the conductors and choirmasters may have been invited.'

This had come as rather a shock to Sally. She was quite sure she had specified only the other seven members of the committee when she'd called Iris to arrange the date.

'Exactly how many extra guests can I expect?' she had asked glaring around the table at her co-members, several of whom shifted uncomfortably in their seats and made mumbled admissions of possibly 'just mentioning' it to a couple of others. It seemed the opportunity to furnish friends and acquaintances with the chance of meeting Justin Trevelyan in person had been too good to pass up.

Grimly, Sally ripped a fresh sheet of paper from her pad and wrote Friday's date at the top. She passed it to Iris on her right, 'I need to know exactly how many people I can expect so I can make sure I'll have enough plates and glasses and things. So, I want you all to write down the names of anyone you've invited.' She had watched in growing disbelief as the list travelled slowly around the table, everyone seeming to write at least four or five additional names on it.

On its return, Sally had crossed out a few names which were duplicated and then totted up the total with a sinking heart. What had started life as an informal supper for eight committee members plus Justin had mushroomed into a fully-fledged party with, at a conservative estimate, around thirty guests. She was then faced with two problems. First, how to physically fit that number of people into her tiny cottage and cater for them. Second, and by the far the biggest worry as far as she was concerned, was how to break the news to Justin.

When it came to it, Sally opted for the stress-free catering option. Unusually for her, she left school on the Friday exactly at three fifteen and, salving her conscience with the argument that the party was as much for Justin's benefit as anyone else's, she dipped heavily into his house-keeping contribution and allowed herself free rein in the supermarket for the second time that week. She now had a car boot full of nibbles, dips, finger food, French sticks, cheeses, pates, assorted fresh fruit and vegetables, and vital additional supplies of paper plates, cups and napkins. Not a big drinker herself, she'd done the best she could on the drinks front and, besides soft drinks and juices, had chosen a few bottles of medium-priced red and white.

Gratefully, she found a parking space within yards of her front door, pulled in and began unloading.

After a couple of hours with a hoover and duster, the cottage was rendered fit for inspection, the downstairs furniture rearranged and all extraneous clutter confined to Sally's bedroom. A further hour of opening packets, washing, slicing and arranging in every dish, platter and bowl she possessed, saw the food laid out attractively. Next, she set out drinks and glasses on the worktop beside the kitchen sink, then strategically placed her full complement of table lamps in the living room and conservatory to create a warmly welcoming glow. Which left her with only the one remaining difficulty......telling Justin.

She had put off breaking the news of the evening's growth from intimate gathering to full-blown party, partly due to lack of opportunity to talk to him about it, but mainly, if she was honest with herself, out of cowardice. He had been reluctant enough to meet just the committee members socially. She couldn't imagine him being overjoyed at this fresh turn of events. Now, she regretted not having tackled him about it before. He was due home any minute. What if he came in, took one look, put two and two together, turned around and went straight back out again? Knowing Justin, that was a distinct possibility and Sally did not want to be left holding the metaphorical baby.

She was rearranging the drinks for the third time when she heard Justin's key in the lock. Peering through the half open kitchen door, she saw the look of horror he cast over the living room and out into the conservatory. For several long moments, he stood stock still. Sally shrank back into the kitchen. Then came the explosion and she knew that the moment of reckoning had arrived.

'Sally!' he roared. He appeared in the doorway, his face like thunder, and folded his arms across the width of his chest. 'Explain,' he ordered curtly.

Instinctively, Sally reached for the strand of hair hanging over her shoulder. Justin reached forward and removed it from her grasp. 'I'm waiting,' he told her, voice like ice and eyes like twin chips of granite.

'Justin, I'm sorry. Things just got a bit out of hand,' she burbled, nervously. 'I only realized on Wednesday when everyone confessed to having invited extra people and by then it was too late to do anything about it.'

'And you didn't tell me, why exactly?' he demanded harshly.

'Well, I haven't seen you to talk to since the meeting and I thought…' she swallowed, risking a glance at the stern implacability of his face, 'you were going to be here anyway, what would a few more people matter?' She tried a chirpy smile but it failed miserably, her lips catching on her teeth in the dryness of her mouth.

'How many?'

'About tw… about thirty odd,' she admitted in a small voice. And waited. She put her hands firmly behind her back to prevent herself wringing them. Justin stared at her. Minutes passed.

'Jesus!' he exclaimed finally, levering himself off the door jamb and making a hasty exit.

So, that was that. Sally moved despondently from the kitchen, to the living room, to the conservatory. It all looked so good; the food, the drink, the lighting, creating the perfect party ambience, all ready and waiting for the imminent arrival of her guests. Absolutely pointless now of course since Justin, unable to stomach the thought of being lionized by village worthies for the entire evening, had just turned tail and fled. Well, there was nothing much she could do about that now but she was blowed if she was going to let all her preparations go to waste, Justin or no Justin. After several pointless but extremely satisfying minutes in which she dwelt on what exactly she would like to do to him at that precise moment and then a few more on what exactly she was going to say to him when she saw him next, she did what she guessed any self-respecting woman would do in the circumstances. She went upstairs to make herself look as good as possible.

Confidence. That was what she needed. A little chutzpah. She rifled through the contents of her wardrobe looking for something that would give her a much-needed boost. If she had to host this party single-handed and explain to everyone who would be coming specifically to meet him that the guest of honour was not, in fact, going to be there, she wanted to look good doing it. Her hand alighted on a scarlet dress. She'd worn it only once when in London for the hen night of an old university friend. Her fingers closed on the silky fabric and itched to pull it out but she hesitated uncertainly. Was it not perhaps a little too…'nightclub'? Insufficiently Country Casuals? On the other hand, she loved that dress and knew it looked good on her. Decisively, she drew it out and slipped it on.

It was very fitted, hugging her figure like a second skin. The neckline plunged dramatically, revealing an expanse of smooth bare skin at the back and rather a lot of cleavage at the front. A deep vent in the hem at the back also afforded tantalizing glimpses of thigh encased in sheer black stockings. As Sally bent to put on the familiar black ballet pumps, the spirit of the dress seemed to take over somehow and she found herself instead slipping her feet into the black satin stilettos she'd bought to go with it. She scooped her hair high into a fashionably messy bun, securing it with a smooth black clasp, and added some dangly jet earrings. Completing the look by slicking on some fresh make-up, she tottered into the bathroom and subjected herself to serious scrutiny in the full-length mirror.

Oh goodness! Her outfit had chutzpah in spades and fairly sexy chutzpah at that. Peter, who professed a preference for the demure look particularly where Sally was concerned, was going to have apoplexy, to say nothing of Bob Helmsworth! Perhaps she should change, put on something a little less revealing? But even as she dithered, a noise at the front door had her flying down the stairs, to greet the first arrival.

'Justin! It's you!' she exclaimed stupidly as she rounded the bottom of the stairs and came to an abrupt halt in front of him.

'So it would appear,' he agreed, thrusting several carrier bags into her hands. 'Take those into the kitchen,' he instructed as he went back outside, reappearing moments later with several more. The bags were heavy and clinked. Sally, placing them gingerly on the kitchen floor, peered inside. Bottles. Lots of bottles.

'If I'm going to have to spend the evening being charming to Pious Pete, Helmsworth and Iris Girton, I am going to have to be fairly well anaesthetized,' Justin told her by way of explanation. 'And I don't intend to achieve it by drinking any of the paint stripper you've bought.'

Ruthlessly, he confined her purchases to the small cupboard under the stairs. Then Sally watched in awe as he unpacked bottle after bottle of his own. He must have spent a small fortune! But aside from the wine, posh red, white and blush, she noted with approval and considerable surprise that he had also bought a couple of cases of beer, sherry, sweet and dry, and an extensive variety of expensive spirits and mixers.

'There!' he stood back and surveyed the tightly packed worktop with satisfaction. 'That should cater for more or less everyone, I think.' He turned to Sally, who was still speechless with surprise. 'Vital ingredients for a good party, Sal. Good food, good booze and good company.' He shot her a wicked grin, 'Well, two out of three ain't bad! Now,' he stowed the carriers out of sight and made for the door, 'I'd better have a wash and brush up. I don't want to let the side down after all.'

Chapter Thirteen

Heavens, he does brush up well, was Sally's first thought as Justin reappeared about twenty minutes later, a dark tailored jacket over spotless white T-shirt emphasizing the width of his shoulders and the almost Hispanic, dark good looks occasionally found in native Cornishmen. Instinctively, she breathed in the citrus tang of his aftershave and smiled her approval as her eyes met his. Then a sharp rap at the door had Sally leaping into action and any chance of conversation between them was lost.

Justin, every inch his mother's son, turned out to be an excellent host. At some point, he had sorted out, courtesy of his iPOD speakers, some discreet but tasteful jazz which gently plugged any awkward conversational gaps. He circulated constantly using the several bottles he managed to hold at one time as his excuse both to introduce himself to people as he refilled their glasses and to take his leave as he moved on to the next willing victim. He plied Harriet Minors and Iris with syrupy sweet sherry causing the former to become quite coquettish and the latter to address him fondly by his Christian name. As Sally predicted, now that he was on his best behaviour, he did indeed have them eating out of his hand before he'd done more than couple of circuits of the room.

Having a common point of interest meant that everyone chatted easily about their pieces and the progress of their rehearsals so far; they were all very excited about the festival. Sally, following Justin's lead, patrolled the rooms, a plate in each hand, making introductions as she went.

Peter was predictably late, having sent Sally a brief text explaining that he was held up at the beside of a sick parishioner. Sally, happening to be standing by the window as he approached, greeted him at the door, offering him her cheek and thanking him for the bottle of what Justin would undoubtedly refer to as paint stripper.

'Good grief, Sally!' he exclaimed as he kissed her hello. 'What are you wearing?'

Sally looked down at her dress and up again at Peter. 'A dress,' she frowned. 'What's the matter? Don't you like it?'

'Well, yes but,' he gave it a longer, more thorough examination, 'it doesn't leave much to the imagination, does it?'

Sally, under the influence of two rather large glasses of wine, was rapidly developing a level of chutzpah to match that of her dress. 'This,' she waved a hand at the throng behind her, 'is a party and this,' she smoothed her dress over her hips, 'is a party dress, and,' she continued defiantly, 'I think I look rather glamorous.'

Peter looked dubious and slightly disapproving. 'There is a very fine line between glamour and vulgarity, you know, and I'm not at all sure that dress falls the right side of it. Can't you put a cardy over it or something?'

Sally, who had had her own doubts about the dress when she'd viewed it earlier in the privacy of the bathroom, opened her mouth to tell him that she would go upstairs and find something suitable to put on as soon as she got the chance but chutzpah took over, 'At least I made an effort, which is more than you have!'

Peter stiffened and replied with something approaching peevishness, 'I have come straight form Mrs. Tregembo's sick-bed, as you well know. I thought you'd rather I did that than waste time going home to preen myself. What I'd like to know is, would you have made so much of an effort if Trevelyan hadn't been here?'

Sally, realizing their furiously whispered conversation was beginning to attract attention, flicked up the latch on the door and pushed him back outside onto the doorstep.

'For your information, I'm dressed like this precisely because I thought he wouldn't be here tonight!' In spite of Peter's barely suppressed tut of disbelief, she continued, 'When he found out how many people were going to be here, he just dashed off without saying anything. I thought I was going to have to host the whole thing by myself. Let's face it, I knew I couldn't rely on you being here to help. So, I dressed to impress just to get me through the evening. As it happened, he'd rushed off because he realized I hadn't bought anything like enough drinks and came back later having spent a fortune on exactly the kind of thing everyone likes.'

'Don't be taken in by overt displays of generosity,' Peter warned. 'It's easy to throw money around when you have plenty. Much more impressive, to give generously of what you only have a little.'

'Like time, you mean? That'll be why Justin's been here holding the fort with me for the last couple of hours? Because he's got nothing else to do, has he? Because he's not really running a whole festival for no money and not much thanks just to save your church, is he?'

Peter looked affronted. 'He's not the only one with commitments, Sally. If you had asked me to, of course I would have been here earlier to help.'

The fresh air was starting to have a sobering affect on Sally and the first few heavy raindrops of what promised to be a spring storm were dampening her spirits as well as her hair. She realized suddenly that their argument was futile and that she'd neglected her guests for quite long enough. 'The point is, Peter,' she told him rather sadly. 'I shouldn't always have to ask. Anyway, I'm asking you now, I've a houseful of people and I'd like us both to go inside and look after them.' With that, she pushed the door open, strode back into the conservatory, grabbed a couple of plates and started handing food around once more, leaving Peter to fend for himself.

But, now that the first rush of activity and the effects of the wine were abating, Peter's words continued to echo in Sally's head. Self-consciously, she hitched her dress up at the front and tugged the hem down towards her knees. She no longer felt glamorous and sophisticated, she felt exposed and vulnerable. Bob Helmsworth's clammy hand on her bare back clinched the matter. She ran upstairs and rummaged frantically through the drawer at the bottom of her wardrobe, unearthing a black pashmina which she draped over her shoulders. It covered her back completely and, if she drew it forward enough, hid most of her cleavage too. Feeling much more respectable, she threw herself back into circulation.

'Sally dear!' Iris hailed her. 'What a splendid party! You really have done us proud.' Sally offered her a plateful of tiny smoked salmon blinis. 'I don't mind if I do. The food is lovely, Sally dear. And you must tell me where you got this sherry. It's delicious!'

'You'll have to ask Justin,' Sally admitted. 'He's responsible for the drinks.'

'Really?' squeaked Harriet, looking rather pink. 'He is such a gentleman, isn't he, Iris?' Sally permitted herself a private smile. His charm offensive had obviously worked a treat, on the ladies at least. Iris, keen to establish the source of the sherry, had already attracted Justin's attention and beckoned him over.

He glided towards them, smiling graciously, 'A top up ladies?' Both Iris and Harriet readily held out their glasses.

'You must tell us what this lovely sherry is and where you got it, Justin,' demanded Iris.

Obligingly, Justin filled them in and promised to get a couple of bottles each next time he was passing the supplier.

'And now, ladies,' he concluded smoothly, taking a firm hold of Sally's elbow. 'I'm going to have to steal the lovely Sally away. Slight crisis in the kitchen, I'm afraid.'

'What's the problem, Justin?' demanded Sally, removing her elbow from his grasp as soon as they were through the kitchen door. 'Have we run out of something?'

'Oh, it's not a catering crisis, Sal,' Justin informed her suavely. 'No, more of a couture crisis.' He reached out a hand and casually flicked the fringe of her pashmina. 'What in the devil's name is that?'

'It's a pashmina,' said Sally, clutching it a little more tightly round her. 'Why?'

'Exactly what I asked myself when I saw it. Why? Why on earth would you suddenly decide to drape a scarf over yourself?'

'I…I was feeling a little chilly,' Sally improvised, a blush deepening the heightened colour of her cheeks.

'Liar! It's boiling in there,' he indicated the living room with a jerk of his head. 'And you're obviously feeling the heat, your cheeks are nearly the colour of your dress. Which, by the way, is quite stunning on you. Bringing us neatly back to my original question. Why would you want to cover yourself up when you look as good as you do tonight?' Without waiting for an answer, Justin took hold of one corner of the pashmina. Keeping his eyes fixed firmly on hers, he pulled on it slowly but insistently so the whole thing slid gently along her arms and across her bare shoulders till it ended up dangling loosely from his fingers. He let it fall. 'Best place for it,' he told her in a confidential whisper, neatly kicking it into a corner. Then he placed a hand in the small of her back and gave her a forceful push. 'Go knock 'em dead, Sal.'

Sally erupted into the living room with such force that the kitchen door flew back against the wall. The resulting thwack resonated like a gunshot. Conversations broke off and heads turned curiously towards the noise. Sally stood stock still in the doorway, bathed in a shaft of light from the kitchen as if in a spotlight. Her eyes darted desperately round the room searching for an escape route. She couldn't retreat to the kitchen; Justin was there. She couldn't go forward with everyone watching expectantly.

'Sally!' She was rescued by a familiar figure to her right. Sally darted forward and kissed Kath warmly on both cheeks. 'I'm so sorry I'm late, Sally. Stupid taxi picking me up went to the wrong address.'

'Never mind, you're here now and it's lovely to see you.' To Sally's relief, chatter bubbled into life around them as she spoke.

'It's lovely to see you too, though I'm dead jealous of that dress, skinny cow!' Kath told her affectionately.

Sally frowned. 'You don't think it's a bit tarty?'

'Well, you know my maxim is if you've got it, flaunt it,' Kath, wearing a tight, low-cut sparkly top, evidently had no qualms about accentuating her very obvious assets. 'And if I wore something like that I'd probably look like Nell Gwyn on the pull. You, on the other hand, just look sickeningly chic.'

'Really?' breathed Sally. 'I was a worried it was a bit OTT. Peter didn't think it was appropriate for this kind of gathering.'

Kath gave a little snort of disgust. 'I don't expect Peter would be happy unless you were clothed neck to toe in a wimple.'

Sally giggled. 'I think you mean a habit. A wimple is the pointy hat thing. But I get your drift and I think you're being a bit unkind. He just likes me to look nice.'

'Nice being the operative word. Iris and Harriet look nice, Sally. But I wouldn't rush to copy their style. Anyway, if Peter doesn't like the way you look in that dress, he needs his bumps felt. Oh, wait a minute,' Kath paused, studying Sally speculatively, as if suddenly struck by an idea. 'Sexy red dress. Justin Trevelyan. I don't suppose the two are linked in any way, are they? Could it be you're going back for a second bite of the cherry after all?'

Sally, still burning from embarrassment at the way Justin had thrust her unceremoniously back into the living room just minutes before, shook her head vehemently. She explained the events leading up to the start of the party.

'You thought he'd done a runner and wasn't going to come back?' Kath wanted clarification.

'Well, yes. I mean, I didn't think he'd gone back to London or anything. I just thought he'd stay out of the way till the party was over.'

'And really he'd just gone out to buy all this lovely plonk?' Kath indicated the large glass of white she had managed to secure for herself in spite of her late arrival. 'But that was so good of him!'

'Well, yes, I suppose it was, but it would have saved me a lot of angst if he'd just explained what he was doing at the time. And don't let him hear you call it plonk. It's posh stuff apparently. Anyway, he didn't just get wine. He bought the most disgusting sweet sherry for Iris and her friends, port and brandy for the Helmsworth set, and loads of mixers. My kitchen looks like an off licence!'

'Oh my god! He is too good to be true. He is THE most handsome hunk and kind and thoughtful too. Please tell me he's got some disgusting habits or I might just die of unrequited love!' Kath, the mistress of hyperbole, begged her.

'Disgusting habits…' Sally mused, honestly unable to think of any.

'Yes, you know, like he snores or picks his nose or,' she lowered her voice, 'farts at the table, or something.'

Laughing, Sally wracked her brains. 'Well, I'm not sure about the snoring,' she stopped as Kath raised her eyebrows questioningly. 'OK, OK. He certainly never used to and if he does now, it's not loud enough for me to hear in my room, and he definitely doesn't do either of the other things, thank goodness. Actually, he's quite a model houseguest. He's learned not to drop towels or dirty underwear on the bathroom floor, he puts the toilet seat down and washes up after himself.'

Kath feigned a swoon. 'I can't bear it. He IS perfect.'

'Haven't you listened to anything I've told you about him?' Sally asked in exasperation. 'Honestly, Kath. One glimpse of a bloke's guns and your brain goes all mushy! Justin Trevelyan has the most awful temper and is quite the bossiest man you're ever likely to meet. He's forever telling me what to do and I swear he doesn't even realize he's doing it.'

'Oooh, gorgeous and masterful with it. C'mon, Sally, you have to introduce me to him properly,' Kath put her arm through her friend's. 'If you're quite sure you and he really are history, I wouldn't mind a crack at him myself.'

Sally nodded emphatically. 'I'm quite sure, thank you, but really, Kath, I wouldn't wish him on my worst enemy.'

'I know, honey. You and he had a bad time of it. But I'm not after his undying devotion, I'll settle for a quick roll in the hay, he's that gorgeous. Or is there something you're not telling me?'

'Well,' Sally was about to fill her in on everything she'd read but something held her back. Was it fair to prejudice Kath against Justin on the strength of rumours she'd found on the internet? Though he'd been abominably rude to her at times since he'd re-entered her life so dramatically, and he was more than a little off with Peter, he'd actually behaved very well to everyone else by all accounts. Even when he'd tackled the committee about her work-load, though Iris clearly felt he'd over-stepped the mark, he'd really just asked some difficult questions. And he had been horribly jet-lagged at that meeting which made the nicest of people a bit cranky.

Her instinct was to tell Kath to avoid Justin like the plague but Kath was an adult, quite capable of looking after herself. Perhaps, Sally's conscience niggled, she was being a bit dog in the manger about Justin? But there was no possibility of rekindling her own romantic relationship with him, of course there wasn't. So maybe she should encourage Kath. Maybe she was exactly the diversion needed to draw Justin's attention away from Sally.

'Evening ladies,' Justin approached taking the decision out of Sally's hands. He splashed a liberal amount of white into Kath's glass. 'No drink, Sally?' he queried. 'We can't have that. Let me go and get you a glass.'

'No' Sally laid a hand on his arm to stop him. 'I'll get myself something soft from the kitchen in a minute. First, let me introduce you to my very good friend, Kath Jordan.'

Justin tucked a bottle under his arm and extended a hand. 'Glad to meet you, Kath.'

'Nice to meet you too,' Kath replied leaving her hand resting in his for considerably longer than necessary. 'I sing first soprano with the mixed choir,' she told him, obviously hoping for a spark of recognition.

'Ah yes, of course,' Justin covered smoothly but Sally would have been prepared to bet all her 'housekeeping' that he didn't remember her.

Kath, determined to make the most of her opportunity, began plying Justin with questions and listening wide-eyed and eager to his answers.

Suddenly, Sally felt decidedly de trop. 'I'll... um... just go and get that drink, then,' she murmured and melted away in the direction of the kitchen.

She closed the kitchen door behind her and leaned gratefully against it. Then she poured herself a glass of water and drank it slowly, sip by sip. Having taken off her watch when she got washed and changed, she didn't know exactly what the time was but she did know that it was well past midnight. The balls of her feet throbbed in the unfamiliar stilettos and she was longing for her bed. As yet though, only those who lived furthest away or who had to get back to relieve babysitters had left; the rest of her guests showed no sign of following suit.

She peeked back into the living room. Things out there were still going with a swing. Peter was deeply engrossed in a discussion with Bob, his wife and some of the male voice choir. Justin had abandoned his bottles on the window sill and was now giving Kath his undivided attention. Something he said seemed to strike her as highly amusing and she threw back her head, wild mess of golden curls rippling down her back, affording him a bird's eye view of her even white teeth, long, smooth neck and generous bosom.

Sally pushed the door to and surveyed the mess that used to be her kitchen. This, she decided was why she didn't throw parties very often. It looked as though a particularly thirsty and ill-disciplined army had run amok in it. Bottles littered the floor and every available space on the work top was taken up with discarded plastic glasses, plates of congealing food and puddles of alcohol seeping into balled up napkins. Sally sighed.

Without really thinking about it, she found herself emptying dregs into the sink and stuffing rubbish into a bin bag. She cleared a space on the work surface, gave it wipe with disinfectant spray then neatly lined up all the bottles which had been opened but not drunk dry. She placed the empties carefully on the floor in the farthest corner. Just as she had decided there was not much more she could usefully do, Peter poked his head around the door.

'Sally! I've been looking everywhere for you,' he said teasingly. 'People want to say goodbye.'

In a cottage this size, thought Sally, you couldn't have been looking very hard. Aloud she said pleasantly, 'Well, here I am.'

Peter came further into the kitchen and attempted to take her arm. 'You're not being very sociable, darling. You should be in the living room mingling, not skulking in here on your own.'

Sally shook her arm free. 'I've been mingling, Peter. For the best part of five hours. Believe it or not, I'm a bit tired now and I thought I'd get ahead with the clearing up while I had the chance.'

Peter assumed a suitably sympathetic expression. 'Of course. But don't worry about tidying up. I'll give you a hand with that later. Come on,' he took her arm again and, this time, Sally allowed herself to be led back into the living room. Whatever Peter had said, it didn't look to her like anyone was in a hurry to leave. Then she spotted Justin and Kath rifling through the coats that had been slung over the newel post at the bottom of the stairs. Catching sight of her, Kath gave a little wave and made her way over.

'Justin's kindly offered to see me home, Sally, so we're going to make a move. Lovely party, thanks so much!' As she leaned in to kiss Sally goodbye, she added, sotto voce, with a very naughty giggle, 'And don't expect to see him back tonight!'

Sally kissed her back with an answering smile and reminded herself she should be grateful to Kath. One, because her leaving had started a general exodus and two, for, as it were, drawing Justin's fire. If anyone could keep Justin sweet, Kath would be able to and if he were involved with her, perhaps he'd be a little less interested in Sally's private life. Admittedly, having your best friend get off with your ex on the strength of a mere couple of hours acquaintance might take a little getting used to but she hoped it would work out well for them, she really did.

Mindful of a clamour of guests waiting to thank her and say goodbye, Sally gave herself a mental shake, fixed her smile back in place and gamely performed the part of the gracious hostess until the last of them had left. At last, it was just her and Peter. Sally kicked off her shoes and collapsed onto the sofa.

'Oh, my feet!' she exclaimed, wriggling toes grateful to be released. Peter came and sat beside her. He lifted her feet onto his lap and began to massage them gently, circling his thumbs along her insteps, up across the balls of her feet and in between her toes. Sally closed her eyes in bliss and gave herself up to enjoyment of the rhythmic motion.

'Mmn,' she sighed, 'Lovely.' For several minutes, Peter devoted himself to the task. His hands strayed from her feet, upwards, along her ankles, then he stopped, kneading delicate fingers into her calf muscles. Sally sank more deeply into the cushions, feeling all the tensions of the evening ebbing away. She began to doze off. Finally, Peter gave her calves one last, long stroke and removed his hands.

'Come on, you. This isn't getting the house tidied.' He lifted her legs off his lap and placed her feet back on the floor. Sally groaned and reached out a hand to him.

'Let's leave it, Peter,' she begged. 'We can do it in the morning. I'm so tired and that massage was so heavenly, I can't move.' Peter laughed, took hold of her outstretched hand and pulled her up into a sitting position.

'Best get it over with,' he told her. 'You'll thank me for it in the morning when you're able to have a lie in. Come on.' He moved into the kitchen and Sally heard him opening the cupboard under the sink and rustling plastic bags. Grumbling under her breath, she followed him, took one of the bags and began trawling the living room. Peter meanwhile collected anything that should be salvaged and carried it through to the kitchen. They worked in silence for some time. By now, Sally felt almost catatonic, going through the motions with the minimum of exertion and thought. Eventually, the two rooms were almost back to normal and Sally, using her knees and bottom, nudged the furniture back into its rightful places. She trundled after Peter into the kitchen where she surveyed the mountain of washing up with dismay.

'Oh, my goodness! This is going to take forever. Please let's leave it. I'll do it in the morning, really I will.' But Peter had said that he would help her tidy and that was what he intended to do. He rolled up his sleeves, handed her a tea towel and seized the washing up liquid. 'I'll wash, you dry and put away, as you know where everything belongs.'

'I wish I had a dishwasher,' Sally muttered.

It took ages. Peter washed up as he did everything else, thoroughly and precisely. Sally was much more lax on this occasion, settling for a brisk wipe round to get the dishes more or less dry before stuffing them back vaguely where they'd come from.

After what felt like years, every glass, plate, dish and knife had been put away. Peter rolled his sleeves down and Sally staggered back into the living room. The house felt strangely still and silent now, empty of guests and bereft of the gently ambient music. Outside, Sally could hear the wind yowling and screeching. Rain dashed against the window panes like handfuls of carelessly flung pebbles.

'Heavens, listen to that!' exclaimed Peter, reaching for his coat.

'I had no idea it was raining so hard,' Sally yawned. 'You'll get soaked walking home in this. Why not stay here and go back in the morning? It might have eased off by then.'

'It's OK. Best if I get back to my own bed, I think, Sally.' Possibly it was due to the lateness of the hour and the fact that she was tired beyond reason, but tonight Sally found his stuffiness, which she usually dismissed as an endearing foible, inexpressibly irksome.

'Oh, for goodness' sake, Peter! I'm not suggesting anything untoward. It's late, there's no moon and the weather's foul. You'll get soaked and won't be able to see a thing. I was just trying to save you from catching pneumonia or falling in a ditch and breaking your leg, but if you'd rather risk it than spend the rest of the night in my spare bed, go right ahead.'

Peter hesitated, the sense of her words sinking in. Then he gave himself a little shake and continued buttoning up his coat. 'I think you've forgotten, Sally, that your spare bed is already taken.'

Sally snorted derisively, already heading for the stairs. 'Justin has taken Kath home. He won't be needing my spare bed tonight.'

'Oh,' Peter digested the implications of this. 'Oh, I see. Yes, of course. All the same, I wouldn't feel comfortable sleeping in his sheets and I don't suppose you want to go changing bedding at this time of night. No, best if I head off, like I said.'

By now, Sally was wishing she hadn't started the conversation and was just thinking she'd be glad to see the back of him when a particularly vicious gust of wind accompanied a searing flash of lightning and, almost simultaneously, a floor-trembling clap of thunder. Her conscience kicked in again. He'd stayed on out of the goodness of his heart to help her tidy up; there was no way she could let him go out in this.

'Alright. I'll sleep in the spare room. You can have my bed. I'm assuming you've no objections to sleeping in my used sheets?'

She didn't have to ask twice. Peter was already out of his coat and hot on her heels on the stairs. 'That's very considerate of you, Sally. I have to admit, I wasn't relishing a walk home in this weather one little bit.'

Sally grabbed her pyjamas from her own room and, without even saying goodnight, nipped briefly into the bathroom for the quickest of washes and a hasty brush of her teeth before gratefully subsiding into Justin's bed and falling immediately asleep.

Chapter Fourteen

An icy blast propelled Sally into full consciousness as the duvet was whipped from her body.

'Fuck!' Justin's voice, as he staggered backwards in confusion, rang out loud and angry in the pitch-darkness.

'Sh!' Sally hissed urgently. 'You'll wake Peter!' In one move, she was up on her knees in the bed, flicking on the bedside light with one hand and clamping the other somewhat desperately across his mouth. A dull apricot glow lit a circle around the bed, revealing Justin, damp-haired and naked save for a rather natty pair of dark blue silk boxers.

Justin ripped her hand away, retaining her arm in a vice-like grip. 'Peter?' he repeated, looking around wildly.

'Ouch! Let go,' Sally writhed within his grasp. 'And keep your voice down.'

'Keep my voi…why? What the fuck's going on, Sal?' he demanded in an angry whisper, lessening his hold only slightly.

'You tell me! You're not supposed to be here!'

At this, Justin subsided onto the side of the bed, swept a hand across his face and turned wearily to face her.

'OK. I'm obviously missing something,' he told her in the voice of one clinging onto his patience by the merest thread. 'This is my room, my bed but you're in it. Very simply, and preferably very quickly, explain why.'

'Alright,' Sally agreed. 'But let me have the duvet back, I'm freezing here.' He subjected her to a slow up-down glance as she knelt, barely dressed, before him.

'So I see,' he retrieved the duvet from the floor where he'd dropped it in his surprise and Sally lost no time hauling it up to her chin as much for decency's sake as for warmth.

'Peter stayed on to help me tidy up and it took ages,' she explained, sotto voce, settling herself crossed-legged on the pillow, a judicious distance away from him. 'By the time we'd finished, the weather had turned filthy so I suggested he stayed over rather than walk back. He didn't want to sleep in your bed, so we swapped.'

His dark brows drew together in frown of pure incredulity. 'The more I hear about that man and his 'principles,' (Sally could hear the inverted commas), the more convinced I am that he is completely round the bend.'

'For which,' she reminded him acerbically, 'at the moment, you should be grateful, otherwise he'd be in this bed not me.'

Justin, recovering from his initial shock and beginning to see the funny side of the situation, greeted this with a wry grin.

'Lovely as it is to have your company in my bed, Sal, I could wish it was in slightly different circumstances. If he wasn't barking, you'd be in your bed with him and I'd have mine all to myself. As it is, it appears I'm stuck with someone in my bed that I'm not even allowed to touch.'

'And whose fault is that?' she snapped. 'If only you'd been true to form and slept over at Kath's, we wouldn't be in this mess.'

'What on earth gave you the idea that I'd be spending the night with Kath?' he turned to face her in genuine amazement.

'Long and bitter experience, maybe?' Sally told him with a glare, pulling yet more of the duvet round herself.

'Well, it seems you don't know me quite as well as you thought, doesn't it?' he drew himself up haughtily. 'Your friend Kath might be that easy but I'm not.'

'Kath is not easy,' Sally leaped to her friend's defence, a martial light in her eyes. 'She's young, free and single, and really likes you. And you have to admit, you were practically drooling over her at the party.'

'I certainly was not! I was just being friendly.'

Sally snorted in disbelief. 'Yeah, right!'

'Ah, I see!' Justin relaxed across the bed, leaning on one elbow and raising an eyebrow in sardonic query. 'What's the matter, Sal? Got a touch of the green-eyed monster?'

'What? Ha! Over you? Don't flatter yourself,' Sally, edging further up towards the headboard and doing her best to drag the duvet with her, was emphatic in her denial. 'As far as I'm concerned, Kath's welcome to you. Besides, you agreed to see her home. What did you think she had in mind? A quick hand of bridge and a cup of cocoa?'

'I thought she meant a gentle stroll to the other side of the village to see her safely to her door. How was I supposed to know it was a forty-minute round trip almost all the way to Truro? And,' he went on, aggrieved, 'as neither of us was fit to drive, I had to wait for taxis both ways.'

'All the more reason for you to have stayed there once you got there then!'

'For heaven's sake,' he remonstrated angrily. 'I only met her this evening. I like to know rather more about someone than their name and their bust size before I jump into bed with them.'

'It never seemed to bother you before. Suddenly acquired some morals, have you, Justin?'

Justin took a quick breath, about to argue the point, then raked a hand through his hair and expelled it slowly. 'Sal, what are we doing? This is no time to be debating my morals. In case you hadn't noticed, you're in the devil of a fix here.'

Sally slumped against the headboard. He was right. She'd been so taken aback by his sudden appearance and the ensuing argument, she'd completely forgotten the circumstances which had led to it. Thank heavens for the thick granite walls of the cottage and the soundproofing presence of her tiny bathroom between the two bedrooms. At least she could be fairly certain that Peter would have, so far, remained in blissful ignorance.

'Oh God!' she whimpered, cradling her head in the hand which wasn't clinging on to the duvet.

'Precisely.'

'Oh God,' Sally repeated glumly. The solution had suddenly become obvious to her. She pulled a pillow from beneath her and threw her legs over the side of the bed. She desperately didn't want to leave its warmth and comfort and would have given anything to have been allowed to just snuggle down and drift off again but, clearly, she had done something very bad in a past life and it was not to be.

'Wait,' Justin laid a restraining hand on her shoulder as she made to rise. 'If I were more chivalrous, I'd doubtless offer you the bed and make myself scarce. As it is, I'm knackered, I have a full day tomorrow and I've no intention of playing the martyr. Your sofa's fine for an afternoon nap but I wouldn't want to spend the night or even,' he glanced at his watch, 'the early hours of the morning, on it. As for your bath, I've seen bigger bidets. You clearly need a decent few hours' sleep as much as I do, so,' he paused, suddenly uncharacteristically diffident, 'I have a suggestion.'

'Which is?' Sally was wary.

'We top and tail.'

'What!' Sally slapped his hand from her arm and stepped away. 'Me spend the night in the same bed as you? I don't think so, thank you!'

'Sofa or bath it is then, Sal.' Was she imagining it, or was he sounding just the tiniest bit smug? But both options were equally unappealing and she was desperately tired. Wavering, she glanced back at the soft, inviting warmth of the bed.

'You'll...you promise you'll behave yourself?'

'You're a sexy lady, Sal, but not completely irresistible, you know. I think I'll just about manage to keep control of myself. 'Course, I can't answer for you. D'you think you can keep your hands off me?' In answer, Sally threw a pillow at him, then slid quickly back beneath the duvet, pulled it up to her throat and resolutely closed her eyes.

''Night, then, Sal,' Justin whispered burrowing himself a space at the foot end.

Barely four hours later, in answer to faint sounds emanating from the bathroom, Sally's eyelids fluttered. She adjusted her position slightly, wrapping her arms more securely round the firm warmth of the hot water bottle. Drifting in and out of consciousness, she smiled sleepily to herself. She was so comfortable, so warm.... Then it struck her. Hot water bottle! What hot water bottle? Her eyes flew open and took in the long, muscled and very definitely male leg she was hugging. With a little squeak, she thrust it away and scrambled into a sitting position.

'Shit!' As her fuddled brain fought its way to wakefulness, all the pieces of the jigsaw dropped into place and she realized the full horror of her situation. 'Justin! Wake up!' she croaked, crawling to the end of the bed.

Justin was lying face down, duvet round his waist, revealing an expanse of smoothly tanned back. One arm was flung carelessly across the pillow whilst his head nestled in the crook of the other, tousled hair starkly black against the pillow. Long lashes lay still along chiseled cheek bones. His breathing continued deep and even. Sally had never seen Peter first thing in the morning but she couldn't help reflecting that he probably wouldn't look as good as this.

Oh God! She thrust the disloyal thought from her mind, stretched out a hand and gave one exposed shoulder a hefty shove. 'Justin!'

He didn't stir. Sally crept closer and shook harder. 'Wake up!'

'Mmn?' Eyes still firmly closed, Justin stirred slightly, rolled slowly onto his back, wrapped his arms loosely round her and showed every sign of drifting back to sleep.

'Justin!' she hissed again, shaking him furiously with one hand and trying to disengage herself with the other. 'You have to wake up!'

Suddenly his eyes flew open, very blue, very lucid and just inches from her own. His arms clamped round her, pinning hers to her sides. 'But I am awake, Sal. Wide awake!'

'You brute! You were awake all along!' She accused, aghast.

'And what a way to wake up it was too.' His gaze moved significantly to her breasts which, clamped hard up against his chest, spilled lushly out of her scanty top.

'Sh!' Sally begged. 'Peter will hear you. I just heard him use the bathroom. He could come in at any moment.'

'Pure Peter? Come in here uninvited and unchaperoned? Unlikely, Sal. And in any case, why should I care? This is, after all, supposed to be my bedroom.'

'Exactly. So he's not going to be overjoyed to find me in here with you, is he? However, innocent last night was.'

'Innocent, Sal?' he allowed his eyes to wander once again. 'You, here, barely dressed and in my bed?'

'I'm not in your bed,' she reminded him. 'I'm on it. There's a double duvet between us.'

'Well, we can soon fix that!' Keeping firm hold of her with one hand, he matched the action to the words and twitched the duvet from beneath her. Immediately, Sally could feel him, warm and hard against her. She caught her breath as an answering wave of heat welled up from deep within. Her breathing quickened and a long dormant pulse beat between her legs. There was nothing innocent about it now.

'Please, Justin,' she begged again. 'Stop being such a pain and help me!'

Wickedly, he laughed down at her, enjoying her plight. 'But Sally, why would I? This is exactly how I like my women, in my bed and begging me!'

Sally swallowed. She could feel his heart beating against her ribs, his breath, soft against her cheek. How many times over the past six years had she dreamed of being with him, just like this? How often had she longed to be in bed with him, in his arms, his lips close enough to brush with her own? Now, here they were, just two scraps of silk separating their eager bodies.

He wanted her, that much was clear. And she wanted him. God, how she wanted him! All she had to do was relax against him, one touch, one kiss…and the rest would be inevitable. But she couldn't.

Unexpected, unbidden, hot salty tears of regret welled in her eyes.

'Sal!' Instantly, Justin released her from his hold. 'Sweetheart, don't!' he implored.

Angrily, Sally rolled away from him and sat, back towards him, on the edge of the bed, scrubbing furiously at her face with a corner of the duvet.

'Sal, I was just messing around. I didn't mean… I didn't realize…' his voice trailed away as Sally turned to face him, eyes blazing.

'Oh, grow up, Justin!' she hissed furiously. 'For god's sake, grow up! Yes, you're a hunk, yes, you turn me on, OK? Satisfied now? We established that years ago, just like we established that you're no good for me and I'm no good for you. So now you've got a choice. You can help me sort out this godawful mess I've got myself into or you can carry on behaving like an ape and blow the best thing that's happened to me in years.'

Justin straightened up abruptly and took a deep breath obviously about to give her back as good as he'd just got. Then, suddenly, he swept one hand back through the tangle of his hair, as realization dawned on him, 'Fuck!'

'Fuck?' Sally tutted in despair. 'That's the best you can do? Fuck?'

But Justin, kneeling now, seized her shoulder and administered a non-too-gentle shake. 'No, Sally, listen. You've got to go and head him off,' he whispered, urgently. 'Otherwise he'll see my coat and shoes by the front door and realize I came back after all. Get him into the kitchen and keep him there. I'll put some clothes on and leave through the front door. OK?'

Sally was off the bed and at the door in less than a heartbeat. Once there, she paused momentarily and glanced back at him.

'Thank you!' she mouthed, drawing an answering nod of recognition from Justin. Then she slipped out, pasting on her best good morning smile, and literally bumped into Peter on the landing.

''Morning,' she stood awkwardly, gripping the handle of the bedroom door tightly behind her. A stab of guilt seared through her so painfully, she was surprised it wasn't visible.

'Good morning, darling,' Peter placed a chaste kiss on her cheek then stepped rather hastily away, indicating her state of undress with a sweep of his hand. 'Perhaps a…um…dressing gown might be a good idea?'

'Yes, of course. You go and put the kettle on and I'll be down in a tick.' As Peter made his way downstairs, Sally whisked into her own room, snatched her dressing gown from the back of the door and belted it firmly round her waist. What she wanted to do was to throw herself onto the neatly made bed, have a good cry in delicious solitude and try, if she could, to sort out her muddled thoughts. But there was no time for that now. Seconds later, she was pulling the kitchen door to behind her as Peter was spooning coffee into mugs, a picture of prosaic normality. He looked up as she entered.

'Sorry if I disturbed you, love,' his look, as he slipped bread into the toaster, was genuinely apologetic. 'I meant you to have a lie in this morning. But I've got the Taylors at 9.30 about christening their youngest and I'm going through wedding arrangements with another young couple straight after that. I've not finished my sermon for tomorrow, either, so I need to get a move on.'

'Don't worry about it,' Sally accepted a mug and gulped gratefully, leaning against the door in what she hoped was a casual pose in order to preclude any premature exit. 'It was good of you to stay so late helping me when you knew you had a busy day today.'

Peter smiled at her. 'No problem. As I couldn't help with any of the preparations, a bit of clearing up was the least I could do.' With the ease of familiarity, he found two plates, butter and jam and began to spread the freshly popped toast. 'What are your plans for today?'

Sally considered this with half her mind whilst the other half tried to work out whether or not Justin had had time to make his escape. She'd been so focused on the party that she hadn't given much thought at all to what she'd be doing the day after. 'Oh, just domestic stuff, you know,' she improvised, killing time. 'Housework, washing, bit of shopping. Maybe even forty winks, if I'm lucky, to catch up on some sleep.'

'And tonight?' Peter had already made serious inroads on his second piece of toast and his mug was nearly drained. Sally strained her ears for footsteps on the stairs. Hurry up, Justin, she willed silently. Aloud, she said, 'No plans. Why? Do you want to do something?'

'Yes, as a matter of fact, I do. I thought it might be nice if we went out for a meal. We haven't done that for quite some time. What about the restaurant at Lawncrest? I've heard very good things about it since that TV chef took over the kitchen.'

Sally was surprised by this suggestion; it was unlike Peter to eat out without the excuse of a special occasion. She considered briefly. Maybe it would be a good idea to spend an evening with him? An evening away from the festival plans, from his parishioners and, most importantly, away from the disturbing influence of Justin Trevelyan.

'I'd like that,' she told him honestly. 'I'll phone and book, shall I, as you're going to be busy? Best not leave it to chance as it's a Saturday, or we might not get a table.'

Peter nodded his agreement. 'Good idea. Thanks.' Then, washing down the last of his toast, he checked his watch. 'I need to get going,' he pecked her cheek. 'Text me later what time to pick you up.' And with that, he took her by the shoulders, moved her bodily out of his way and went to get his coat.

Sally peered anxiously after him. Justin should be long gone by now she reckoned but was aware, even so, that she was holding her breath expectantly. Just as Peter reached for the latch, there was the sound of a key being inserted from the outside and Justin appeared, shaking rain from his hair and stamping mud onto the doormat.

'Peter!' he acknowledged, feigning surprise and adding, Sally supposed, for authenticity's sake, 'I wasn't expecting to see you here at this hour of the morning. Good night, was it?'

The colour rose in Peter's cheeks as Justin's meaning sank in. 'Yes, thank you. That is… me being here at this time isn't quite how it seems, you know.'

'Oh, I believe you, Peter.' Justin assured him with a wry smile. 'Strangely, me being here at this time isn't quite how it seems either.' Then, as Peter struggled to make sense of this enigmatic statement, Justin opened the front door and held it wide. 'Well, don't let me keep you. I'm sure you've got places to be and people to see.'

'Good timing,' observed Sally from her post in the kitchen doorway, as the front door closed behind her fiancé.

Justin removed his coat and shoes. 'Something of an essential quality in a conductor,' he replied, adding darkly, 'shame the same thing can't be said of you.'

'No, well, I'm sorry about...' she flapped a hand somewhat helplessly, 'all this,' adding impulsively, 'Let me cook you breakfast to say thank you.'

'I'd rather not, actually. I need a shower before I get dressed properly, then I've got a full schedule. I plan to be out for the rest of the weekend.' He took the stairs two at a time and headed straight into the bathroom.

Brilliant! He muttered under his breath, masochistically standing under a freezing cold shower. Not content with winding her up at every available opportunity, you have to reduce her to tears and then fling her offer of breakfast back in her face. What is the matter with you, man?

Furiously, he lathered his hair and ducked his head back under water so cold it made him gasp. He knew exactly what was the matter with him. Sally Marsh! No-one else had ever got under his skin the way she had. The way she still did. But, whilst in the heat of an argument, he might very well feel like throttling her, the last thing he wanted to do was to hurt her. Incomprehensible as it might seem to him, if Sally had truly found happiness with Peter, then who was he, Justin, to reappear suddenly in her life and spoil things?

Seemed to him the solution was the same as it had been six years ago. Cold showers, lots of runs and something, or rather someone, to take his mind off her. He could only hope this time he would be more successful.

Chapter Fifteen

Throughout Saturday, people phoned thanking Sally for the party and asking her to pass their thanks on to Justin. She promised them all that she would though she had no idea when or even if she'd be able to. He'd made it quite clear she needn't expect to see him over the next couple of days. Who knew when she'd next get to have a civilised conversation with him?

In the event, it was actually Monday evening before Sally saw either Justin or Peter to speak to again.

Mrs Tregembo had taken a turn for the worse late on Saturday afternoon and, inevitably, Peter had the best part of the evening with her in hospital. He'd phoned Sally to explain just as she'd been putting the finishing touches to her make-up, leaving her all dressed up with nowhere to go. Biting back her disappointment, she'd called the restaurant to cancel their reservation then, on an off-chance, she sent Kath a quick text to see if they could get together.

Unusually for Kath, several minutes passed before her reply pinged into Sally's inbox.

Soz, sweetie. J called me out of the blue! Coming round 2nite after reh. Have urgent appt with bath and Ladyshave!! Maybe this time...???? X

Sally didn't dare explore the various emotions she felt on reading that. Stoically, she'd texted back.

Good Luck…be gentle with him! Txt me how it goes. Xxx

Then, she'd wiped off her make-up, changed out of her glad-rags and resigned herself to an evening of SATs paper marking.

Sally heard nothing more from Kath that evening. She wasn't surprised. What did surprise her was the sound of Justin's key in the lock shortly after midnight. She lay on her back in the darkness listening to the sound of him getting ready for bed. It was strangely comforting having someone else around.

Her eyes flew wide open and she stared at the ceiling in horror.

She hadn't felt lonely or scared here before! So why did she find it comforting having someone else around now? Not someone else, she corrected herself, Justin. It was comforting to know Justin was around. It was good to know he was back. And that he hadn't spent the night with Kath.

Sally rolled over and groaned softly into her pillow. What was going on with her? Justin Trevelyan might appear to be the perfect romantic hero; tall, dark, handsome and successful, but she, of all people, knew the pitfalls of being in a relationship with such a man. He put himself and his career first and everyone else came a very poor second. Heaven help anyone naïve enough to fall in love with him!

Besides, she reminded herself firmly, she had no business to care one way or the other if Justin was back. She should be disappointed for Kath that things hadn't panned out the way she'd wanted them to and definitely not thinking that having Justin in the next room was 'comforting'.

It should be Peter she was thinking of in that way, not Justin. Peter, who always put others' needs first, who was always steady, reliable and supportive. Peter had been there when she and her mother were coping with her father's unexpected death. Peter had seen her through the long, agonising illness which had eventually claimed her mother. Peter had helped her sort out the funeral, the sale of the bungalow and the bureaucratic nightmare that was probate. It was Peter who, with help from Kath and Iris, had scooped her up and pieced her back together when she had been at her lowest ebb.

Where had Justin been through all of that? Shagging his way round Europe, leaving a trail of broken hearts behind him. Justin had been her first love. But she was very different now from that wide-eyed, love-struck teenager. There would probably always be something between them, some special attraction, some reminder of their younger selves but she had different needs and priorities now which couldn't be met by someone like him. It was with Peter that, from the solid foundations of mutual respect, admiration and friendship, a deep affection has grown into an abiding love. It was with Peter that she'd built a solid relationship, a richly fulfilled life in the warmth of their community. Peter was her fiancé. And she loved him far too much to risk throwing it all away. She really did.

The hours she'd spent during the night thrashing out her emotions had not been wasted for, when Sally woke on Sunday morning, she felt refreshed, calm and more settled in herself than she had for ages. Now, safe in the knowledge that Justin was already up and out, she wandered into the conservatory, coffee in one hand, phone in the other. Sally smiled wryly as she reread Kath's text which, sent in the wee small hours, showed she'd had even more difficulty getting off to sleep than Sally.

*******! What is the matter with him? Kxxx

Sally pressed call, curled up in her favourite chair and settled down for a comfortable chat.

'Sally!' Kath answered almost immediately. 'Normally I'd kill you for calling at this time on a Sunday morning but, as I was tucked up in my PJs by half eleven last night, I'm glad of the distraction.'

'What happened?'

'What didn't happen, is more to the point!' Kath was aggrieved. 'We went for a drink at The Quantum which was a total treat. I usually have to make do with a night in the pub or a film and a curry. We had posh cocktails and nibbly things and it really seemed we were getting on well. He was sooooo lovely, Sally. He was attentive, gentlemanly, thoughtful, funny, sooo nice.'

Yep, Sally agreed silently. She knew only too well that Justin could soooo be all of those things.

'Then,' Kath went on, hardly drawing breath, 'about half ten, he started muttering about having a full-on day today and before I knew what was happening, we were back at mine. We had the briefest of kisses on the doorstep and then he legged it! I might not have the best relationship record but this is the first time I've failed even to get someone over the threshold after two dates. What am I doing wrong, Sally?'

'Oh, Kath,' Sally sighed, torn between sympathy and exasperation. 'How would I know what's wrong or right where Justin is concerned? What I do know is, he's selfish, arrogant, moody and unpredictable and if you've got any sense, you'll steer well clear.'

'As you've said. Lots of times,' Kath reminded her dryly. 'But that's not going to happen, is it, Sally? I can't help myself. I'm like a moth to a flame.'

Sally couldn't help laughing. 'Moth or not, you're quite incorrigible, that's for sure. Still, if you're hell-bent on pursuing him, nothing I can say is going to stop you.'

'Yep, like you said, I'm incorrigible.' Kath agreed good-naturedly. 'So if you do have any pearls of wisdom you'd care to share....?'

'Well, he clearly likes you so my best offer is, when you see him again, just be yourself. You are seeing him again, I take it?'

'Yes... no... I don't know,' admitted Kath. 'He did mutter something about giving me a ring in the week just before he turned tail and ran. But I'm not holding my breath. Should I call him, d'you think?'

'No,' Sally was grateful that, at last, she was able to give her friend some concrete advice. 'Don't ring him. If he said he'll call you, he will. Just wait it out. Interrupting something he considers important with a random phone call, is a sure way of getting in his bad books.'

'Mnn, you might be right,' Kath conceded reluctantly. 'I suppose I'll just have to be patient. But what if he doesn't call?'

Sally was quick to reassure her. 'He likes you, Kath. He'll call. And like I said, when you do see him again, just be you. If he can't see how lovely you are, then he doesn't deserve you.'

Kath gave one of her trade-mark, full-throated chuckles. 'I don't want him to deserve me, Sally, I just want him to sha....'

'Ew, stop! Enough!' Sally yelled, laughing. 'I know exactly what you want him to do to you without you spelling it out!' In spite of her laughter, she thought it was time to draw their call to an end. 'And now, I'm going to wish you luck and ring off before you can sully my ears with any more sordid details!'

109

Sally spent the rest of the morning catching up on some mundane chores and trying to put Kath's call out of her mind. Her bedroom was still a mess from being used as a dumping ground during the party so she put that to rights, gave it a thorough clean then did a couple of loads of washing, a few bits of ironing, an hour or so prepping lessons for the coming week. There was just time for a sandwich before heading across to the church to tidy up the vestry after the morning's creche and then help with the afternoon's Sunday School class. After that, she drove over to Truro to see Mrs Tregembo as she knew Peter would be too busy with Sunday services to fit in a visit.

Just as she was pulling into a parking space, her phone beeped. It was Peter, in a brief gap before Evensong, calling to apologise for letting her down the previous evening and suggesting they reschedule for tomorrow. He had, he told her mysteriously, something specific he wanted to talk to her about. Sally couldn't help but think that sounded rather ominous. What could Peter possibly want to discuss with her that merited a 'diner a deux'?

Chapter Sixteen

Sally chose her outfit carefully; a high-necked, black dress which skimmed her slender finger and swirled around the calves of her black boots.

Her efforts were rewarded as Peter let himself in and, watching her come downstairs, told her, 'You look nice, love. Very elegant.'

'You too. Very smart.' Sally was pleased that he'd also made an effort wearing a smart dark green jacket and tailored chinos instead of his clerical collar and black suit. 'How was your day?' Sally slipped into the passenger seat of his Polo listening with half an ear as he filled her in on various meetings and Mrs Tregembo who seemed to be holding her own.

'But I didn't ask you to dinner to talk about parish work,' Peter broke off, turning towards her with a self-deprecating smile. 'There's something I want to discuss with you.'

Sally made face, 'Should I be worried?'

'Not at all,' he reassured her. 'At least, I hope you won't think so.'

'Well, go on, then,' she urged. 'Don't keep me in suspense.'

'Patience, Sally,' his tone was teasing. 'Wait till we get to the restaurant.'

For the rest of the journey, they were silent, Sally wracking her brains over what he wanted to talk about, Peter concentrating on driving along the high-hedged lanes. Then, the road dipped towards the sea and Peter pulled a sharp left into a narrow entrance.

'Here we are then, Sally,' he shucked off his seatbelt and came round to open her door.

Lawncrest was the most prestigious hotel in the area. Tastefully converted from the original manor house, it boasted 24 bedrooms of various degrees of opulence, its own golf course, swimming pool, health spa and a restaurant which had recently gained a Michelin star.

Even though it was early on a Monday evening, the tourist season was already well underway and there were only a few unoccupied tables. A graciously friendly maitre d' greeted them at the door, guided them smoothly to their table and produced large, leather-bound menus. A lesser being appeared to take their drinks order which arrived minutes later. Sally, though puzzled to know what Peter was up to, was distracted by their glamorous surroundings. Chandeliers, crystal and silverware gleamed and shone all around. Dark suited waiting staff slid unobtrusively between tables. In every corner, huge urns spewed exotic flowers, their scent mingling with the delicious aromas wafting from the kitchens.

Sally leaned across the table, 'Heavens, this is posh. We should buy shares in silver polish. They must get through tons of the stuff! And these carpets are inches thick. You could lose a small dog in them for days!'

Peter laughed, 'It's certainly impressive,' he agreed. 'If the food and hospitality is as good as the décor, it should please the most exacting critic.'

Sally's enthusiasm died abruptly. Ah, now she understood. Lawncrest would meet with approval from anyone with any taste. Even someone well-travelled and used to the best. Like Justin Trevelyan. Perhaps Peter was right? Perhaps it would be better if Justin took himself off to a hotel?

A waiter appeared. Sally, who'd barely looked at the menu, ordered at random. She was heartily glad that the table next to them was not yet taken; this was a conversation she didn't want overheard. Even so, she found herself whispering, 'So what was it you wanted to talk to me about?'

Peter poured more wine into her glass, then water into his own tumbler. He cleared his throat and lined his cutlery up a little more exactly.

'Peter?' Sally leaned in, demanding eye contact. Eventually, he looked up.

'I wanted to know what you thought about this place,' he told her. 'We could see one of the rooms later, perhaps?'

'Why would we want to do that?' She straightened up, eyes narrowing. How was Peter going to explain what he clearly had in mind?

'I'd want to know everything met with your approval before I went ahead and booked anything.'

'Why, exactly,' Sally demanded, determined not to make this any easier for him. 'Would you be booking something?'

This time Peter met her gaze full on. 'We've waited long enough now, Sally.' He reached out and took her hand. 'We...I... can't go on like this indefinitely.'

'It won't be indefinite!' Sally snatched her hand away, then, catching his expression of hurt, covered the movement by breaking her roll. 'Once the festival is over, everything will go back to normal.'

'Exactly! Hopefully we'll have raised enough money to get all the building work done and then we can go ahead as planned.'

Suddenly aware that the conversation had taken an unexpected turn, Sally put the roll down and gave him her full attention.

'Go ahead as planned?'

'Of course!' Peter was positively animated now. 'Ideally it would be sooner but we wouldn't want to get married in a building site, darling, would we?'

'Married?' Sally echoed.

Peter laughed at her confusion. 'Yes, married! I think it's high time we set a date for the wedding.'

'But...but...,' she gestured at their surroundings. 'What's all this got to do with it?'

'I've got a little nest-egg,' he admitted diffidently. 'We'll want some for a honeymoon but there should be enough to cover the reception too even if we have it here.'

'The reception? Here? Oh Peter!' her face flooded with colour as she realised she'd attributed him with entirely the wrong motives.

Mistaking her embarrassment for disapproval, Peter rushed on, 'Only if you like it, Sally. You see, if the repairs are all finished by the summer, you'll be on holiday and so will your teacher friends. It's short notice for booking a wedding reception but they do still have weekday availability here.'

Sally stared at him stunned. He'd clearly given this a lot of thought. But she'd had no inkling.

'Actually,' Peter threw caution to the winds. 'I've taken the liberty of sounding out the bishop too and August 15th would be a pretty good date for everyone. How does that sound?'

'August 15th?' Sally repeated, dazed. 'I suppose that would be OK.'

Peter gave her hand a little squeeze. 'You could sound a bit more enthusiastic, love,' he chided her.

'Oh, I am!' said Sally, trying to sound it, adding truthfully, 'Just shell-shocked, that's all. When you suggested a meal, setting a date for our wedding was the furthest thing from my mind.'

'Sally!' She jumped at the piercing squeal and found herself smothered in a huge hug.

'Kath! My goodness! What are you doing here?' Bemused, Sally returned the embrace. Over Kath's shoulder, her eyes met first those of her fiancé, looking as bewildered as she felt, then Justin's inscrutable gaze.

Peter rose to his feet. 'Kath, Trevelyan.' To Sally's amazement and, she guessed, Justin's chagrin, he said, quite uncharacteristically, 'We've got some rather splendid news to celebrate. Won't you join us?'

There was a flurry of activity as Peter and the maitre d' got in each other's way supervising the rearrangement of the tables and the arrival of a bottle of champagne.

'So,' when at last they were all seated, Justin raised his glass. 'What are we toasting?'

Peter half rose then settled for raising his own glass in response. 'Sally and I,' he declared, 'have set the date!'

'Sally!' Kath issued another of her speciality squeals. They chinked glasses. 'That's wonderful! When? When?'

Sally squirmed self-consciously. Frowning, Justin drained his champagne; he had no idea what Peter was talking about.

'The wedding,' she took pity on him, 'is to be on August 15th. That's why we're here. Doing a reccy.'

Justin topped up his glass and raised it towards her, 'Rather belatedly, congratulations. To Sally and Peter. May you get all the happiness you deserve.'

Kath, taking a large gulp, echoed, 'Sally and Peter.' Then she rose and tugged at Sally's arm. 'Sally and I need to powder our noses. Talk amongst yourselves, boys.'

'Excuse us,' grateful for the reprieve, Sally didn't need asking twice.

As the restroom door closed behind them, Kath seized Sally giving her a shake, then gathering her into a warm, congratulatory embrace.

'You lucky cow! An actual wedding date! That's so exciting!' Kath stood back, regarding her expectantly. She seemed much more excited than Sally was.

114

'Yes,' Sally responded with as much enthusiasm as she could muster. Peter's news seemed to have had a strangely disorienting effect on her. 'It's going to take a bit of getting used to but, yes, it is rather exciting.'

'God, Sally!' Kath placed her hands on her hips and rolled her eyes in exasperation. 'If the love of my life had just set the date for our wedding, I'd be dancing on the table tops. And if he'd said we could have the reception at a joint as swish as this one, I'd probably be doing it naked! You can carry 'cool' too far, you know.'

Sally rubbed her forehead. 'I know. It's just I've been so focussed on the festival for so long, I haven't even thought about our wedding. This is all a bit of a surprise.'

Hands still on hips, Kath cocked her head to one side watching Sally closely. A long and not entirely comfortable silence engulfed them. Then Kath asked gently, 'Surprise, as in nice surprise, or surprise as in nasty shock?'

Sally stared hard at her engagement ring whilst her emotions, which seemed to have been on a rollercoaster ride all of their own, finally came to a halt. Suddenly, she straightened up, looked Kath in the eye and smiled broadly.

'Nasty shock, of course! I don't want my reception here, I want it in the village hall with catering by the WI and drinks by Andy and Lou and the whole village in attendance. But, realistically, although Peter's right that the basic structural stuff might well be finished in four months, there's no way the whole refurb will be so I suppose I will just have to resign myself, somehow, to a reception in this swish joint, as you put it. And,' she went on, raising an expectant eyebrow at her friend, 'I'd like you to be my bridesmaid!'

Kath squealed again at a pitch and volume that made Sally fear for her hearing, grabbed her friend by the arms and began the promised jig, bouncing up and down on the spot.

'Oh my god! I've never been a bridesmaid before. Thank you, thank you.' Abruptly, she stopped as a further thought struck her. 'You know what would be completely brilliant?

'No, what?' Sally indulged her.

'If… if Justin was to be best man…' Even knowing Kath as well as she did, Sally could scarcely believe she'd had the nerve to suggest that, but at least she had the grace to blush as she did so.

'Get real, sweetie. That's not going to happen is it? Peter gets to pick the best man, his brother or his best friend. Justin doesn't qualify on either count.'

'But it's tradition!' Kath persisted, an edge of desperation in her voice. 'The bridesmaid gets to cop off with the best man.'

'I'm pretty sure that tradition only applies when the best man and the bridesmaid haven't already copped off with each other, which, if you haven't already, you definitely will have done by then.'

'If only,' Kath moaned darkly. 'That's part of the reason I was so glad you were here tonight. I still don't know what's going on with him.'

'What do you mean? He's brought you here, hasn't he?' Sally didn't like seeing her normally ebullient friend looking so crushed.

'Well yes, but he keeps blowing hot and cold. I never know where I am with him.'

Join the club Sally thought to herself. Aloud she said again, 'What do you mean?'

'OK,' Kath settled herself back against the sink unit. Sally, recognising this was probably going to take some time, did the same, folding her arms across her chest and waiting expectantly. 'So, he takes me home after your party and couldn't be nicer. I'm convinced he's going to stay the night but he leaves me at the door and heads off. He calls me Saturday. Like he's desperate to see me and look how that panned out. Then yesterday, in between whatever it was he was doing all day, he's texting and calling and really twists my arm to come out with him tonight. I greet him at the door, and I'm not quite ready…'

'Kath! You didn't!' Sally already knew the punch-line to this story.

'It wasn't my fault if he caught me not quite dressed, was it?' Kath protested her innocence, although they both knew better.

'And?' Sally prompted, though she scarcely needed to ask.

'He'd booked a table here and wasn't about to cancel. Honestly, Sally, I practically laid it on a plate for him. What is his problem?' Clearly torn between frustration and anger, Kath produced a comb from her bag and dragged it viciously through her curls.

Sally too turned towards the mirror, touching up her lip gloss and reflecting on the irony that Kath, who never had trouble getting any man she wanted, should be asking her advice on Justin for the second time in two days. Irony too that Sally, who could normally be relied on to give the most sensible advice on almost any subject, was completely at a loss when it came to understanding what made Justin tick.

'Well,' Kath regarded herself critically. 'I think I've done the best I can with the raw materials provided. If he's not interested, he isn't and there's not much more I can do about it.'

'That's the spirit,' Sally popped her lip gloss back into her bag. 'Now, I think we've left those two making polite conversation for quite long enough. Let's go and rescue them.'

The meal was not a success. The food was delicious, the service prompt and discreet but the conversation was sadly lacking. Peter, having finally got Sally to agree the date, was keen to hear her opinions on all things wedding related. As Sally seemed to have left her enthusiasm in the ladies' powder room, it was left to Kath, who'd clearly already given the subject a lot of thought, to respond to his ideas. Justin applied himself stolidly to his food. His sole contribution was when applied to to adjudicate over the choice of wedding music when he sided with Peter's preference of Widor's Toccata over Grieg's Wedding March with the proviso that it needed a first-class organist.

Finally, dessert was cleared, coffee refused with some relief all round and the bill requested. Sally shifted uncomfortably in her seat, dreading the total and knowing that, as Peter had invited Justin and Kath to join them, he should really pay the whole. But Justin casually tossed his gold card onto the platter and insisted on paying as his way of congratulating the lucky couple. After some demure, and a quick glance at the final sum, Peter graciously accepted and they rose to go.

Sally and Peter's journey home was accomplished in almost total silence. Though it wasn't an unpleasant silence, it wasn't exactly companionable either. Sally had the uncomfortable feeling that was her fault. As they pulled up outside her cottage, she unclipped her seatbelt and moved closer to her fiancé in an effort to make amends.

'Thank you for a lovely meal, Peter,' she murmured, kissing him softly on the lips. 'Come in and have a coffee with me.'

Peter didn't answer but cupped her cheek, returning her kiss and deepening it, his tongue finding hers as his hands travelled greedily over her body.

'Don't you think we're a little old for making out in the car?' Sally whispered, drawing back slightly. 'Why don't you come in so we can snuggle on the sofa in the warm?'

Immediately she'd spoken, Sally cursed herself. Peter froze then straightened up. The spell was broken. Stupidly, she'd reminded him of who they were, what they were doing and what it could lead to. He set her away from himself, cleared his throat and looked pointedly at his watch. 'I think not, love. You've got school tomorrow and I have a busy day too. I think we'd both function better after a good night's sleep.' Then, as an afterthought, he added in a whisper of his own, 'But I do appreciate the offer, Sally.'

Whether he really wanted to get a good night's sleep or whether he doubted their ability to remain suitably chaste, Sally couldn't be sure, but she resigned herself to his decision. This time there had been no party, no cleaning up and no thunderstorm to sway him; there was no way he'd change his mind.

'Ah, well,' she reached into the footwell for her bag and got out, calling a goodnight over her should as she let herself into the cottage.

She slipped off her boots and pottered into the kitchen to flick on the kettle. Up till now, Sally had willingly accepted Peter's strict views on pre-marital intimacy but, tonight, she couldn't help but feel rather cheated. They'd set a date for their wedding, for heaven's sake. Surely that should have been celebrated with a little more passion than a quick fumble in a decidedly chilly polo? And whilst intellectually she could admire Peter's iron-willed self-restraint, it wasn't entirely flattering to have a fiancé that found it quite so easy to resist her.

On the other hand, the atmosphere during dinner had been so strained, she did feel rather wrung out. Maybe she was better off settling for a cup of cocoa and an early night? She could certainly do with some time to process the fact that she would now definitely, actually and finally, be marrying Peter in a little under five months' time.

Sally realised that, having gratefully accepted his offer of marriage, she'd always put off discussing the exact details of the matter with him, using her recent bereavement as an excuse. Having lost both parents in quick succession, she'd barely been able to think one day ahead let alone plan the rest of her life.

So now, she reflected as she washed her face and cleaned her teeth, she had no idea what marriage to Peter would really involve. Their discussion at dinner had focussed very much on the day itself, the number of bridesmaids, who the ushers would be, which parishioners would or wouldn't take offence at being left uninvited. But it was rapidly dawning on

Sally that they had so much more, of so much greater importance, to talk about.

She threw herself into bed and subsided onto the pillows, desiring nothing more than to become immediately unconscious. But for the second night running, it was not to be. After the large meal and several glasses of wine, she might feel physically enervated yet mentally she was buzzing. She lay as still as she could manage, concentrating hard on slowing her breathing and relaxing her limbs but her disobedient brain whirled with unanswered questions. Where would they live? Would he move in to her little cottage or would she be expected to decamp to his miserable, grey box? And what about work? Was he expecting her to give that up to become a full-time vicar's wife, or would she continue with her teaching career? And children? It had been tacitly agreed that, at some point, they would have some but when? And how many? And what about his living? Sally knew that the Church could require him to move to a new parish, almost at the drop of a hat. Would she get any say in that? Or just be expected to up sticks and move with him?

Desperately, knowing how dreadful she'd feel the following day if she didn't drop off soon, she pummelled her pillows, tossed the duvet off and pulled it back on again, tried lying on her back, her front and her sides, but to no avail. Finally, on her third trip to the bathroom, this time for a drink, Sally heard Justin's key in the lock. She paused on the landing, toying with the idea of joining him downstairs for a chat. Heaven knew she could do with mulling things over with someone. Then she heard his step on the stair and fled back to her own room knowing that she'd missed her chance. Just as well. There was no way she should be having that kind of chat with him. Her eyes slid to the clock. 2.46 am. The last thing she thought of before she finally drifted into an uneasy doze was that it had taken Justin nearly three hours to see Kath home. But he hadn't stayed.

Chapter Seventeen

As she parked the car in her usual space and unloaded her school bags from the back seat, Sally noted the sleek hire car hugging the pavement a few yards further down. Justin was at home, then. She wasn't sure, at that moment, whether that was a good thing or not. The last day of the school term was always utterly exhausting. Even though they finished early, it was always ages before they got rid of the last, over-excited children and lingering parents, and then there was the obligatory end-of-term get together in the staffroom for thank yous and goodbyes. By the time she got home, Sally felt fit to drop and ready to welcome the holidays with open arms.

Right now, she was looking forward to a nice cup of tea and her feet up for ten minutes of peace and quiet. She just hoped Justin's presence wouldn't get in the way of her doing that.

Sally opened the door to find him lying full-length on her sofa, i-pod attached as usual, eyes firmly closed, wearing his jogging bottoms and nothing else. She watched him for a moment, trying to judge whether he was just concentrating or actually sleeping. The long, clean line of his body, rock hard chest rising and falling with the regular rhythm of his breathing, was having a most peculiar effect on her pulse rate. Averting her eyes, she pushed the door to gently and crept past, putting her bags down carefully so as not to disturb him. Not quite carefully enough; Justin's eyes flew open and he struggled to a sitting position.

'Sal!' he croaked groggily, squinting at her in an effort to focus. Obviously, he had been well and truly asleep. He rubbed the flats of his hands up over his face and, somewhat unsteadily, got to his feet. 'What time is it?'

'Sorry, I didn't mean to wake you.' She checked her watch. 'Twenty to six.' Sally slipped off her shoes and moved towards the kitchen. 'Fancy a cuppa?'

'Uh no!' Justin fairly leaped towards her putting himself between Sally and the kitchen door.

'Why not?' She regarded him, suspiciously. 'Whatever's the matter, Justin?'

His assurance that it was 'nothing, nothing at all' was hardly likely to allay her suspicions or improve her patience.

'Look,' she told him squarely, arms folded and eyes narrowed. 'I've been out since the crack of dawn and at work all day. I really would like a quiet sit down in my own house with my feet up for five minutes, if that's OK with you.'

Justin gripped her arm and steered her firmly towards the stairs. 'I'll make the tea. You get changed and come back down in, let's say about fifteen minutes?'

Sally resisted. 'What's going on?' she demanded. 'If you've done something terrible to my kitchen, Justin, just spit it out. I'd far rather you told me straight up.'

'I haven't broken anything, Sally,' he promised. 'Quite the opposite. Now please, just for once, do as you're told.' He'd got her to the foot of the stairs and stood, frowning down at her. With his size and strength and sheer implacability, he was barring her way as effectively as a brick wall.

Sally gritted her teeth, about to give in when Justin sniffed theatrically, adopted a stricken expression and fled to the kitchen. Mystified, Sally followed him.

As Justin removed a blackened dish from the oven, Sally stopped on the threshold, staring in disbelief. The worktops were littered with pans and utensils in various stages of sticky messiness. The draining board was covered with vegetable peelings, some of which had escaped to the floor where they nestled cosily amongst breadcrumbs and pools of tomato juice. Several carrier bags lurked in the corner by the bin which itself dripped with stains. The only other time her kitchen had looked this bad was on the night of the party. And it had taken upwards of thirty people to achieve that!

Momentarily, Sally was stunned but the sight of Justin, naked to the waist, barefoot, wielding her flowery oven gloves and doing his best to salvage what had once been a lasagna, got the better of her. She clapped her hand to her mouth and dissolved into laughter. Justin looked up and shrugged apologetically.

'What can I say?' he asked ruefully. 'I meant to have everything ready and the mess all cleaned up by the time you came home. Thought you might be tired with it being the last day of term and everything...'

Sally, regaining control of herself with difficulty, was surprised and touched that he had gone to so much trouble. Not touched enough to offer to help tidy up though.

'Fifteen minutes, Justin,' she told him sternly. 'Then I want my kitchen back to normal and a cup of tea in my hand.' With that she turned abruptly and stomped up the stairs.

'Fifteen minutes, Sal,' he corroborated from the kitchen. 'But don't come down a minute sooner.'

I'll come down when I like, Justin Trevelyan, she muttered to herself as she reached her bedroom. Amusing as the sight of him scraping desperately at burnt lasagna had been, Sally's mood had not been improved by being denied her much longed for cup of tea and a sit down. Grumpily, she changed into jeans and a soft V-neck sweater, washed her face and brushed her hair, then decided she could hold out no longer. Her stomach was rumbling and her tongue was cleaving to the roof of her mouth.

She padded back downstairs and found Justin in the living room. He'd put on a tight, white sports T-shirt over which he was wearing her blue-striped apron. He looked up and grinned, customary sangfroid regained.

'You can go through now, madam,' he indicated the conservatory with a sweep of his hand.

Sally obeyed and was impressed. The table was set with cutlery, plates and a jug of iced water. Glancing through the open doorway, she saw he had also managed to do a pretty nifty clean-up job in the kitchen.

Justin followed her in carrying the lasagna, then returned for warm focaccia and salad.

'Justin, this looks wonderful!' Somehow, he'd rescued the lion's share of the meal and Sally found her mouth watering. 'I'm so hungry!'

'Tuck in,' he invited, pleased at her reaction. 'It's nothing special but I thought you deserved a little 'end of term' treat.'

'I'm sure you deserve a treat just as much as I do with the hours of rehearsal you've been putting in but I'm not going to complain. I could get used to having a meal waiting for me as soon as I get home,' she took the plate he offered her, loaded with a generous portion of only slightly over-crisped lasagna.

'Things went a bit astray,' Justin explained, helping her to salad and bread. 'I thought, whilst the lasagna browned, I'd have a quick sit down with the scores of the pieces I'm doing with the Philharmonia straight after the festival. Then I went and fell asleep.'

'Been a hard week has it?' Sally asked conversationally, tucking in with relish.

'Not especially. I'm used to this kind of routine, don't forget. It's just I'm,' he hesitated, busying himself with dishing lasagna onto his own plate. '… finding it a little hard to sleep at the moment.' He poured some water into both their glasses.

'Perhaps,' she suggested, waspishly, 'you should try going to bed a little earlier.'

Justin raised a querying brow, 'Oooh, Sal! Been keeping tabs on me?'

'As if!' her denial was swift. 'The stairs creak. I wake up.' Every night since the meal at Lawncrest, Sally had heard him returning home in the wee small hours. What Justin didn't know was that Kath had been like the cat who'd got the cream all week, more than happy to fill Sally in on all the graphic details.

'Well, we can't have that. You need your beauty sleep. It won't happen again,' he assured her.

'Thank you,' Sally replied politely, inwardly feeling anything but courteous. What did he mean she needed her beauty sleep? And what did he mean 'it won't happen again'? Was he going to stay out all night in future?

'More salad?' Justin proffered the bowl.

'No thanks,' Sally glanced down at her plate where the remnants of her meal lay congealing. Her unreliable appetite had fled. She pushed the remaining food around for a while, then gave up. 'That was surprisingly tasty, in the circumstances. But I'm sorry, I can't manage any more.'

Justin rose and began, rather briskly, to clear the table. 'No, I'm sorry, Sal. For waking you up and for ruining the meal.' Sally noticed he didn't specify exactly how the meal had been ruined but had a suspicion he wasn't just referring to burning it slightly. Justin glanced at his watch. 'And for being stupid enough to fall asleep and get behind schedule. I have a rehearsal at half seven.'

Sally too got to her feet. 'Don't worry, I'll clear away.'

He put a hand on her shoulder, pressing her back into her seat. 'The point was to treat you a little, Sally. Not leave you with a load of washing up.'

'Justin,' she adopted her best teacher voice. 'It was lovely to come home to a meal someone else had cooked for me but sometimes the best laid plans go awry. I promise I won't hold it against you. And I can cope with a bit of washing up. Stop making a mountain out of a molehill and go and change.'

For a moment, Sally thought he was going to continue to protest. She looked pointedly at her watch and, swearing softly under his breath, he gave in and turned away abruptly.

Sally waited till she heard the shower running then began taking things through to the kitchen. She covered the lasagna and put it in the fridge, with the remaining salad. Neither of them had eaten very much. No need to cook lunch tomorrow, then. The shower noises stopped. Sally ran water in the sink to wash up and, a very short time later, she heard the front door slam.

As she washed the dishes, very slowly and carefully, enjoying the soothing nature of the mundane task, she wondered if Iris had any idea of what a can of worms she had opened up.

Sally was not very sexually experienced. But she knew enough to recognize that the physical attraction between herself and Justin had been particularly intense. And apparently still was. On her part at least.

Justin was not the only one going short of sleep. Her unconscious self and her body were apparently oblivious to her decision to focus her energies and emotions on Peter. Too often, Sally was still awake when she heard the click of the front door on Justin's return. Still awake and deprived of sleep by her treacherous body reliving the pressure of his lips on hers, the feeling of his hands upon her skin. When she did finally drift off, he came to her in her dreams, his kisses tormenting her, his caresses leaving her aroused and yet unsatisfied.

If she had known this was how it was going to be, would Iris have been quite so eager for Sally to invite him? And if Sally had known how susceptible she still was to his mere physical presence, would she still have agreed to do so?

That lack of blatant physicality was one of the things that had first drawn her to Peter. She had sworn she would never go through again what she had been through with Justin. Those terrible months when it had felt as if her heart was literally ripping apart. When she had truly believed she would never be happy again. Sally had immersed herself in caring for her ailing parents and her teaching and, somehow, supported by Peter's steady companionship, she had got through it. He had been so different to Justin, so calm, so measured, so peaceful to be with. She had been truly content since they had become engaged. His gentle, undemanding caresses had made her feel comfortable and safe. She knew that Peter would never leave her or do anything to hurt her.

Sally felt suddenly that she needed the reassurance of seeing him. She finished washing up, left everything drying on the draining board, picked up her handbag and left through the conservatory. Peter had agreed to open the church ready for that evenings' full rehearsal; he might well still be there.

She hurried along the footpath and into the churchyard. Minutes later, she was creeping in through the heavy porch door.

Peter was standing at the back of the church, watching the orchestra tuning up. He turned as she approached, his welcoming smile balm to her agitated feelings.

'Hi, love,' he whispered. 'Come to listen?'

'No, I came to find you, actually. Can we go outside for a minute?'

Peter did not need to be asked twice. He followed her along the path and further into the churchyard. As soon as they were out of sight of the main entrance, Sally turned to him.

'I need a hug, Peter,' she rested her head on his chest and allowed his arms to come tightly round her.

'Sally love, are you alright?'

'I'm fine. I just haven't seen you for a while and I wanted to spend some time with you, that's all.'

'I'm not going to complain about that,' he planted a kiss on the top of her head. 'I was beginning to think you'd forgotten I existed.'

'Silly,' she chided gently.

'I can't stay long though, Sally,' he told her, regretfully. 'I was just about to leave when you came in. Mrs Tregembo is back in the care home but still quite poorly and I promised I would go down and spend the evening with her.'

'Poor Mrs Tregembo,' Sally sympathized. 'If you're going tonight, I'll try and get over there tomorrow sometime.'

'Would you, love? She'd appreciate that. And I'll try and pop round to your place later. Trouble is, they tend to get a bit miffed if I show any favouritism, so I'll have to speak to everyone once I'm there. With that and the drive there and back, it could be quite late.'

'Oh,' Sally couldn't hide her disappointment.

Peter fished in his pocket and produced the heavy church keys. 'Actually, you could help me out there. If I'm not back before this lot finish,' he jerked his head in the direction of the orchestra, 'could you lock up for me?'

Sally nodded and drew away. 'Of course. You go and do what you need to do. Give Mrs Tregembo my best wishes.' She gave him a quick, dry-lipped kiss. 'I'll see you later.'

Bereft, Sally wandered back to the church, drawn inside by the luscious orchestral sounds. What with marking, end of term events and committee meetings, she hadn't had chance to get along to any of the rehearsals so far. Now, she slipped into the back pew and allowed the music to wash over her.

It was heavenly. They might all be amateur musicians but many were of a very high standard and all had been practising their parts hard. Justin, in his trademark black T-shirt and tight blue-black jeans, was a dark commanding presence at the front. For a moment she was transfixed by the gorgeous sounds filling the church from the flagged stone floor to its vaulted arches.

Justin lowered his arms, rapped the lectern and the orchestra stopped obediently. He made some comment, causing a ripple of amusement, then addressed one of the brass players who raised a hand acknowledging his error. Justin raised the baton once more, brought it down smartly and the music sprang again into life. Sally felt suddenly transported back to her student days. How many hours had she spent like this, listening to Justin rehearsing?

After their first inauspicious encounter, it hadn't taken long for Justin and Sally to become inseparable. He had allowed her to see the sensitive musician behind the laddish, rugby-playing exterior. And it was only with Justin, that the usually quiet and bookish Sally would feel comfortable enough to really let her hair down. Both, it transpired were studying in London; Sally reading English and Justin, on a scholarship, at the

126

Royal College of Music. At the time, it had seemed the most natural thing in the world for them to graduate from friends to live-in lovers.

Even whilst still at college, Justin had begun to be offered work conducting various groups around the country, putting in hours listening to pieces, studying scores, travelling all over, sometimes even abroad, learning his craft. Sally had kept him grounded and sane. He stopped her working too hard and took her on wild, spontaneous jaunts. It had been blissful.

A strange rustling, tapping noise brought Sally back to the present. The musicians were shuffling their feet and rapping their bows on their music stands, as a sign of their appreciation of the conductor. Justin was praising their efforts and thanking them, saying how much he was looking forward to the next rehearsal.

'Good job, everyone,' he concluded. 'I know you're all busy people but if the brass and woodwind could just have a look at those solos by Wednesday, that would be brilliant. I'll see you then.' He closed his score, stepped off the rostrum and headed down the aisle. A smile lit his face as he noticed Sally.

'Hi!' he was clearly surprised to see her. 'I thought you'd be at home with your feet up.'

She rattled the keys in her pocket. 'Peter asked me to lock up for him.'

'Ah,' the smile in his eyes dimmed. 'There was me thinking you had come to listen to the rehearsal.'

'Well, that too. It's sounding very good.'

'Yes, I have to tell you I'm relieved. I wasn't quite sure what I was letting myself in for.'

'I wouldn't have got you involved in anything too dreadful,' she assured him. 'Surely you knew that?'

Justin gave a short, dry laugh. 'I'm never too sure of anything where you're concerned, Sally.'

'An uncertainty which is entirely reciprocated, believe me,' she retorted swiftly.

Justin shrugged. 'That should keep us both on our toes, then.'

Sally didn't reply. It was too confusing having this kind of conversation with Justin. And it was perfectly correct what she had said. She didn't ever know where she stood with him. One minute their relationship was almost back to the easy camaraderie of their earliest days together. The next moment, and she could never seem to tell exactly what would trigger the dramatic change, she was walking on egg-shells as Justin turned into the prickly, authoritarian maestro she had dreaded he would be. And now, all the time, on Sally's side at least, was that undeniable physical attraction that she was fighting so hard to keep at bay.

She leaned on the back of the pew watching as the stragglers packed their instruments away and drifted out. Although their conversation seemed to have ended, Justin did not move. The leader of the orchestra called out to him that they would see him in The Pump shortly. He raised a hand in acknowledgement.

'Join us, Sally?' he invited casually as they followed the last of the musicians down the aisle and into the porch. He pulled the heavy door closed and Sally turned the key in the lock.

'Uh, no.' Though a drink with the orchestra, many of whom she knew anyway, would have been nice, she was tired. And Peter was coming round once he'd done his duty at the care home. 'Thanks, but no thanks.'

'Peter?'

Sally nodded. 'He said he'd try and catch up with me later.'

'He could always join us in the pub,' Justin suggested, then added rather pointedly, 'Might be nice if he got to know some of the people working so hard for the benefit of his church.'

Sally resented the implied criticism. 'He knows most of them already actually,' she told him, her tone sharp, 'from other events. And he's very busy. His parish is a big one. Anyway,' she tried and failed to visualize Peter drinking and chatting Justin and the other musicians, 'He's not really a pub person. I'll wait for him at home.'

'Please yourself,' as he turned to go, Sally had no clue as to whether he minded her turning down his invitation or not. With a deep sigh, she rummaged in her bag and produced a torch. Justin stopped, looked from the torch to the black depths of the churchyard and back to Sally. He echoed her sigh and, frowning, took the torch from her slack grasp.

'I'll walk you back.'

'There's really no need, Justin,' Sally protested. He appeared cross again for some reason and she had no desire to spend the next ten minutes bickering. 'And it's out of your way.'

'Nonsense,' he contradicted curtly. 'I can't let you go back along that footpath on your own at this time of night.'

Sally couldn't help but laugh at his reluctant chivalry. 'Justin, I've been wandering round this village on my own at night since I was in my teens. I really don't need an escort.'

'Not entirely true, Sally. And if it was, it shouldn't be.' He tightened his hold on the torch and shone it ahead. He draped an arm loosely across her shoulders and steered her towards the lichgate. Sally slipped from his hold and moved ahead. Darkness and physical contact with Justin were the last things she needed right now!

'Really, Justin. I'm fine. Anyway,' she paused, turning to look back at him. 'Won't Kath be expecting you?'

Justin too stopped in his tracks and faced her squarely. 'I have no plans to see Kath tonight,' he told her quietly. 'And even if I did, I'd still walk you home.'

'Oh,' Sally digested this in silence for a moment, trying to read his expression. Then, she whirled away from him and broke into a run. 'OK,' she challenged recklessly. 'You want to see me home? You'll have to catch me first! Race you!'

She had a head start and long legs. She heard a muttered oath from Justin, then he lengthened his stride and was hot on her heels. Suddenly, it mattered very much to Sally that he didn't catch up with her. Suddenly, it seemed imperative that she reach home before he did. She put on a spurt, dodged into the undergrowth to cut off a loop in the path, coming out well ahead only a hundred or so yards from her own back garden. Justin, taken by surprise, fell back slightly but was soon back in contention. As she lifted the latch on her gate, she could hear his measured breathing just behind her.

She slipped through and made to slam it behind her, but Justin was too quick, staying it with an iron hand.

'Not so fast, you little vixen!' he panted laughing and, with a hip shimmy a county level winger would have been proud of, squeezed through after her. He stretched out a hand, grabbing her wrist and jerking her roughly back towards him. Sally fetched up abruptly against him as his arms fastened round her like steel springs.

The night was very dark, the air still. For a moment, Sally could hear nothing but the wild beating of her own heart, could feel nothing but the answering rhythmic pounding from Justin's chest. He looked down at her, as she stood, motionless within his embrace.

Gently, he reached up a hand, lifting a tendril of hair which had caught on her lips. He stroked it away, his fingers following its length till they came to rest, twined in its silken length, cradling the back of her head. He tilted it back, forcing her to look up at him. Very quietly, he told her, 'I won, Sal!'

'Justin...' his name, when she said it, was scarcely more than a breath.

Slowly, reluctantly, he relaxed his hold, his arms sliding down, coming to rest loosely by his sides. Sally lowered her eyes and cleared her throat. A long moment passed.

Then, anxious to relieve the moment of intimacy, she whisked away and pretended to stagger the last few paces to the conservatory door. Melodramatically, she swept the back of her hand across her brow in mock relief.

'Wow! Phew! Just made it! Lucky I had you to beat off all those nefarious characters lying in wait for me.'

'Ungrateful woman!' he accused, following more slowly, but there was no anger in his voice.

Sally unlocked the door and stepped over the threshold. Justin remained resolutely on the bottom step.

'I know you thought I was being ridiculous,' he told her self-mockingly, 'but it made me feel better to see you safely home. Humour me, OK?'

'Actually, I think it was very sweet of you. Thank you.' She wanted to say more but found she couldn't.

Justin raised a hand in a dismissive half-wave and turned away. ''Night, Sally.'

He was almost at the garden gate when she called out softly to him, 'Justin?'

'Hmm?' he turned back to look at her, framed as she was in the doorway, the light from the conservatory glinting on the smooth length of her hair.

She dimpled mischievously. 'I had no intention of going through the churchyard, you know. I always go the long way round if it's dark.'

Justin threw his head back and laughed. 'I did wonder. That churchyard always used to spook you.' He opened the gate and went through. 'At least I saved you a longer walk. Good night, Sally. Enjoy the rest of your evening.'

The room was spinning! Sally, fighting for consciousness from the depths of a very deep sleep, could not understand what was happening. She appeared to be hard up against a very warm wall on one side but with nothing on the other. Bands of steel were fastened around her arms and under her knees and she was aware of being raised then swung around to the left. She took a long steadying breath. The scent of lemons triggered a forgotten memory. She opened her eyes. And found she was staring directly into the deep, dark gaze of Justin Trevelyan.

'Sh...' he admonished her in a whisper, hugging her more securely to him. 'Go back to sleep, little one. I'll just carry you upstairs.'

Obediently, Sally closed her eyes once more but was now sufficiently awake to work out what was going on. She must have dropped off on the sofa whilst waiting for Peter and, rather than leave her there to risk a stiff neck and aching body in the morning, Justin had taken it upon himself to carry her up to her room. She should tell him she was awake now, tell him to put her down so she could walk upstairs. But somehow, she just couldn't.

This was how it had been used to feel. Justin's firm, warm body wrapped around hers. His breath lightly fanning her cheek. The steady beat of his heart beneath her ear. She could smell the old familiar smell of him, that light, lemony fragrance overlaying the male muskiness, and a faint tang of alcohol on his breath. Then he would turn his head, his lips would find hers and that delicious, pervasive, all-encompassing warmth would spread through her body...

Sally eased one arm free and slid it round his neck, her fingers coming to rest in the soft, springy curls at his nape. She felt his breathing quicken, his muscles tense. Then, too soon, they were at her bedroom door, Justin nudging it open with his knee. In two long strides, they were beside her bed. He bent slowly and gently laid her down.

Sally opened her eyes and looked fully, imploringly, into his. She did not want this to end. Slowly, so slowly neither were aware of any movement, the distance between them narrowed. His face was moments from hers, his skin grazing the downy softness of her cheek.

His lips were cool, slightly salty as he brushed them lightly across her mouth, sending a sensitizing tingle through her.

As he eased away, Sally parted her lips. Her tongue, tentative at first, sought his. Justin groaned, a harsh and tortured sound deep in his

131

throat. Then, unable to hold back a moment longer, he crushed her against him and his mouth conquered hers. Dizzy with lust, with longing, Sally returned his embrace with all the pent-up passion she possessed. Her hands roved over him, seeking, stroking and exploring.

Justin peeled her jumper over her head, revealing the scanty bra she wore beneath. He freed one aching breast, cupping it in his hand, his thumb expertly teasing the nipple to bullet hardness. His mouth abandoned hers to follow the trail his skilful fingers had blazed, nibbling and sucking. Sally gasped, waves of sensation rolling over her. Her body arched under him.

Suddenly, Justin stilled. He raised his head, looking down at her,

'Are you sure about this, Sally?' he asked quietly, his lips almost touching hers. 'I won't do anything you don't want me to. It's your call.'

They both knew if he had not stopped at that moment, they would have made love then, all the way and it would have been wonderful. But he had stopped, and in that moment, Sally's conscience kicked in and she knew that she could not, they should not, allow this to happen.

Her hand on the warm solidity of his chest increased its pressure infinitesimally, holding him at bay. Justin froze.

'I see,' was all he said, rolling away from her and heading for the bedroom door. 'Don't worry, Sally. I won't bother you again.' He closed it quietly behind him.

Sally curled onto her side, hugging her knees to a body still pulsating with desire, her heart wracked with pain and her mind with indecision. Footsteps pounded on the stairs, the front door opened and then closed once more. Sally squeezed her eyes tight shut and vainly willed herself to sleep.

Chapter Eighteen

Sally spooned coffee into the mug and added boiling water. She needed caffeine. Fast. Long after she'd heard Justin come in, she had lain awake, the shameful events of the evening going round and round in her mind like some hideous carousel. She had only herself to blame. Justin had simply been sweet, again, carrying her upstairs so that she could spend the rest of the night in comfort. He'd kissed her, yes. But the rest? That had been down to her. She'd turned his kiss into something more, something that could have had devastating consequences. What on earth had possessed her?

The answer to that was simple. Lust. Justin Trevelyan was one of the most attractive men you were ever likely to meet. She hadn't needed the reactions of Lou or Kath to confirm that for her. But lust was not a trustworthy emotion. You couldn't build a life with someone based on lust. Lust was to be avoided at all costs. Justin Trevelyan was to be avoided at all costs.

Which, of course, was impossible.

Today they were starting rehearsals for 'Joseph and His Amazing Technicolour Dreamcoat' with the massed children's choirs. Today, Sally, who had coached the primary choirs, and Steve Archibald, the music teacher from the local comprehensive who had coached the secondary choir and soloists, were due to spend the whole day in the church with all the children. And Justin. After last night, Sally had no idea what mood he'd be in.

133

Coward that she was, Sally had no intention of waiting around to find out. She intended to head for the church as soon as possible. Hopefully, having sixty-odd children and at least one other adult around would force Justin to curb his temper.

Earlier, hurriedly showering in near silence, she'd considered throwing a sicky. But, today's arrangements were far too complicated to dump on someone else at short notice. Sally had the names, addresses, pink medical forms, signed parental permission slips and emergency contact numbers for all the children. Sally knew who couldn't be trusted to stand by whom, who was likely to need emergency toilet breaks and whose hay-fever meant they had to be kept well away from the flower arrangements. Sally had the break-time biscuits and squash and an additional supply of sandwiches for those who had forgotten their packed lunches. She was also first aid trained and female; there was no way she could leave all those children to the not-so-tender care of Justin and Steve. So she bolted down her coffee and toast, loaded up her car with the bags of supplies and was away before Justin had surfaced.

The church was cool and calm in the early morning quiet. Sally made her way straight to the vestry to set out the squash and paper cups. They'd get far more done if the children were kept fed, watered and regularly toileted. Stashing some packets of biscuits away for later, Sally heard a noise coming from the church. Then the magical opening chords of Joseph floated through the air, making her stop and listen. Justin had arrived.

Sally couldn't leave the vestry, couldn't face him. Not yet, not on her own. Pointlessly, she moved packets and cups from one end of the table to the other and then back again. Get a grip, Sally Marsh, she chided herself.

Only when the beautiful music was drowned out by children's excited chatter, did Sally feel able to leave her hiding place.

'Miss Marsh!' a knot of girls broke apart, running to fling their arms around her middle in greeting.

'Hiya, girls,' Sally smiled a welcome as she chivvied them into their places. She raised her voice in a general command. 'Come on now, guys. No time to waste. Park your stuff in one of the front pews and go and stand in the positions we practised. Let's get you ready, please.'

Justin was already at the lectern, impatiently flicking over pages of his score. Surrounded by children, he seemed even larger, more forbidding than ever. Or was that just her guilty imagination?

A tap on her arm distracted her.

'Wish me luck, Miss,' Laura, the slight fourteen-year old who was singing the intricately difficult Narrator's part, had been in Sally's class a few years previously. 'Mr. Trevelyan's well scary!'

Sally gave her a hug but found she couldn't contradict her. 'You'll be fine. You're brilliant and you know it. Just do it as you usually do and he'll be very impressed,' she reassured her hoping she sounded more confident than she felt.

Laura was excellent and all the youngsters had been thoroughly well-drilled but Sally had no idea if Justin had any experience with children. He could be short on patience at the best of times and snapping and carping at kids was the quickest way to turn them off. She gave Laura a little pat and ushered her forward. Steve Archibald appeared and took his seat at the piano. Sally sat down next to him. In addition to everything else, she was official page-turner for the day.

At that moment, Justin looked up surveying the seething mass of youth before him. He glanced round, giving a slight nod as his stern gaze rested momentarily on Sally then he turned and rapped the lectern with his baton. An expectant hush fell. Sally swallowed nervously.

'Right, you lot. I'm Mr. Trevelyan. I've only got two rules. One, you do what I say as soon as I say it. Two, you're here to sing and that's all.' He glared at a couple of older boys at the back to emphasize the point. Sally held her breath unsure of how the children would respond to this kind of straight talking. Then he smiled, instantly gaining the undying devotion of all the females over twelve.

'So that's the lecture out of the way. Now let's have some fun!' He jumped down from the podium and took Steve's hastily vacated place at the piano. Justin didn't sit however, but looked over the top, keeping eye contact seemingly with the whole choir at once while he played. He bashed out a catchy jazz riff and demonstrated a warm up exercise that went with it. 'Vowels, first starting with A,' he instructed.

The children sang with gusto. Each exercise he played was jolly and energetic, sometimes loud and hearty, sometimes in a dramatic stage whisper. Sally needn't have worried. In no time at all, he had them following his every movement.

They rehearsed Joseph hard until lunch-time with only a ten-minute break in the middle. Then Justin decided he needed to concentrate on the key parts with Steve to iron out some of the trickier entries.

'Right,' he announced as the children took their places after lunch. 'Narrator, Joseph, the brothers and the other soloists stay here with Mr. Archibald and me. Everyone else file quickly and quietly into the side room with Miss Marsh.'

Sally couldn't believe her ears. 'Excuse me, Mr. Trevelyan, what would you like me to do single-handed with forty children in the small room?'

He looked at her bemused. 'Anything you like, Miss Marsh. I'm sure you will come up with something productive.' And he turned away, immediately immersing himself in the intricacies of the narrator's part.

Sally filed numbly into the side room with her troops. Fleetingly, she wondered if this was a subtle way of Justin exacting revenge; being cooped up in a confined space with forty lively youngsters was no-one's idea of a good time. She dismissed the idea. He was wholly focused on perfecting the performance and wouldn't let anything get in the way. He was probably expecting her to rehearse their parts but Sally wasn't a musician and didn't even have a score. She gave up.

'OK, then kids. Who feels like a game of hunt the teacher in the churchyard?' she called, leading the way out of the rear door.

At least it was sunny. For over an hour, the older children lay on the grass engrossed in their phones, the younger ones raced round maniacally as Sally hid everywhere she could think of but, when high-spirits threatened to turn into horseplay, she decided enough was enough. She lined them all up quietly then marched them inside, up the aisle and back into their places. She had the dubious pleasure of seeing Justin looking quite confounded.

'What the….?' he turned on Sally, his expression thunderous, as Laura was cut off by the stomping of forty pairs of feet.

'Time for another full rehearsal, Mr. Trevelyan,' Sally told him brightly. 'I'm sure you'll agree that the soloists, particularly Laura, need to rest their voices for a while.'

For a split second, it looked as though he was going to disagree, big time. Then, as Sally slid into her seat by Steve, Justin swallowed whatever pithy epithet had come to mind, raised his baton and commanded brusquely,

'Number Seventeen. Jacob in Egypt, without Laura, Mr. Archibald, please.'

The rest of the afternoon flew by as Sally did her best to follow the music and turn the pages at the right time. At exactly five o'clock, Justin shut his score and congratulated the children on their excellent work.

Physically exhausted from her heroic efforts in the churchyard, mentally drained from concentrating so intently and emotionally wrung-out after the previous evening, it took all Sally's willpower to smile and be civil as she paired children up with appropriate adults and saw them safely off. At last, the church empty, she made her way over to Steve to thank him too. She rubbed her temples, trying and, she suspected failing, to ward off her gathering headache.

'You alright, Sally?' Steve asked as he made a few notes in his score.

'Yes, I'm fine,' she replied automatically. 'Why?'

'Oh, nothing. You just look a bit peaky, that's all,' he said kindly. 'And you're not your usually sunny self.'

'Sally is exhausted,' Justin interrupted having picked up on the tale-end of their conversation from halfway down the aisle. 'She's been running herself ragged. But the only way she'll get a break is if someone actually kidnaps her and carries her bodily away.'

Sally gave a wry smile. 'I'm sure that was not intended as any kind of a compliment but I'm going to take it as one, even if it was a bit back-handed.'

'It wasn't intended as anything other than the unvarnished truth,' Justin told her baldly. 'You take on far too much and, it appears, everybody here just stands by and lets you.'

'Yes, they do, don't they?' Sally agreed with saccharine sweetness, hands on hips, staring him down. 'I expect that's why I spent over an hour running round like a lunatic keeping forty kids occupied this afternoon. Oh wait, no, that was OK though, wasn't it? Because that was your idea.'

'It most certainly was not my idea. I simply asked you to remove them so we could rehearse. I can hardly be blamed if you took them outside to play and then discovered it was too much for you.'

'Too much for me?' Sally couldn't believe the cheek of the man.

'Children, please!' Steve cut in, hastily. 'You two sound just like me and the misses after a long day at school.' He looked from one to the other, shaking his head. 'I probably should stay and referee but Mrs. A is expecting me to wine her and dine her tonight to make up for having been out all day, so I'm going to have to love you and leave you. Justin,' he extended a hand which Justin gave a cursory shake.

Sally, already regretting he had heard her sounding off, gave him a quick hug. 'Bye, Steve, and,' she called after him as he strode quickly away, 'thanks so much for today.'

He turned and waved. ''Bye, guys. Have fun. Just don't draw blood, OK?'

Justin waited until the porch door was firmly closed, then he turned on her, eyes glinting like two chips of flint. 'Don't blame me if you bit off more than you could chew, Sal.'

'But it was your fault! You never said you'd need to split the children up. If you'd told me, I'd have arranged it properly. Instead you did what you always do, just changed the rules to suit yourself. How could you land me with all those children to look after in that tiny little space all by myself?' To her consternation, Sally felt tears pricking her eyes. She was tired and overwrought, all right. If it wasn't enough that Steve Archibald had witnessed them squabbling like a couple of school kids, now she was going to embarrass herself by breaking down in front of Justin. Again!

'Sally, please, I…' he stretched a placating hand towards her.

'Don't!' she all but screamed, hanging on to the last shreds of her self-control by a whisker. 'Don't you come over all kind and caring now when it's too late. And don't, don't touch me!' Violently, she pulled the church keys from her handbag. 'Lock up. I'm going home to bed.' She threw them towards him, adding vehemently in case he was in any doubt, 'alone!'

Chapter Nineteen

Sally's eyes hurt. She blinked experimentally a few times then closed them again firmly, settling for watching the coloured lights dancing on the inside of her eye-lids.

She'd been late to bed again last night having remembered when almost at her front door that she'd promised to pop in on poor Mrs Tregembo. By the time she'd done her duty by the old lady and driven back, Sally had been way beyond exhaustion.

In bed at last, she'd given in to a good old cry but she was regretting it now. Her head ached; her eyes stung. She'd bet they were red and puffy, her skin blotchy. She was hungry and thirsty having skipped last night's dinner. She struggled into a sitting position and ran her hands through the tangle of her hair. That needed washing this morning too!

Sally grabbed her dressing gown from the foot of the bed, wrestled herself into it and coiled her hair into a loose knot. Then she eased her legs over the edge of the bed and stood up tentatively. Her head pounded. Her stomach grumbled loudly.

It was no good. She couldn't face a shower until she had a cup of tea and some toast inside her, even if it meant facing Justin first. Reluctantly, she made her way downstairs.

Justin, catching up on some overdue e-mails, glanced up as Sally rounded the bottom of the stairs. She looked ash-pale, almost plain. His heart constricted as he fought an almost overwhelming urge to scoop her into his arms. Take care, Justin, he warned himself. It was imperative he got today right.

He tried a tentative, 'Hi,' and nervously awaited her reply.

She managed a strained half-smile in return, swayed slightly and clung more tightly to the newel post.

'Sally…' hastily, he set the laptop aside, rose and went towards her, placing a steadying hand under her elbow. 'Listen, Sal, don't take this the wrong way, but you look God awful. Come and sit down.' He steered her to the sofa and gently pressed her back into the warmth of the cushions he'd just left. 'Are you sickening for something?'

She shook her head, then frowned deeply, as if moving her head was a bad idea. 'I'm OK. Just need something to eat,' she confessed piteously.

'Right, well, I've just put some toast on.' Justin was relieved. This was OK. The practical stuff he could do. It was the other stuff he kept messing up. With her anyway.

He vanished into the kitchen and made a cup of strong tea and a plate of toast, thickly spread with margarine and jam, just the way she liked it. Sally accepted both with gratitude, put the plate on her lap and tucked in. Justin resumed his seat on the sofa, carefully leaving a generous gap between them.

After a moment, she asked,' Shouldn't you be somewhere, doing something?'

Justin shook his head. 'It's Sunday, the day of rest,' he informed her. 'Everyone has been working so hard, I gave them the day off. That goes for you and me too.'

'I'm going to church later,' she mumbled through a mouthful.

'No, you're not,' he told her firmly. 'You're having a rest, even if I have to tie you up to make you.'

Sally eyed his laptop. 'You're not resting.'

'E-mails. Mostly from Max. Not exactly taxing. He says he may come down for the final concert. Anyway, I was just killing time till you emerged. Now, I'm going to make you another cup of tea and another piece of toast, which you will eat,' he glared at her sternly. 'Then I am going to run you a hot bath which you will spend at least half an hour in. After that, well, we'll see how you're doing. I might feel the need to make you lie on the sofa and feed you grapes.'

Sally smiled wanly. She ought to object to being bossed around like this but it was almost as nice having someone else take charge as it was being cossetted indulgently. She took a second helping of tea and toast upstairs to the bathroom, applied a face mask she found in the cupboard and allowed herself to wallow at leisure in the hot, frothing water Justin had drawn for her.

When she emerged a lot more than her allotted half hour later, she allowed herself the luxury of a thorough pampering. She moisturised her feet and her legs, already shaved in the bath, massaging in a sweet-smelling lotion for several minutes. She filed and painted her nails, both hand and toe. She cleaned her teeth, flossed thoroughly and used mouthwash for the full, recommended minute. She carefully dried her hair, styling the front to fall softly away from her face. She plucked her eyebrows and stroked her most expensive face cream into the puffy blotchiness beneath her eyes, then added both foundation and blusher before applying full eye make-up. She put on a clean, newish pair of jeans, her favourite vest top and a soft, cashmere cardigan in a dark, claret red. She regarded the result in the mirror. Not bad. At least no-one was going to accuse her of looking 'God awful'. And she felt better than she had in days.

Justin, once more engrossed in the laptop, looked up as she approached. 'God, Sal!' he commented appreciatively. 'That's quite a transformation.'

Sally, flattered but uncomfortable with another of his back-handed compliments, took refuge in humour, 'Bambi's not at death's door any more, then?'

He put the laptop to one side and rose to his feet, hands on hips, silently appraising her. 'No sign of Bambi at all. But I think maybe Bambi's older, much, much sexier sister just dropped by.' He allowed his words to sink in for a moment or two, then clapped his hands together, saying briskly, 'Right then. You obviously don't need to languish on the sofa and you've missed church by miles anyway, so I'm kidnapping you as threatened.' Correctly interpreting Sally's expression of consternation, he added easily, 'Don't worry, Sal. There's a strict 'look, don't touch' policy in operation today. Just friends, no strings attached. Think you can handle that?'

'I can,' she assured him swiftly. 'The question has always been, can you?' The minute the words left her mouth, she regretted them. Yes, he could be moody and unpredictable, he teased her, called her out and argued black was white with her but, since her wedding date had been set, he had proved that she could trust him implicitly. Could she really be so sure of herself?

Justin had turned away, plugging in the laptop charger. She couldn't see if she'd upset him but knew she had to make things right between them. 'I'm sorry, that was unfair. And ungrateful. You're being very sweet. Again. So,' she coaxed, 'what's the plan?'

He straightened up and looked at her. Her heart sank. For a moment, she thought he was going to tell her that, actually, he couldn't be bothered with her today after all. Then he threw her a grin, 'Mystery. Get your coat and put your shoes on.'

The hire car was sleek, spotless and smelled of leather and car wax. Sally lay back in her seat which reclined so far she was almost lying down and watched from this novel perspective as the familiar scenery flew past. Sunlight, filtering through the trees arching high overhead, tinted the world a strange apple green. Along the hedgerows, pale fronds of montbretia pushed their way through mossy layers and, beneath them, tiny delicate primroses peeped shyly from their leafy rosettes. Sally sighed with satisfaction. It was nice to be driven for a change.

'OK?' Justin asked, glancing over at her and smoothly changing gear.

Sally nodded, 'Mmn, this is lovely. I could get used to being chauffeur driven.'

'Sorry, I forgot the peaked cap but I can address you as m'lady if you like.'

'Idiot!'

'But I would!' he protested and she believed him.

As the high hedges and tunnels of branches gave way to flat down land, Justin flicked the indicator and pulled over.

'Anyway, enough chauffeuring, we're here now.' He jumped out and opened Sally's door for her, taking her hand briefly as she stepped down.

Sally, jamming both hands into her pockets for safety's sake, looked around for some clue as to what the day's entertainment would be. They were parked in a small gravelled area just back from the road. There was one other car there already, its owner heading off across the downs towards the as yet invisible sea, a collie puppy frisking at his heels.

Justin answered her querying look, 'I toyed with the idea of flying us both over to Le Touquet for lunch but….' He paused. God, he hoped he'd got this right! Taking a deep breath, he went on, 'So, first we're going to work off all that tea and toast with a walk across the cliffs. Then we're going to find somewhere nice for lunch, secluded but with a sea view.'

Sally was relieved. Maybe, on another day, she would have loved a private plane and a posh French restaurant. But today, she didn't want to have to be glamorous or gracious or grateful. Today, she wanted to just be herself. And now she could. Perfect. She smiled. 'Let me guess, you have the very place in mind?'

'I might have,' he reached for her hand. 'Come on, this isn't going to blow those cobwebs away.' He yomped off with Sally in tow.

They came over the rise and were greeted with the most spectacular view. Sally had lived in this area all her life but had never before looked across the wide, sweep of the bay from exactly this position. She really should walk the coast more often.

'Isn't this great?' Justin called back at her, the wind whipping the words from his mouth. He took a huge lungful of air. 'Breathe, Sally,' he instructed. 'Doesn't that smell good? And look how far we can see.'

He stopped for a moment and pointed, 'Godrevy Lighthouse, still standing, I'm pleased to see. Then all the way round, Hayle, Carbis Bay, St Ives, just tucked in over there. What a view!'

The surf was up, rolling in and crashing on the flat, golden sand. They watched, in awe, as black clad figures rode their boards atop the waves.

'It's good surf today, by the look of it,' Justin mused. 'Even, high, not too messy. Lucky guys.'

'Do you miss it? All this?' Sally asked.

'It's great now I'm here, but not really. I suppose I'm not the kind of person to miss places and things. Just as well, the amount I'm travelling at the moment. And that has its compensations. I've surfed Bondai and Waikiki.'

'Lucky you.' But Justin was already heading off once more across the towans. Sally did not think of herself as being particularly out of shape. She coached the school athletics team in the summer and the netball and gym clubs in the winter. But keeping up with Justin rapidly rendered her breathless and had her removing her coat. Gratefully, she pulled up beside him as he stopped at a cutting in the cliff top.

'Remember this, Sal?' To her consternation he started descending the other side. 'We used to have to climb down the cliffs here but they've put in steps, of a sort, now for the holidaymakers. Come on, we'll walk back across the beach.'

Sally followed him down the roughly hewn steps, taking his hand for the last few feet where the rocks had been left in their original form.

The sand was wet, firm under foot. Justin retained her hand and continued his blistering pace. Sally trotted along behind him.

She was just about to beg for a break when they rounded a small promontory and she could see the beach rising before them, up to meet the towans in a tangle of marron grass and sea holly. Justin lead the way back onto the scrubland, guiding her to a small hollow in the dunes.

'Your table awaits, m'lady,' he told her with a sweep of his hand.

Sally laughed. 'Hmn, what's the special, sand soup with grass salad?'

'Patience,' he chided. 'I can see you're fit to drop, as Iris would say, so you wait here and I'll be back in five.'

Mystified but happy to obey, Sally sank down onto the sand, stretched out her legs and rested her back against the wall of the hollow. She hadn't done this since she was a student, not since, in fact, the last time she'd come here with Justin….

As if conjured by her thoughts, he reappeared, carrying two huge bags and sporting a backpack.

'Up you get,' he instructed, producing things from the bags at lightning speed. 'Rug to sit on, plates, cutlery, condiments. Here,' he passed one of the bags to Sally. 'That one's got the food in it, you set that out. I'll sort the drinks.'

Smoked salmon roulades, tiny crustless sandwiches, morsels of sushi, asparagus wrapped in slivers of roasted beef and firm slices of quiche soon covered the blanket. When he'd had chance to put together such a lavish picnic, she had no idea but she was more than ready to do it justice. She peeked further into the bag; there was fruit, cheese and crusty bread to follow.

'Cheers,' Justin captured her attention once more by handing her a glass of champagne. 'I got a half bottle of champers for you and some of that ghastly fake bubbly stuff for me as I'm driving,' he told her as they clinked glasses.

'This is getting to be a bit of a habit, you feeding me.'

'Well, somebody has to. I saw what was in your fridge when I arrived, remember? Admit it, you mostly live on bread and apples.'

Sally protested but there was some truth in what he said. If she wasn't cooking an evening meal for Peter, she made do with a sandwich and fruit. She certainly never made feasts like this one.

'Oh, my goodness,' she sighed at last, lying back on the rug and closing her eyes. 'I am so full! Wake me up in about three years.'

'Three years?' Justin laughed. 'Think what you'll miss.'

'Well, the music festival for one thing. I could certainly do with waking up the other side of that.'

'Nonsense!' he told her firmly. 'It's going to be a huge success. You will be the saviour of the village. They'll probably make you mayor!'

Sally snorted. 'I'd better stay asleep then. Not sure I could handle mayorship.'

'I think you could handle pretty much anything you put your mind to, Sal.'

A silence fell during which Sally thought, 'anything except you, Justin'.

As if reading her mind, he asked suddenly, 'What happened to us, Sally?'

Sally shrugged noncommittally. Was it really worth raking it all up again?

'No, really,' he insisted, his voice quiet and serious, while he studied her face intently. 'Where did it all go wrong?'

Sally sighed heavily and raised herself on one elbow. 'You dashing off to Stockholm and sleeping with every woman in sight wasn't helpful.'

'You telling me the quicker I left the better and that if you never saw me again it would be too soon for you wasn't much help either.'

'I was hurt and upset. I didn't mean half of what I said.'

'Ditto.'

'Ha! It's one thing saying things in the heat of the moment,' she told him as she sat up angrily. 'What you did was something else entirely. Dad was desperately ill and all you could think about was leaving the country. You left me when I was at my wits' end and immediately started a string of affairs.'

'I'd already signed the contract! I had no choice but to go. The Stockholm job was my first as an associate conductor. I was so pleased, so excited. I wanted you to be part of that, Sal, but you'd made it quite clear you no longer wanted me around.'

'And the women?'

'I was young and stupid. I thought the best way of getting over you was by replacing you as soon as possible. For what it's worth none of it meant anything. None of it was even particularly enjoyable. Replacing you just wasn't that easy.'

'It felt like you were making me choose between you and my parents, Justin.'

'It felt like you were making me choose between you and my career.'

There was a pause. They sat shoulder to shoulder gazing out across the ocean, a gulf just as wide between them. Then Sally said sadly, 'As it was, Dad didn't live to see the end of your first season.'

'I was sorry, you know that, to hear about your father. He was a good man. I sent flowers as soon as my mother phoned and told me.'

'We got the flowers,' Sally told him.

'You never acknowledged them.'

'That was nothing personal. It was a difficult time. No-one got any thank you letters.'

'I didn't know about your mother being so ill for so long though. My parents had moved by then. I'm sorry.'

'That was difficult too.'

Silence fell again, each thinking their own thoughts.

'So,' Sally said finally, lowering her eyes and picking at a thread on the rug. 'We both made our choices.'

'Yes,' Justin turned to look at her. 'You happy with yours?'

Sally shrugged and sighed. 'Pretty much. All choices involve some kind of compromise though, don't they?'

'Such as?'

'I've never visited Stockholm and I don't suppose I ever will now.' She smiled a small, wry smile. As if Stockholm mattered.

'Why not? You could go anytime you like. You can go anywhere, do anything, Sal, anytime you like.'

'Hardly! I work. I'm engaged. Vicars don't get much holiday. Or pay either for that matter.'

'You can't let Peter stop you doing things. Relationships should enhance your life, Sal, not limit it.'

'The same could be said of careers,' she reminded him. 'Is there no-one special in your life, Justin?'

146

'Not so's you'd notice. The life-style's not really compatible with emotional commitment.'

'Other people manage it.'

'Maybe they're better at compromise than I am, then. Or maybe they're better at choosing the right partner.'

'Yes, perhaps you just haven't met the right woman yet.'

'Perhaps I did once, but let her get away. Or perhaps I just thought she was the right one. Anyway, you and Peter are lucky to have found each other.'

'He's a good man.'

There was no disputing that. Another silence fell.

Then Justin asked quietly, 'Why did you ask me down here, Sal?'

'You know that. Iris made me.'

'Sounds like you didn't really want to.'

'No, I didn't.'

'Why?'

'I thought... I thought I still hated you. Then I thought I didn't and that was worse...scary even.'

'And you don't?'

'No.'

'And is it scary?'

'No. At least, not when....not when you're being like this. When you're behaving yourself. Anyway, I didn't think you'd come. Why did you?'

Justin half-turned and fixed his gaze on the distant light-house, leaving Sally studying his profile. 'I told you,' he said flatly. 'Curiosity. I guess I felt the same way you did. I thought I still hated you. Then I was scared in case I didn't.'

'And?'

'And I don't. Hate you, I mean. And yes, it's scary.'

'Why?'

'Because I find it so damned hard to behave myself!'

'Oh,' Sally was quiet for a moment, whilst she digested this. She felt the need to lighten the mood. 'Plus ca change...'

'I meant with you, not in general.' He turned back and subjected her to the full force of his intense blue stare.

'That's not how it reads on the web.' It was Sally's turn to avert her gaze. 'You're not exactly a model of good behaviour, making cellists cry, cavorting with married women.'

'My, you did do your homework.' His tone was acerbic.

'You're not denying it then?'

'No, but you really shouldn't believe all you read, Sally. I made one cellist cry and she deserved it.'

'Huh! How can you say that?'

'Because it's true! She was the principal cellist. We were rehearsing for the Last Night of the Proms. It's a big programme and there's not much time. One expects instrumentalists who know they have solos coming up to have prepared properly. When it came to hers, she simply wasn't up to it. I bawled her out, made her swap with her desk partner who played it perfectly and saved the orchestra the embarrassment of an appalling performance.'

'Even so. To humiliate her in front of everyone like that…'

'Actually, she got off lightly. The vital piece of information we made sure didn't get into the papers was that she was married, to a really nice BBC producer and the reason she wasn't on top form at the rehearsal was that she'd spent the previous night catting around with someone in the chorus.'

'When did you get so puritanical? You've had your own fair share of married women!'

'Woman singular. The lady in question was in a train-wreck of a marriage with a career in the same state. She was an empty-headed clothes horse, with fading good looks, desperate for any kind of publicity. I was young, photogenic, highbrow by her standards. She latched on to me like a limpet and made sure everyone saw us together. And yes, before you ask, I did sleep with her. After all, I'm a man not a monk.'

'I wasn't going to say a word.'

'I slept with her once and pathetically grateful she was too.'

Sally grimaced. 'I don't need the gory details, Justin.'

'The point I'm making, Sal, is that I'm a just conductor. How many paparazzi have you noticed dogging me? None. I'm not Zak Efron or Richard Madden or someone. I don't tweet, I don't blog, I'm not trending. I'm not hot news. Stories about me only get into the media when someone particularly wants them too. The specialist press might mention when I've won a Grammy or a CD goes platinum. The gutter press confine themselves to the more salacious items.'

'Right, so nothing I read about you was true then?' She found that hard to believe.

'I'm not saying that. Most of it has some basis in truth. Like I said, I'm a man not a monk. Why shouldn't I date who I want? And I work hard to give the best performances I can, so I accept nothing less from other professionals. But I don't throw my weight around for the sake of it and I don't set out to hurt people.'

'Yes,' Sally admitted grudgingly. 'Apart from that awful committee meeting, you've got on really well with all the festival musicians,'

Justin acknowledged this with a shrug. 'No point doing otherwise. They're all doing their best. They don't deserve for me to be too hard on them.'

'True. And you do seem to be getting fantastic results. I'm nervous about the festival but only from an organisational point of view. I know the performances will be great.'

'Well, thank you!' Justin inclined his head, accepting the compliment. Away in the distance, a church bell chimed for evensong. He stood up and held out his hand. 'Come on, it's starting to get chilly. Time to head back.'

They packed up the remains of their picnic and soon were bowling along back to the village. As they turned off the main road, Justin said, 'What do you say we finish the day with a pint in The Pump?'

Sally was tempted. It would have been the perfect way to round off what had been, for the most part, a lovely day. But she knew it was a bad idea. She smiled, regretfully, 'I don't think so, thanks. It wouldn't be fair.'

'Fair?' he queried, looking puzzled for a moment. Then the penny dropped. 'Oh, you mean on Peter. Would he mind?'

'He would be very understanding, I'm sure, but think about this from his point of view. I've been pleading tiredness all week, I missed the services last week and this, I spend the whole day out and about with you and then we go drinking together in the evening.' Misquoting Justin's own words, she added, 'He's a vicar, not a monk. It would be reasonable for him to be a bit peeved.'

'Point taken. I'd feel the same in his shoes,' he admitted.

'But I've had a lovely day, Justin. I really do feel revitalised. Thank you.'

The car glided to a halt outside her cottage. As Sally went to open the door, Justin laid a restraining hand on her arm. She tensed, hoping he wasn't going to do or say anything to spoil her peace of mind.

'I had a great day too, Sal. I'm glad we're friends again.'

149

So that was it. Sally Marsh and Justin Trevelyan were friends again. 'Me too, Justin,' she told him softly. 'Me too.'

Chapter Twenty

The church was in chaos. Or appeared to be. The Pump teams had done themselves proud at the beginning and end of each day ensuring that the correct number of chairs and music stands were set out in the correct places for whatever rehearsal was taking place next. On this occasion, it looked like they had used every moveable chair within a ten-mile radius. The nave was packed with people. Instrument cases blocked the aisles. Today, several choirs, the orchestra, assorted children and adult soloists would be rehearsing together for the first time.

Sally picked her way towards the vestry where the choirs would congregate. As she opened the door, a wave of guilt passed over her. She'd spent all the previous day with Justin enjoying herself so much, she had completely forgotten about tidying up after the crèche and Sunday School. Now the place was a tip!

Although the helpers did their best, it wasn't easy to clear up with their own children still around. On this occasion, it looked as though they'd given up trying. Toys, crayons and scraps of paper littered the floor, puzzles were tipped out willy-nilly, children's chairs lay upended where they'd fallen. Sally sighed and set about instilling some kind of order. She'd got as far as stacking all the chairs, when the door opened and Iris peeked in.

'There you are, Sally dear…Oh my goodness!' Iris regarded the mess with dismay. 'Well, we can't have this, can we dear? Not with people coming from as far away as Launceston to help us out.' She strode in and began gathering armfuls of toys to put into the chest.

Sally paused in what she was doing and smiled her gratitude. 'I didn't get round to it yesterday. I had a bit of a break, actually. But I've never seen it this bad before.'

'I heard you'd been out for the day,' Sally was about to justify her day off when, to her surprise, Iris went on, 'Yes, I've told Justin what a good idea it was to make sure you had a day off and, I must say, dear, you are looking a lot perkier. And, it's not really so bad in here, we'll soon get it straight with the two of us.' Purposefully, she bent again to restore a set of wooden shapes to their tray.

As she did so, Sally yelled a warning, 'Iris!'

Too late, she'd seen the round plastic figure rolling beneath Iris's heel, too late she'd cried out. Iris's ankle turned awkwardly, she lost her footing, stumbled forward, came up sharply on the corner of a bookcase, landing in a crumpled heap against the far wall.

'Iris!' For a split second, Sally froze. Then, as she shot across the room, the door flew open and Justin came hurtling through.

'What happened?' he asked curtly, as Sally, First Aid training coming instinctively to the fore, spoke quietly to Iris and gently probed her limbs.

'She turned her ankle on a toy. I don't think she's broken anything but she's out cold and she has a nasty gash on her forehead,' Sally looked up at him, tears welling in her eyes. 'I couldn't bear it if anything happened to her,' she whispered.

Recognizing Sally's sudden vulnerability, Justin immediately took charge.

'I'll call an ambulance,' Already Justin had his phone out and was dialling. 'Where's the First Aid box? She needs something to staunch that bleeding.'

'Over there, top cupboard.' Sally took it as he handed it down, and pressed a large gauze pad to Iris's head. 'I'm really worried how long an ambulance will take. The nearest hospital is Truro. It'll be at least twenty minutes each way. And she's still not come round.' There was a marked note of desperation in her voice.

Justin raked a hand through his hair. 'Can she be moved, do you think?'

As Sally nodded uncertainly, Iris uttered a groan and her eyelids fluttered.

'Iris?' Sally touched her free hand to her friend's check. 'Iris, can you hear me?'

Iris groaned again before closing her eyes and relapsing into unconsciousness.

'Right,' Justin came to a decision. 'We need to get her checked over as soon as possible. I'll pull the car up as close as I can to the porch, then we'll take her ourselves.'

By this time a considerable number of people were crowding into the vestry. With a single instruction, Justin cleared the room of everyone except Sally and, sensibly, Andy from The Pump who had a lot of experience in dealing with rugby injuries and could be relied on to keep calm.

As he strode through the church, Sally could hear Justin giving a brief explanation of what was happening and instructing Steve to take over.

It felt like hours to Sally but was in fact only minutes later that he returned, scooped Iris into his arms and, with Sally scurrying along beside them, pad still pressed to Iris's head, carried her out to the car. Sally got into the back first and cradled Iris's head onto her lap as Justin gently disposed the rest of her frail body onto the back seat. Then, shouting to Andy to follow behind, Justin leaped into the driver's seat and they sped off.

Luckily, Justin knew the roads. His nocturnal forays to Kath's had reacquainted him with the narrow Cornish lanes and the layout of the new bypass. Luckily, Royal Cornwall Hospital was well signposted. Luckily, they weren't stopped for speeding.

He pulled up outside A&E and jumped out, reappearing very soon with a porter, a nurse and a trolley. Sally was only too glad to hand Iris over to the professionals. She herself was shaking by this time with a mixture of delayed shock and fear that she may have been wrong about moving Iris.

Justin put a consoling arm around her shoulder, tossed his keys to Andy with the instruction to park the car somewhere and put a good few hours' worth in the machine, and lead Sally to the reception desk. There seemed to be a lot of details required. She answered as best she could, Justin filling in when she faltered. They were instructed to take a seat and wait.

'Couldn't I go with her?' begged Sally. 'I'm the nearest thing to a relative that she's got.'

The receptionist was kind but firm. 'I'm afraid not. It's best to leave it to the triage team at this point. Your friend is in very good hands. Someone will be out to let you know what is happening as soon as possible.'

Miserably, Sally subsided onto one of the bare plastic chairs. Almost immediately a nurse carrying a clipboard came out to them and asked Sally a lot of questions about how long Iris had been unconscious.

'I'm not sure. About two minutes?' She glanced at Justin for confirmation. 'Then she came round briefly but fainted again. She was coming and going in the car too.'

'And, up till now she's been in good health?' Sally nodded, unable to remember the last time Iris had had as much as a sniffle. The nurse smiled. 'Don't worry. We always take extra precautions with head wounds but your friend is back with us now. A bit woozy but more or less lucid. You should be able to see her in a little while, once we've patched up the cut.'

Sally, realising she had been clutching Justin's hand practically since their arrival, let go suddenly and hugged her knees to her chest instead.

'Don't worry, Sal,' he said gently. 'She'll be OK. Iris is tough as old boots under that blue rinse.'

'Oh, Justin, she looked so frail, lying there and..' a large tear welled, trickled down over the softness of her cheek and blobbed wetly onto her hand. Justin reached over and dried her cheek with his thumb. 'I feel so guilty,' she whispered.

'Guilty? What have you got to feel guilty about? You did everything right. The nurse said so.'

'I don't mean then. It's… it's my fault she fell. I hadn't tidied up. She stood on a toy and ricked her ankle, that's what made her fall. If I hadn't gone out with you yesterday…' her voice trailed off.

'Stop it!' he ordered, making the receptionist glance up sharply. He shot her a charming, reassuring grin, she smiled back and pretended to be engrossed in her computer screen. But Sally could tell her ears were straining. 'Stop right there,' Justin continued quietly. 'None of this is your fault. You might as well blame me, or whoever it was who should have tidied up, or the toddler who dropped the toy in the first place.'

'But…'

'Or even Iris herself. No-one could make Iris do anything she didn't want to. I'm hazarding a guess that she insisted on helping you?' his voice raised in question and Sally nodded numbly. 'Well, then. It was just an

154

unlucky accident. And anyway, I'm sure she would be the first to say that you are as entitled to a day off as anyone else is. In fact…' he paused as if about to disclose something which he might later regret, 'to be honest, I know she would. She gave me a bit of a nudge in that direction actually.'

'Oh?' the receptionist wasn't the only one with her ears pricked. 'You mean the walk, the picnic…all that, wasn't your idea?' She felt she ought not to mind; they'd had a lovely day anyway but she knew that if he told her the whole thing was down to Iris, she'd feel cheated somehow.

'No! That was all me. I'm not sure a picnic on the cliffs was what Iris had in mind…' he paused musingly, then gave himself a little shake and returned to the subject in hand. 'No, she just happened to mention that she thought you looked a bit peaky and that someone with some 'gumption', as she put it, needed to take you out of yourself a bit.'

Sally digested this in silence for a moment then hastily scrubbed her tear-stained face with her sleeve as Andy approached. He noted her panda eyes and looked at Justin in consternation.

'Any news?'

Justin filled him in. 'They said we could see her shortly.'

Andy was visibly relieved. Iris might have her faults but she was a bit of a village institution and the locals were very fond of her.

'Oh well. That's good, then.' He took the seat next to Justin and lowered his voice, 'I can keep an eye on things here, Jay, if you need to get back to rehearsals,' he offered. 'Lou's holding the fort at The Pump.'

Justin shot a meaningful look at Sally who still had her arms wrapped tightly round her knees and was rocking slightly back and forth, her face and expression of anguish.

'No, you're alright, Andy. I'd like to hang on here at least till I've seen Iris for myself and know she really will be OK. But,' he rubbed a hand across his brow. 'You're right, the timing's not great. What would help is if you could take a message down to Steve Archibald?' Andy nodded in agreement. 'Ask him to just keep everything ticking over till I get back?'

'Sure, no problem. Best write it down though if it's anything musicky. You know I'm the biggest cloth ears as ever lived.'

'Yeah, but a good mate, all the same,' Justin agreed, rising to beg some paper from the receptionist who was only too happy to oblige the handsome 'foreigner'. Armed with several sheets, he scribbled a long list of instructions, at the bottom of which he wrote, 'Find Peter and get him here asap.'

Andy frowned and looked once more from Justin to Sally and back again. 'You sure, mate? Only, the news is that you two...' In the face of Justin's furious frown, he let the sentence die.

'You should know better than to take any notice of the village gossips. What they don't know, they make up.' Justin heaved a huge sigh then straightened his shoulders. 'Whatever. I know they've said Iris will be fine but I'm worried this is far too soon after Sal's mum. She'll want Peter to be here.'

Andy raised his eyebrows doubtfully, 'Really?'

In answer, Justin clapped him gratefully on the shoulder and gave him a shove towards the automatic door.

Peter arrived just as the nurse was explaining that Iris's cut had been dressed and, though the doctor didn't think her ankle was broken, they were going to send her up to radiography as soon as possible. Iris would like to see them while she was waiting for that to happen. Sally, Justin and Peter formed a subdued line and filed through into the curtained cubicle.

Iris was lying very straight in the bed, sporting a rather spectacular dressing across her forehead and an unwieldy lump towards the foot of the bed. Her eyes were closed and her skin had a worrying yellowish pallor. She looked very small and vulnerable. Sally gasped and plunged forward to take her hand.

Peter turned to Justin and said, 'I appreciate everything you've done, Trevelyan, but I know you're busy. I'll take over from here.' He placed a possessive arm across Sally's shoulders.

Justin thrust his hands deep into the pockets of his jeans, watching as Sally gently stroked Iris's thin, liver-spotted hand. 'Sure, but I'll just have a quick word with Iris before I go.' He stepped forward, casting a dark shadow the length of the bed. Iris opened her eyes.

'Goodness, I must be much worse than I feel, if you three are visiting me all at the same time!' she exclaimed.

'Oh, Iris, you're awake,' exclaimed Sally in delight. 'I thought you were unconscious again.'

'Just resting my eyes, dear,' Iris reassured her, before continuing briskly, 'Now, I don't want you fretting, Sally, dear. As you can see, I'm in the best possible place and I don't want you wearing yourself out trying to fit in visiting me, with everything else you've got to do. And that,' she turned a penetrating gaze on Justin, 'goes for you too, young man. Much as I appreciated that nice bottle of sherry, there's no need for you to be coming to see me again either.'

Sally frowned, puzzled. 'Sherry?' She looked from Iris to Justin just in time to catch his slight, warning shake of the head.

'Yes, dear,' Iris replied, either missing or ignoring Justin's silent message. 'He popped over between rehearsals on Thursday with a bottle each for me and Harriet. And I'm very grateful, Justin. Both for the sherry and for today. I dimly recall being swept into your arms like some Victorian heroine,' she smiled rather wistfully. 'A pity really that I wasn't sufficiently compos mentis to enjoy it.'

'Iris!' Sally giggled in spite of her confusion.

'Well, dear, the most attractive man I usually get to associate with is Bob Helmsworth. At my age, you have to take your pleasures where you can. Still, they say I'll have to stay in here for a couple of days for observation, whatever that is,' she sounded rather pleased than otherwise.

At that, Justin let out an irreverent hoot of laughter earning himself a look of reproach from Peter. Unabashed, he said, 'Iris, you wicked woman, you're enjoying this, aren't you?'

'Of course, dear. It's quite an adventure, isn't it? And there are some really very nice young doctors here,' Iris replied with a twinkle.

'Nurses too, I'll bet,' answered Justin. 'How about you put in a good word for me?'

'Justin!' Sally exclaimed, more shrilly this time.

'Careful, Sal,' Justin warned. 'You're shrieking again.'

'Well!,' she expostulated plonking herself down on the bed with a thump. 'If you two don't take the biscuit! I've been worried sick about you, Iris, whilst you've been chatting up the doctors and having a high old time. As for you,' she turned her wrath on Justin. 'I suppose it was too much to expect you to behave but you could at least be civil to Iris.'

'Ah, Sally,' he gave her arm a comforting pat. 'I'm afraid I've exhausted my meagre reserves of good behaviour, sweetheart. I've been minding my Ps and Qs with you now for nigh on three hours and, as you well know, all good things come to an end. Speaking of which, Iris, now that I can see you really are on the mend and in good spirits, I'm going to have to love you and leave you.' He bent quickly and, to everyone's surprise, kissed her gently on the cheek. 'And as far as the nurses are concerned, I hear there's a vacancy for a petite blonde.'

'Really, dear boy?' Sally could have sworn Iris was actually enjoying sparring with Justin. 'I was under the impression you harboured a penchant for willowy brunettes.'

'Iris!' Sally was reduced to shrieking again, cherishing the vain hope that Peter wouldn't recognise the significance of that last comment.

'You know me, Iris,' Justin retorted easily. 'I like to keep my options open. The proverbial rolling stone, that's me.'

Iris reached for his hand and clung to it for a moment. 'You may be able to pull the wool over everyone's eyes, including your own, young man. But you don't fool me. Keep a firm hold over that pride of yours or you could end up regretting it for the rest of your life.'

Fleetingly, Sally worried how Justin was going to respond to being spoken to like that but he took it in good part.

He gave the old lady's hand a last squeeze before laying it gently back on the covers. 'Just you keep your eyes open for that blonde, Iris.'

With a wink and a grin, he turned on his heel and strode off, leaving Sally to wonder what exactly, if there was a vacancy for a petite blonde in Justin's life, was the situation between him and Kath.

Peter, who had remained silent through these exchanges with a look of utter bemusement on his face, took advantage of Justin's disappearance to express his own sympathy to Iris.

'I was so sorry to hear what had happened to you, Iris. I'm sorry I wasn't there too.'

'Yes, well, we've already established there was no need for you to have been. Justin and Sally coped admirably. There was nothing else anyone could have done. And I'm going to be fine very shortly. They're only keeping me in because of this,' she touched a tentative hand to her head, 'and the double vision.'

'Double vision?' Sally leaped on this fresh symptom in a panic. 'That's not good, is it?'

'Quite usual,' Iris told her calmly, 'when one has been unconscious. And it's resolving itself nicely already. At this rate, they'll be packing me off home by tomorrow.'

'In the meantime,' Peter made another attempt at asserting himself, 'what do you need us to do for you? Would you like some of your own clothes? Any toiletries?'

158

'If I have need of anything, I'll let Sally know,' Iris told him acidly, 'as no doubt it will be Sally who actually goes and gets it for me. But, there is something I'd like you to do, Peter.'

'Yes?' eagerly he moved closer to the head of the bed.

'Take Sally straight back to church and make her stay there till the rehearsal is over. And be sure to give Justin all the help and support you possibly can. They're both going to have a lot on this week.'

'Well, yes,' Peter agreed unenthusiastically. 'That goes without saying.'

Iris fixed him with a stern look. 'Does it? I'm glad to hear that. No leaving Sally to lock up on her own or wearing herself out visiting your parishioners late at night. Now,' she slumped back suddenly on her pillows, 'I'm really feeling rather tired, so I'd be very grateful if you would both leave me in peace to have a little doze.'

Sally bent and kissed her, then she and Peter, rather like two chastised children, tip-toed away.

As instructed, Peter returned Sally to the church where, Steve having done sterling work in Justin's absence, the massed musicians were well into a rehearsal of the hauntingly beautiful Lachrymae from Verdi's Requiem. Briefly, Peter hovered over her solicitously, fetching her a mug of hot sweet tea from the vestry and asking periodically if she was sure she wouldn't prefer to go home. Sally shook her head. Being on her own at home worrying about Iris and the rehearsal was the last thing she needed.

As it was, Justin called a break soon after her return and after the initial flurry of interest in the current state of Iris's health, Sally soon found herself almost rushed off her feet, directing people to the toilets in The Pump, supervising the rearrangement of the chairs for the next pieces, providing teas and coffees and generally making sure that everything that needed doing was done in the short time available.

Chapter Twenty-one

Sally got up at five-thirty am. She hadn't needed to get up that early. Everything that could be done had been done. Everything that still needed to be done had someone's name allotted to it and everyone with an allotted task had been briefed till they could have recited their duties backwards, in Arabic, in their sleep. But sleep was the one thing Sally appeared to have no control over. It had been evading her since about two o'clock. Finally, having tossed, turned, thumped her pillow, sipped water, counted sheep, tried meditation and added up the income from ticket sales repeatedly in her head, she had admitted defeat, put on her dressing gown and slipped silently down the stairs.

She made a cup of tea as quietly as she could, fetched a throw from the sofa in the lounge and curled up in the conservatory to watch the day dawn. The sky was already high and light, the sun just blooming on the horizon. The merest hint of a breeze stroked the treetops where optimistic chaffinches were telling each other what a perfect day it was going to be.

By eight o'clock, having convinced herself that seven was not too early to shower and risk waking Justin, Sally was in the church wielding a duster and a jar of beeswax, polishing the pews to a shine that was almost dangerous. By nine, the flowers were tweaked, refreshed with water and the merest hint of droop or decay ruthlessly eradicated. At ten o'clock exactly, half a dozen stalwarts of the WI arrived bearing a variety of covered platters and serving dishes, by which time Sally had worked herself into such a state of nervous anticipation that she practically threw herself sobbing into their arms, so grateful was she that they had arrived, on time, exactly as planned.

Financially, Cornwall is not the richest county. Since the closure of the tin mines and the depletion of the fishing industry, it's had more than its fair share of deprivation and unemployment. But, due to its very shape and structure, tapering into the ocean like a gnarled hand pointing towards America, its views, arts and sports opportunities exercise an irresistible pull on those with time and money to spare.

Space in the church was restricted, the numbers limited. After hours of speculative messaging and calling by Max and Sally, the preconcert lunch and talk events had achieved considerable cache. People were willing to pay premium prices for the privilege of dining with Justin and listening to him talk knowledgeably about the music.

The lunch, largely made from donated local produce, looked fit for a king with individual Cornish pasties, their melt in the mouth pastry filled with flavoursome steak and vegetables, minute lobster patties whose sweetness lingered on the tongue, seared scallops in mead and starry-gazey pie with the fish heads pointing skywards through the fluffy pie-crust. The tickets were all sold out and a tidy profit guaranteed.

Justin, gorgeous in a beautifully cut pale grey Paul Smith suit and black silk shirt, worked the room like the professional he was, thanking, flattering, cajoling, deferring and generally ensuring that everybody present felt they were his personal guest. Legendary charm in overdrive, he chatted easily to his neighbours during the meal and then, whilst the guests were served coffee, delivered an amusing, erudite and very well-received talk on the composers and pieces which were to be played later that day.

Meanwhile, in the church, the first ensemble had already arrived and set themselves up in readiness for the afternoon concert.

On top of everything else, Sally had somehow remembered to reserve two easily accessible seats for Iris and Harriet, who was staying with her on her return from hospital. Though still too fragile to take part, Iris insisted on attending every concert. And now, there they both were, happily ensconced in the front row, studying the programme most of which Sally could have recited by heart.

'Don't worry about me, Sally dear,' Iris said as she approached to check they were both comfortable and that Iris's crutches weren't going to pose a health and safety risk. 'Everything looks absolutely lovely, you've saved us splendid seats and Harriet has everything I might need, haven't you, Harriet?'

Harriet twittered in agreement. 'Oh, yes, painkillers, a little bottle of barley water to wash them down and that nice mobile phone Justin gave Iris in case she needed to call anyone and couldn't get to the real phone under her own steam.' Sally raised an eyebrow at this, yet another example of Justin's unobtrusive thoughtfulness.

Aloud she said, 'Make sure it's switched off while you're in here, won't you? We don't want it going off in the middle of a performance!' Seeing a look of panic cross Harriet's flustered face, Sally gently took the phone and switched it off. As she did so, she caught sight of the time and felt a little lurch of nervous anticipation. 'There you go,' she handed it back. 'When you want it on again, just press that button there. Now, time for me to get things underway, I think. Enjoy!'

Sally planted a gentle kiss on Iris' brow and slipped into the vestry to give Justin his cue. Precisely on schedule, he lead the VIPs to their seats in the front seats of the church already full of an expectant audience.

In the week leading up to the festival, Sally and Justin had been thrown even more closely together and, somehow, in spite of the pressures of the hectic schedule, they had managed to remain friends. The days had passed in something of a blur for Sally who, when she looked back on it afterwards, was sure she didn't eat, drink or even sit down for the entire time, so busy was she chasing up every last detail. But, in the moment before he brought his baton down for the start of the first concert, Justin glanced over at her, their eyes met, she felt the familiar tightening in her stomach and knew everything was going to be fine.

A huge weight lifted from Sally's shoulders as the last notes of the Verdi Requiem died away late into the evening on Easter Monday. A brief silence descended on the church, then Justin lowered his baton for the final time and the audience broke into rapturous applause. The festival was officially over.

Justin himself applauded each of the four soloists in turn, the orchestra and the choir, then he dropped a low and dramatic bow before springing lithely from the podium and heading off to the vestry, the singers following in his wake. Rising as a man to its feet, the audience called them

162

back repeatedly, bow after bow. Eventually, Justin mounted the podium once more and turned to make an address.

'Ladies and gentlemen,' his deep voice, resonating around the body of the church, commanded their attention. 'As you are aware, this concert brings to a close the first ever St Piran's Festival. It truly has been an incredible team effort and I'm sure you would like to join me in thanking all those whose hard work and commitment have made it possible.' A further spontaneous round of applause greeted this statement. Justin held up his hands for quiet, pausing theatrically and allowing his gaze to roam the packed church, 'I'm not going to attempt to name everyone who has contributed as I'm bound to forget someone and Sally will kill me!' An appreciative ripple of laughter swept through the pews at that. 'Instead,' he continued. 'The festival committee has asked me to invite you all to join them for a celebratory drink and nibbles in The Pump.'

No-one needed asking twice. Audience and musicians streamed across the green into the pub and, in a very short space of time, the church was empty apart from Sally and Peter.

'You go on, love,' he jangled the keys. 'I'll lock up and follow you over.'

Sally had been at the church since early that morning. She felt hot and dishevelled and was sure that her make-up had run all over her face.

'Actually,' she told him rummaging in her bag for her hairbrush. 'I'd quite like five minutes to myself to tidy up a bit. I feel like a piece of chewed string.'

Peter laughed doubtfully. 'You don't look like anything of the sort but if you'd like to freshen up, I'll wait.'

'There's no need,' she held out her hand for the keys. 'I'll lock up and see you over there.'

'If you're sure?' Sally nodded and waved him away. 'I'll get you a drink,' he promised heading for the door.

Sally regarded herself in the vestry mirror. As she'd thought, her hair was a knotty mess, she had panda eyes and not a vestige of lip gloss left. She freshened up with some wet wipes, brushed her hair and reapplied her make-up. Then she gave herself a liberal squirt of perfume.

She was just heaving the door to when a sound caught her attention. Sally stopped, held her breath, listened. There it was again. Surely not, someone crying? She moved along the path towards the source of the sound.

163

And saw Peter, his arms wrapped round Kath, one hand cradling her head against his shoulder, the other patting her back with the soothing, rhythmic gentleness one might use to comfort a child. Sally, seeing her friend's very obvious distress, started towards them but Peter, looking up and seeing her approach, made a small moue of discouragement and shook his head. Sally stopped in her tracks and backed up. Then made her way slowly over to The Pump.

As she stepped over the threshold, Bob Helmsworth thrust a cool glass of something clear and sparkling into her hand.

'Well done, Sally! Splendid job!' he enveloped her in an overly enthusiastic
embrace. 'The whole thing went off brilliantly. Drink up. The champagne is courtesy of Justin's agent.'

Obediently, Sally took a large gulp. She disengaged herself, her eyes meeting Justin's across the crowded room. He raised his glass to her and inclined his head slightly before turning away immediately to resume his conversation. Sally found she really wanted to talk to him, and to Max too of course, to get their take on how things had gone.

The bar was heaving. There was barely room to move. Justin was surrounded by a tightly packed crowd of admirers. Sally attempted to fight her way towards him but the revellers closed in around her and everywhere she turned there were people topping up her glass and clamouring for her attention. She gave up turning back to Steve Archibald who was giving a note by note analysis of that evening's performance. Sally worked her way down another glass of champagne.

A few minutes later, Peter appeared at her elbow and, anxious to hear what was wrong with Kath, she allowed him to lead her into the comparative quiet of the corridor by the toilets.

'Well, I think we both knew it would end in tears,' he commented quietly, pulling the bar door closed behind them. 'Kath and Justin,' he explained in answer to her frown of query. 'Although, I have to say I think he did the decent thing in this instance.'

Sally leaned back against the wall and gave him her full attention. 'Is that why Kath was crying? He's finished with her?'

'Yes, at least, according to Kath, they never were officially dating, as it were. But he ended it at the beginning of the week. She's been pretty miserable ever since but things came to ahead this evening when she realised she'd probably never see him again.'

'Poor Kath.' Sally had known they were seeing less of each other but hadn't realised Justin had ended it completely. 'But what makes you say he's done the decent thing?'

'Well, again according to Kath, Trevelyan told her that he's not looking for a long-term relationship, his career always has to come first, and he thought it was better if they cooled things down before either of them became too involved. He said that as there could be no future in their relationship after he returned to London, he didn't want to risk either of them getting hurt. As I said, decent of him, in the circumstances.' Peter took Sally's glass and helped himself to a sip.

'But she seemed so upset!' Sally had never known Kath actually cry over a man before. And though she hadn't seen much of her friend in the frenzied week running up to the festival, Kath had given Sally no cause to suppose that what she felt for Justin was enough to make her do so now.

'Unfortunately, it appears he left it a little too late. They'd both got rather more involved than he'd intended. At least Justin can immerse himself in his career. Kath, on the other hand, seems quite devastated. Yes,' mused Peter, 'it's going to take her a long time to get over this heartbreak.'

'Hmn, heartbreak?' Sally voiced her scepticism. 'Hurt pride more like.'

'Sally!' Peter remonstrated, shocked. 'Kath was genuinely upset. She's going to need a lot of support to get over this love affair, from both of us.'

'Love affair?' Sally wasn't sure that half a dozen dates quite merited the term. 'Peter, they'd only known each other a couple of weeks.'

'When it's the right person,' he told her meaningfully, 'falling in love can take much less time than that.'

Sally had to admit that this was true; it had taken her younger self just one minute to fall in love with Justin. She thrust this unwelcome thought out of her mind.

'Are you sure,' Peter continued, 'you're not being just a little mean-spirited here, darling?

'What's that supposed to mean?' her tone was sharp.

'You may not be interested in Trevelyan any more, but perhaps,' he suggested cautiously, 'you're finding it just a little difficult admitting that he and Kath might have feelings for each other?'

'Don't be ridiculous, Peter!' Sally declared, all the more indignant as she had asked herself much the same question just a few short weeks ago.

'I couldn't care less what Justin does, or who he does it with.' But she found she did care, very much indeed. Perhaps Kath and Justin had had more than just a casual fling? Who could blame them? Kath was extremely attractive, intelligent, funny and very good company. Justin was a catch on anyone's terms.

Sally snatched her glass back from Peter and tossed down what was left. 'I sincerely hope,' she assured him fervently, 'that Justin and Kath haven't fallen for each other, because, as he has so rightly pointed out to her, he puts his career first, always has and always will. So, if they have, nothing but misery will come of it. And, trust me, I should know!'

'Sally….' Peter laid a placatory hand on her arm. 'I'm sorry. I shouldn't have said anything. You're tired and overwrought. And I'm sure Kath will make a much better job of explaining it all to you than I have. Please, don't let's fight.'

He drew her to him and gently put his arms around her. Sally resisted the urge to push him away. Peter was right, she told herself. She was emotionally and physically exhausted and that was why she was getting het up. She rested her aching brow against his shoulder.

Suddenly, the bar door flew open. Sally raised her head and found herself looking straight into Justin's steely blue eyes. He took in the scene in an instant.

'Excuse me,' he said suavely. 'Apologies for the intrusion.' He glowered at Sally momentarily, then turned on his heel and left.

Champagne on an empty stomach is not a good idea; Sally knew that. Back in the throng of the public bar and halfway down yet another glass she began to realise that champagne on an empty stomach, when you're dog-tired and have been living on adrenalin for seven days straight, is a very bad idea indeed. With the noise, the heat and the dreadful crush, it wasn't long before the dull ache in her head had metamorphosed into full-scale pounding and she felt more than slightly sick.

Peter was ensconced in a corner with Kath, deep in conversation. Iris, delighted that her idea had paid such handsome dividends, was holding forth to Bob, Harriet and anyone else within earshot. Max and Steve appeared to be getting on like a house on fire. Of Justin there was no sign.

With difficulty, Sally edged her way towards the back door and slipped out into the cool, velvety darkness of the pub garden. She sank down gratefully at one of the wooden tables and rested her head on her arms. After a few deep, slow breaths, the dizziness receded slightly and she sat up gingerly. As her eyes grew accustomed to the darkness, she became aware of a still and solitary figure a couple of tables away.

She hesitated, then whispered, 'Justin?'

'Sal,' he answered flatly, without looking around. After a minute, he picked up the glass and bottle at his elbow and threaded his way, slightly unsteadily towards her. 'Mind if I join you?'

She pushed a chair towards him with her foot. 'Be my guest.'

He sat down heavily, stretching his long legs out in front of him. He filled the glass and pushed it towards her, 'Drink?'

'No thanks,' Sally knew she'd already had more than enough. 'But don't let that stop you.'

Justin leaned back in his chair and took her at her word, drinking deeply straight from the bottle. With only the moon filtering through the clouds and the occasional star for light, Sally found it impossible to read his expression. He was a deep, dark, brooding presence beside her. They sat, at the same table yet worlds apart, in silence.

'So, that's that then,' he said at last. 'How're you feeling, Sal?'

'Me?' Sally scooped her hair off her face and gathered it into a heap on top of her head, enjoying the feel of the cool night air caressing her neck and shoulders. She assumed he was referring to the festival.

'Oh, you know. Exhausted. Delighted. Relieved.' She turned and grimaced at him. 'I have no idea how you survive doing this for a living.'

He gave a soft bark of laughter. 'It's not so tough once you're used to it. And I have it easier than you've had it, remember. Normally I just rock up and conduct. Max arranges everything else.' He paused, considering. 'This has been a bit of a one off though,' he admitted.

'How so? You've done festivals before?' Sally was curious.

He laughed again. 'True, but they don't usually involve doing my own cooking and laundry....'

It was Sally's turn to laugh. 'You insisted on staying with me, remember? You have only yourself to blame there!'

He slanted the bottle towards her acknowledging her point. 'It's not just that though. I'm not really used to being with the same crowd for quite so long. And I don't usually work with amateurs,' he hesitated, refreshing himself again from the bottle.

'So, you'll be glad to get back to London, then?' Sally prompted.

He took another long, slow drink. 'I didn't say that.'

'It's what you meant.'

Justin shrugged. 'Maybe....' Another long, still silence developed between them. It was Justin who broke it. 'So, what's the final total then? Have we done it? Reached the target?'

Sally noticed the 'we'. Perhaps he wasn't quite as detached as he'd like her to believe. 'Actually,' she told him after a moment's thought. 'We're a bit further off than I'd like. We'll be able to get the structural stuff sorted but that's about it. The bulk of the interior refurbishment will have to wait till someone has another fundraising brainwave.'

'Do another festival,' he suggested. 'Make it an annual event.'

'You offering?' Sally wished she could see his face properly. Did he mean it? And if he did, could she really go through all that again?

'Maybe,' he sounded as though he didn't much care one way or the other. 'Or maybe I'll just get Max to send a cheque.'

'A cheque?' What did that mean?

'Why not?' he was nonchalant. 'Tell him exactly how much you need. He'll sort it. Less trouble than going through all this again.'

'But, Justin,' Sally was incredulous now. 'It's thousands!'

He shrugged again. 'Max tells me my complete Beethoven has just gone platinum. That'll probably cover it.'

Sally sat up straight and looked him in the eye. 'You're drunk, Justin Trevelyan. Drunker than I am! You don't know what you're saying.'

'I'm not drunk, Sal. At least, not drunk enough,' he took another deep pull at the bottle. 'And you know me. I don't like being beaten. I said I'd come down here to raise the funds for your hall to be finished and that's what I'm doing. Does it matter exactly how I do it?'

Sally frowned at him. 'You really are serious, aren't you?' she marvelled. 'We'll have to put up a plaque or something, in your name.'

'God no!' he repressed a shudder. 'The press would have a field day with that. Tell you what, Sal, give me an invite me to your wedding and we'll be quits.'

'What?'

168

'You heard. An invitation to your wedding.' He moved at last, leaning forward to study her face intently in the glimmer of moonlight. 'It is still on, I take it?'

'Yes! Yes, of course it is!' His words had jolted her. The last-minute preparations for the festival had been a convenient excuse to forget all about her pending nuptials. Now, she supposed, she'd really have to start planning it. Should be a piece of cake after the past few weeks.

'Then invite me,' he persisted.

'You're kidding me, right?'

'Not in the slightest,' he informed her coolly. 'Think of it as a return on my investment.'

'But...' Sally tried and failed to visualise Justin at her wedding. In fact, just imagining the wedding was proving pretty difficult.

'What's the matter, Sal?' he taunted. 'Scared my presence will rock the boat?'

'No!' Sally scorned this suggestion.

'Well then,' his eyes met hers, openly challenging. 'Invite me.'

'OK,' Sally submitted in exasperation. 'You're invited.'

'No, properly.' He held out a hand, palm upward. 'In writing, so you can't renege on the deal.'

Sally had no idea how he'd managed to manoeuvre her into this but she was damned if she would let him think she was too chicken to have him at her wedding. At least she'd enjoy it more than he would! She dug a pen and a scrap of paper from her bag and scrawled;

Justin,

August 15th, 12 noon.

St Piran's Church

U R invited.

Signing it with a flourish, she slapped it into his hand. Justin read it through solemnly then folded it carefully and put it in his pocket. As he did so, the pub door opened and Sally looked up to see Max silhouetted in the doorway.

'Car's here, Justin!' he approached rapidly. 'Your stuff's all loaded and we're ready to roll.'

Sally frowned. Had she missed something? 'You're leaving? Now?'

Justin kept his eyes fixed on the bottle in front of him. 'The festival's over. There's nothing to keep me here, is there, Sal?'

Dumbly, Sally shook her head, 'No, I suppose not.'

'That's one of the reasons I came down,' Max was saying. 'I had to make sure J.T. made it back to London tonight.' Deftly, he removed the bottle from Justin's grasp. 'Just as well I did. There's no way he could fly himself back in the state he's in and he's got a ten o'clock rehearsal with the Philharmonia in the morning.' He set the bottle on the table and gave his client a nudge. 'Come on, old chap. Five hours sleeping it off in the back of the car should have you right back on top form.'

Sally realised with a shock that this was it. The festival was over. Justin was leaving. Tonight.

Suddenly they were all standing up, a rather awkward little triangle.

'Well,' said Sally uncomfortably. 'I guess this is goodbye then.' She turned to Max. 'Thanks for everything.' They kissed cheeks and he enveloped her in an avuncular embrace.

'You did a great job, Sally,' he told her as he released her. 'You should be really proud of yourself. Keep me posted on the renovations, won't you?' He turned to go. 'Justin?'

'Give us five minutes, Max,' Justin instructed. He turned to Sally, who, desperate to have the goodbyes over and, at the same time, to prolong these last minutes as long as possible, avoided eye contact.

Max headed off towards the door. Justin waited till they were once more alone, then reached out, slowly drawing her towards him.

'For old times' sake, Sal,' he said as his arms came round her. This time there was no hesitation, no resistance. Her lips beneath his were warm and pliant. Justin uttered a soft moan and tightened his embrace, crushing her to him. Sally gave herself up to him completely. In that moment, she realised there was nowhere else she wanted to be, no-one else she wanted to be with. She wanted this to last forever.

They broke apart, breathless. Sally raised her palms to her flaming cheeks and realised she was shaking. Justin gave a long, shuddering sigh then took a step backwards. The empty silence stretched out between them. Eventually he raised his hand in a half-wave and let it fall again, heavily, to his side.

'Bye, Sal.' She watched, wordless, motionless as he turned and walked away.

Seconds later, the stillness was shattered by the roar of an engine as a car sped out of the village.

Chapter Twenty-two

Sally opened her eyes. Sunlight filtering round the edges of the curtains lit the bedroom. She smiled. Sunshine! A good omen, surely?

Throwing back the covers, she eased her legs over the side of the bed and faced the wardrobe. She opened the door and withdrew first an off-white dress of soft lace over shimmering satin, then one of dark red silk. As she hung them on the curtain rail, Kath erupted into her room, shattering the early morning quiet.

'Sally!' she squealed taking her friend by the shoulders and bouncing excitedly. 'This is it. Today's the day!'

Sally, a pang of nervous anticipation knotting in the pit of her stomach, knew Kath was right. This was it; today was the first day of her new life.

The hairdresser arrived. She tamed Kath's unruly curls into a rippling cascade. Then she smoothed Sally's shining lengths upwards and back into an intricate French plait. She was just spraying some wayward strands into their final position when Kath, nose to the window, shrieked, 'Flowers, Sally. The flowers are here!'

Sally ran downstairs and received two bouquets of deep red roses and gypsophila before instructing the florist to take the button holes up to Peter's house. The groom, the best man (a cleric friend of Peter's), Andy, Kath's brother and the ushers should all be there by now. Then, showered and clad in her best undies, Sally slipped into her dress then helped Kath into hers.

The next shriek heralded the arrival of the wedding car. Holding their hems, they went carefully down the stairs and out into the street. Sally pulled the door shut behind her and posted the key back through the letter box. She wouldn't need that again for a while; the agent already had the spare. She turned away quickly, following Kath down the path. The chauffeur carefully arranged Kath, Sally and their dresses in the back seat of the limousine then drove them, smoothly and sedately, the short distance to the church.

Iris and various members of Kath's family greeted them as they arrived, tweaking their hair, straightening their dresses and giving last minute words of advice. One of the ushers appeared and, at his signal, the bustling women melted away.

Kath held Sally away from her and subjected her to a last, long, critical look. 'Are you sure, Sally?' she whispered.

'You?' Sally shot back.

Kath nodded emphatically. 'Absolutely.'

Sally took Kath's hand and squeezed it hard. 'Come on, then,' she gave her friend an encouraging smile. 'Let's do this!'

They moved together into the porch where, in the absence of fathers, Kath's brother and Andy were waiting for them. They linked arms, Kath gave the nod to the usher and, as the first joyful chords of the Wedding March filled the air, they stepped through the doors and began their stately journey down the aisle.

Ahead of them, Peter, smartly attired in a new clerical suit, and shoulder to shoulder with his best man, turned slightly to watch their progress, an expression of delighted pride lighting up his face. Just as they drew level with him, the heavy panelled door at the back of the church creaked ajar then slammed shut. There was a brief hush, then a ripple of whispers washed over the pews reaching the group at the altar as a barely audible flurry of speculation.

Easing her head fractionally to the right, Sally watched from the corner of her eye as the latecomer burst in, tossed his order of service onto the back pew and flung himself down beside it. A gasp of recognition escaped her.

Justin, arms folded across his chest and wearing an expression more fitting to an execution than a wedding, lounged in the corner of the

172

farthest pew, glowering resolutely ahead oblivious to the hundred or so pairs of eyes watching him in anticipation. Please, Sally begged silently, please don't say or do anything to spoil things, Justin, please.

There was a brief pause whilst the Bishop scanned the assembled guests with wise and experienced eyes, Then, apparently assured that there would be no further interruptions, he raised his voice to address them.

'Dearly beloved,' he began solemnly and Sally dragged her mind back to the matter in hand. 'We are gathered here today to celebrate the marriage of Peter and Kathleen...'

A hymn book clattered to the floor. A startled child began to grizzle. Sally, back to the congregation, could only cling tightly to her bouquet and will the Bishop to continue. He cleared his throat, increased the volume and ploughed on.

The hymns were sung, the vows exchanged, the rings slipped onto waiting fingers and the bride duly kissed. As the bells rang out, the wedding party took their positions and processed slowly back down the aisle. Drawing level with the last pew, Sally, hanging onto Andy's arm for dear life, risked a glance at Justin. He looked absolutely furious.

As they emerged into the glorious summer sunshine, handfuls of rice and confetti rained down on them, settling in Kath's curls and lying like epaulettes along Peter's slender shoulders. Andy was claimed by Lou to replace the battery in their digital camera. The bride and groom were claimed by the photographer. Sally, temporarily at a loose end, waited quietly by the porch entrance.

Suddenly her wrist was seized and her arm jerked nearly out of its socket as Justin dragged her round the corner of the church tower into relative seclusion.

'What the fuck is going on?' he demanded, as soon as they were out of earshot of all the guests.

'Justin!' Sally wrenched herself from his grasp and rubbed at her reddened wrist. 'We're in a churchyard! For heaven's sake mind your language.'

'Mind my language?' he repeated, incredulously, catching her by the upper arms and administering a hefty shake. 'What kind of language do you expect me to use?'

'Justin!' Sally implored for a second time. 'Let me go! You're hurting me!'

Abruptly he released her and thrust her away from him. 'I'm hurting you?' he thundered. 'The boot's on the other foot there, Sally, surely?'

'What?' Sally stared at him in disbelief. 'I have no idea what you're talking about. Come to think of it, I've no idea why you're even here!'

Justin thrust his hand into his pocket and produced a crumpled piece of paper. Sally recognised the scrawled invitation she had given him after the final concert. She opened her mouth to reply but before she could form a coherent sentence, Peter came round the corner at a run.

'Sally! There you are!' he skidded to a halt. 'Oh, Trevelyan!' The appearance of Justin threw him off guard. He clearly had no more idea than Sally why his wedding had been crashed by the last man on earth he'd want to be there but, after a brief internal wrangle, he decided there were more important things to attend to. Pointedly, he turned to Sally. 'Kath is absolutely refusing to have any group photos taken without you and if we don't get started soon, we'll be all behind with everything at Lawncrest.'

For the second time that day, Sally found her wrist firmly grasped as she was towed round the corner of the tower and man-handled into position beside Kath's brother.

Justin, it became clear, had no intention of causing a public scene. Apart from a brief and, apparently, mono-syllabic conversation with Andy, he spoke to no-one but remained, on the periphery of the milling throng, leaning moodily against the trunk of an oak tree, watching the scene through narrowed eyes. He made no move to approach any of them again until they had arrived at Lawncrest and Sally was standing next to Kath in the receiving line. The last of the invited guests were just filing past, when Sally found her arm grabbed once more as Justin staked his claim.

'Kath, Peter,' he nodded dismissively to the bewildered couple, ignored Kath's outstretched hand and turned on his heel, practically dragging Sally in his wake. 'We need to talk,' he told her, overriding her protests and physical resistance as easily as if she had been a recalcitrant toddler.

'OK, OK!' with difficulty in her high-heeled shoes, Sally stumbled after him. 'I'll come, I'll talk. Just stop pulling me around, will you?'

To her relief, he did just that. He stopped by the lifts and called one with a swift, angry jab, bundling her in before him as it arrived and punching the button for the third floor, maintaining all the while an iron grasp of her wrist, and a tight-lipped silence. Sally seethed inwardly trying to make sense of Justin's behaviour. She had no idea why he was there, why he was so furiously angry or why he felt they needed to talk quite so urgently. What she did know was that his treatment of her was making her every bit as cross as he was.

The only explanation that made any sense to Sally was that he had turned up hoping to rekindle his relationship with Kath. That would at least account for why he was so angry. Imagine coming all the way down from London feeling sure of a warm welcome only to find the object of your affections was the bride-to-be.

The lift drew bumped gently to a halt and opened with a swish. Justin made a bee-line for one of the doors, inserted the plastic card he produced from his pocket and let them both in.

He wheeled Sally round to face him and, momentarily, she recoiled from the look of sheer fury on his face. When he spoke, his voice was unnaturally quiet, but Sally was in no way fooled. He was barely managing to contain himself.

'Right, so, where were we before Peter so rudely interrupted us?' he asked almost conversationally. 'Oh, yes, I remember. Peter and Kath have just got married. I repeat, what the fuck is going on?'

'You know what's going on!' Sally did not trouble to keep her voice down. She let rip with relish. 'Peter and Kath just got married!' She gestured at her own attire, 'posh frock, fancy hairdo, bunch of flowers? I'm their bridesmaid! You know all that. What I don't know is what you want me to do about it!'

'Explain!' Justin, released from his self-imposed restraint, yelled back at her. 'I want you to explain to me why, when I turned up fully expecting to see you and Peter tie the knot, to be able to put you behind me once and for all, so maybe I can finally get on with my life, why you're still here, unmarried, free, single and looking so bloody beautiful it hurts! What the hell happened? And why, whatever it was that did happen, didn't you think to tell me about it?' He subsided suddenly onto the bed, looking at her expectantly. 'Well?' he growled as Sally stared down at him open-mouthed. He pushed a hand roughly back through his hair. 'Why didn't you tell me, Sal?'

Sally opened and shut her mouth, desperately trying to make sense of his outburst. What did he mean put her behind him and get on with his life? Had he really called her beautiful? But he'd said... he'd told her...

175

Suddenly, she found her voice, all the emotion of the past few months bubbling furiously to the surface. 'What did you expect, Justin? 'There's nothing more for me here, Sal,' you said,' she flung his words back at him. 'Just before disappearing out of my life for the second time.'

'Well, what did YOU expect, Sally?' He sprang up from the bed and started towards her, then thought better of it, turning instead to the mini-bar. 'You must have known how I felt about you…'

'How you felt about me? Oh yes, I knew that alright,' her voiced dripped with sarcasm. 'You were desperate to get into my knickers; you seldom passed up an opportunity to make that clear to me!'

'So what if I did, do, want to make love to you?' Looking very much as if he wished it were her neck between his fingers, he snapped the top off a miniature scotch and shot it into a glass. 'You're gorgeous, for God's sake! Any man in his right mind would feel that way about you. At least I was honest enough to admit it! But you, you told me, over and over, you loved Peter and wanted to make your life with him.' He downed the shot in one and immediately poured himself another.

'I thought I did love him! I truly believed that was what I wanted.'

'Exactly!' he tossed back the second scotch as quickly as the first. 'And if that was what you wanted, how could I do anything else but leave? Leave and try to forget all about you? Well, I tried.' he slammed the empty glass onto the table. 'God knows I tried. But I couldn't do it the first time and I couldn't do it this time either. Like I said, that's why I'm here, hoping to see you married and out of reach once and for all.'

'I never dreamed you'd take that stupid invitation seriously.'

'Me neither,' Justin gave a mirthless laugh. 'Then, there I was sitting in the church.'

'When you turned up today, I thought you'd come back because of Kath,' Sally told him in a small voice. 'I thought that was why you were so angry.'

'Kath?' he queried in disbelief. 'God no! There was only one reason I ever showed any interest in her and that was you.'

'Me? Don't you go blaming me for the way you treated Kath!'

'I'm not blaming you, Sal. I'm just trying to explain. Look, I'm not proud of the way I behaved towards her. I used her to try and make you jealous. Then I used her to try and get over you. I just hope she didn't get too hurt in the process…oh, well, clearly not, as she's just hitched up with

176

Peter.' He stopped abruptly, frowning, as a thought struck him. 'Kath and Peter, they weren't… when you and Peter were still…'

Sally gave an exasperated laugh. 'This is Peter we're talking about, Justin,' she reminded him. 'No, I think they started to get close after you dumped Kath but they didn't actually get together till Peter and I were well and truly over.'

Justin digested this in silence for a few seconds. He shook his head disbelievingly. 'To think I drove down here this morning, really believing that, by the time I drove back up again, you'd be married to him.'

'Well, I'm not,' she confirmed abruptly.

'No, you're not.' Justin rubbed a hand wearily across his brow and revisited the mini-bar. 'Well,' he said, searching through the remaining miniatures. 'We seem to have come full circle, don't we? We've established you're not married and I'm surprised. What we haven't yet established is why. So, to repeat one of my original questions, Sally, why? What happened?'

'What happened, Justin?' Surely, she didn't need to spell it out for him? 'You. You happened. I realised that what I had with Peter wasn't enough for me. In fact, my whole life wasn't enough for me. So…' Sally took a deep breath. 'I broke it off with him and…'

'And?' he prompted quietly.

'I handed in my notice and rented out my house,' she told him in a rush. 'I'm…I'm off to Stockholm first thing in the morning.'

Justin spluttered into his glass 'My god! You don't do things by halves do you? And why Stockholm?'

'Well, it seemed as good a place to start as any,' she told him in a small voice.

'Ironic.'

'What is?'

'Last time it was me rushing off to Stockholm leaving you behind. Now it's your turn.'

'I don't have to go.' Sally found she couldn't quite make eye-contact.

Justin stood up, placed his glass carefully on the coffee table and came over to take her hand. 'I think you do, Sal.'

A tear formed in the corner of her eye, welled and trickled slowly downwards over her cheek. So, after all that, were they really going to just slip away from each other again?

177

Justin tipped her chin up so he could see her face properly. He smudged the tear away with the ball of his thumb.

'I think you do need to go, Sal. It's time you started living a few of your dreams.'

'Justin...' Sally began. He placed a firm finger on her lips quelling her protest.

'You need to go. But I don't need to stay.' He caught both her hands and pulled her to him, looking deep into her eyes. 'Let me come with you, Sally.'

'Oh, but... how can you? Surely... your work?'

'My work has made me money, made me famous. It hasn't made me happy. I've a feeling there's only one thing, or rather one person who can do that,' he paused, anxiously watching her face as his words sank in. 'Oh, for God's sake, let's not waste any more time! I love you! Say the word and I'll come with you to Stockholm. I'd go to the ends of the earth for you, Sal, surely you know that?'

Sally was silent, hardly daring to believe what she was hearing. The last four months had been utterly bloody for her. She'd parted with Peter and faced gossip, recriminations and criticism. She'd given up a job she loved, rented out her darling cottage and prepared to say goodbye to all her friends. However hard it had been, she'd known it was the right thing to do and, however much she might try to deny it to herself, she'd known too exactly why she'd had to do it all. Because she loved Justin! She'd realised once he'd gone that she'd never stopped loving him, that hurt and pride and anger had got in the way and hidden the fact from her, but deep down, her feelings for him had remained the same. She'd loved him then just as she'd always loved him, as she loved him now and always would. And he loved her!

She opened her mouth to reply but the words dried on her lips as someone knocked authoritatively on the door. Unwilling to release her, Justin kept his arm around her waist, guiding her with him as he went to answer it.

'I'm sorry to disturb you sir,' the duty manager apologised discreetly, 'but the wedding party is about to eat and the bride and groom would like to know if you are intending to join them.'

'No,' Justin's answer was unequivocal. 'No, we won't be joining them. Please convey our regrets and inform them that...' he paused just long enough to glance at Sally who beamed her agreement, 'we're going to

Stockholm.' Unheeding of the manager's feelings, Justin closed the door in his face and turned once more to the radiant woman in his arms. 'Sally, my darling, my angel, will you marry me?'

'Yes!' Sally, not needing to think twice, threw her arms around his neck and had the satisfaction of almost having the breath squeezed out of her by the man she loved. Minutes passed, then Justin raised his head at last and looked significantly from Sally to the super king-sized bed and back again.

'In that case,' he growled meaningfully, 'there's just time to attend to a little unfinished business….'

Printed by Amazon Italia Logistica S.r.l.
Torrazza Piemonte (TO), Italy

12747994R00105